From the Land of Genesis

A Short Story Collection

From the Land of Genesis

A Short Story Collection

Stephen J. O'Shea

Attention schools and businesses: for discounted copies on large orders, please contact the publisher directly.

For information contact:
Unsolicited Press
Portland, Oregon
www.unsolicitedpress.com
orders@unsolicitedpress.com
619-354-8005

Cover Design: Sean Ficht
Editor: S.R. Stewart

ISBN: 978-1-950730-58-2

For those who have served and are serving.

TABLE OF CONTENTS

INTRODUCTION

I have not fought in a war. I've never served in the military, either. This book, then, comes as a result of over six years of research, including dozens of interviews with veterans from across the United States, the United Kingdom, and the remote territory of Guam. All references to experiences of war are taken directly from these source materials and transcripts, sometimes verbatim. Depictions of veterans in the civilian world, however—of soldiers returning home and adjusting to their new lives—are of my own invention.

This collection, like all good fiction, is a fusion of the real with the truth: of what happened with what didn't happen, but is still "truer than the truth" (Tim O'Brien, *How to Tell a True War Story*). Some of these stories are true to one veteran's experience, while others are true in a broader sense, encapsulating themes that pervaded the narratives of veterans from across three continents and numberless wars.

There is always the question of authority, though: one I've asked myself countless times, and that I still struggle with today. "How can you write about war without having experiencing it?" And the only answer that's ever really satisfied me is the simplest one: you don't.

Instead, you write about human beings. You write about their many complexities, their shortcomings, and their ideals. And, by the end of it, you reach the same conclusions that I found at the end of every interview, and at the bottom of all of my research: that even the most hardened among us, and the most broken, all want for the same things—all feel regret and shoulder burdens—and we all go to great lengths to remember some moments, to forget others, and to face (or to put off facing) the inevitability of death.

But the beautiful part of it is that we can reach across the aisles that separate us—by class, or race, or experience—and grab a hold of someone in an entirely different world and time. This book, for instance, connects veterans and civilians. It spans across two decades, encapsulating the longest war in American history (and counting), and it grabs hold of two worlds: the new world and the old; America and Mesopotamia; the "land of opportunity" and the land of Genesis.

A FIELD PARTY

When Brittany Bloomsbury said that she wanted to throw a party for him, and at such short notice, Terrance thought she was kidding. "Friday at my stepdad's barn," she told him. "It'll be a field party, like old times."

She winked when she said this, and Terrance laughed because Brittany Bloomsbury was beautiful, but also because the last field party he'd gone to was well before he'd gone to war and in a part of town that Brittany would have never set foot on. Years had passed and now she wanted to throw him, Terrance MacElvaney, a party. "For coming home safely," she said, touching his arm in their Winn Dixie parking lot.

The next day, he received a Facebook message with a pin for the location of her stepdad's barn. "See you tomorrow!" Brittany said. There was no one else included in the message, and it was hard to imagine a party being thrown just for him. Especially considering the fact that the only person to meet with Terrance since he'd returned from rehab was Ricky Lang—and that for a single pint on bar trivia night—so the next day when Terrance pulled up a little late and a little drunk to find a dozen or more cars parked alongside Brittany's step-dad's barn he was, well, surprised.

It was cold for December in Louisiana and when Terrance stepped out of his car, frozen grass crunched beneath his good leg. Floodlights ignited a half-mile of empty grassland. Music and voices murmured inside of the barn. Terrance grabbed his Abita beers, locked the door to his old Subaru and made for the entrance. A group of silhouettes huddled against the barn wall and their cigarette ends moved like glowing stars. Terrance couldn't recognize their voices and he smelt marijuana, which usually meant out-of-towners, so he walked past them to find Brittany Bloomsbury.

It was bright inside the barn. It was also warm. A dozen pairs of eyes bore into Terrance and the high walls slanted inward with the only exit behind him. Terrance began to worry that, since Brittany led a different crowd in high school, there might not be a single person he really knew there. But then she was standing in the middle of the barn and Terrance remembered that she had thrown this party for him—that she would've invited Ricky Lang and other people he knew—and that, even if she didn't, they weren't in high school anymore. They were adults, now.

"Brittany," he called, but there was music and she was talking to somebody. It was warm and he walked up beside her. "Brittany," he said, this time in her ear.

"Oh!" she said, wheeling around. "Terrance! I thought... I was worried you wouldn't come." She held a Smirnoff Ice in one hand and after a moment she remembered to smile. She had a disarming smile. Ricky, who was infatuated with Brittany Bloomsbury, once told

4

Terrance that every year her mother bought her teeth-whitening solution. He also said that Brittany wore a metal retainer when she went to sleep.

Brittany hesitated and the man she'd been talking to stepped forward. "Hey, Terrance," he said. He was white and had shaggy brown hair that reached the collar of his polo. "How's it going?"

It took a moment for Terrance to remember his name. When he remembered, he said, "Jesse – Jesse Kieschnick." He said this in a voice that was too loud.

"That's right," said Jesse, then to Brittany.

"Oh Jesse," she said, flashing him the same smile. Brittany's blouse appeared loose and thin, even though it clung to her waist. It was transparent in the back and the side where Terrance could make out her ribs. Her thinness should've been the result of malnourishment, but they weren't in Iraq and things were different here. "Let's get a beer," she said, leading him by the wrist.

"I brought my own," said Terrance. He was holding a six-pack of Abita Amber, his father's beer, but two of the cans were missing. He'd finished them on the drive over.

"Here," said Brittany, lifting the lid of an ice chest. It was full of Miller High Life and Michelob Ultra. Brittany gave him a Miller.

"Some setup you've got here," said Terrance, opening the can without setting down his Abitas. He looked for Jesse, who hadn't followed them to the ice chest, and when Brittany didn't reply he said, "What's up with Jess?"

"Jesse? What do you mean?"

Terrance turned to where they'd been standing but Jesse had slipped off to a further group. They were gathered around a pair of neatly arranged hay bales, standing and talking like adults. "I dunno," he said. His jacket was on and he began to sweat. "Seemed weird."

"Oh, that?" she said. "He majored in international studies."

"He what? —"

"But I'm sure you'll want to mingle," said Brittany. She was looking at the entrance where the group from outside had just walked in. "I bet you haven't seen most of these people in years."

"Like you," said Terrance.

"Me? But I saw you just the other day!" She patted his arm and laughed. "I'll leave you to it, darling. Let me know if you need anything."

Brittany crossed over to the group from outside. There were three of them, all men and all dressed like out-of-towners. When Brittany walked up to them she went to the one that was tall and wore skinny jeans. Terrance lifted the beer in his hand. It was cold and when he drank it the taste was sharp and biting. He took off his jacket, and his shirt stuck to his back. Still, he was much cooler now and the beer made him more comfortable. It helped that, except for the group from outside, most of the faces scattered around the barn were familiar. But when Brittany didn't return and nobody else approached him, Terrance set out to find Ricky Lang.

"There he is!" said Ricky. "Terrance MacElvaney."

He came from a side of the barn where bales of hay lined the wall and people were gathered around a heat lamp. "See, I told you he'd show." Ricky was talking to a girl that trailed him. The girl following Ricky was tall with dark skin and wavy black hair. "Didn't I tell you he'd show? I told you he'd show."

Ricky was Asian-Canadian, and often said things that didn't fit. "Terrance," he said. "This is my girlfriend, Mariana."

Terrance set down the Abitas to greet her. She was taller than him, and her fingers wrapped around his entire hand. "Great," he said with a smile. Then it was quiet and he didn't know what to say so he nodded at the speakers on the loft above them. "Some setup they've got."

"No joke," said Ricky. "Brittany's turned this barn into a vintage nightclub. She's taken the 'field' right out of 'field party.'" He laughed and then shook his head. "She's an event planner now. You know that?"

Brittany was still flirting with the strangers by the entrance. Just then she was being lifted at the waist from behind, screaming and thrashing about. The one holding her wore jeans that clung to his legs. He was lanky and when he set her down they were both laughing.

"That's how they met," said Ricky. "Band from Chicago. Brittany hired 'em for a company retreat. Her father's company. Apparently, they've got a gig in New Orleans next week. God knows why they're passing through this shithole." Then he made a circle with one hand and poked through it with the other.

"And on that note," said Mariana. She turned and walked back to their group by the wall.

Ricky watched her go. "Something else, isn't she?" he said.

Terrance thought her legs were too long for her body, but he was looking mostly at Ricky. When they were in high school, Ricky'd had the tendency to obsess over women to the point of physical illness. He once showed Terrance an entire notebook filled with writing about a girl he'd never spoken to. Eventually, he asked her to homecoming. She agreed, they kissed at the dance, and he never spoke to her again.

"Is she from Clayton?"

"Mariana?" said Ricky, turning back. "Shit no. She's international, doing her post-grad at LSU. Half-German, half-Gibraltarian."

"Gibraltarian?"

"Yeah, that island outside of Spain. Between Spain and Africa."

"Gibraltar."

"That's where the exotic look comes from. She's worldly, you know?" He didn't seem to notice the correction, watching Brittany cross the barn to join their old classmates. She began talking to a man that Terrance recognized when Ricky said, "Hey! Mark Chalupski's over there. You remember Mark?"

Terrance shrugged.

"He was asking about you," said Ricky. "I mean, I told him you might come to the party and he asked what you'd been up to."

"That's nice."

"I told him to ask you himself," said Ricky. "He thought you were off working on an oil rig this whole time. I told him, 'Don't you have Facebook?' I told him, 'That guy's been off fighting a war. He's been fighting the war in Afghanistan—"

"Iraq," said Terrance.

"That's right, Iraq. 'He's been off fighting the war in Iraq. He hasn't had time for our—"

Terrance finished his beer. The bottom of it was warm and tasted like water from an unwashed canteen, so he switched back to the Abitas. This was warm, too, but the taste was better.

"Let's go say hi," said Ricky. He grabbed a few beers from the ice chest and swayed a bit when he walked. When they came up to the group, he introduced Terrance as an Iraq war hero.

There were three others after Brittany moved on. Mark Chalupski, a girl named Sarah—who Ricky began flirting with—and Mariana. Terrance had gone to middle school with Sarah. He remembered her reputation for watching horror movies on mute. She couldn't handle the sounds of suspense, and she always sat cross-legged during the movies because she was afraid of someone grabbing her ankle. She was sitting that way now, even though there was nothing to be scared of.

Sarah and Mark said hello to Terrance and welcomed him home and asked cordial questions about his life since the war. In turn, Terrance asked them questions about their degrees and work and lives since high school. It was all very cordial and after a while there were more people in the circle all talking like adults. Terrance sat on a hay bale that was too stiff, like it had been made for sitting on. But he stuck his legs out and let his back slouch into a comfortable lean. He enjoyed hearing about Mark's work as a business analyst for an IT services company. He made it sound very important and difficult. Sarah was an accounts manager for a New Orleans manufacturer and when Ricky, who was finishing a master's in urban Developmental Planning, said that he was unemployed, Terrance laughed. Nobody asked about his job clerking for Miles' Liquor Store, but he was glad about that and he was comfortable.

The only unsettling bit was where everyone stayed. It was strange to think that he was living with his parents again, but it was even stranger to think that many of them didn't even live in Clayton: that they might be visiting for the holidays, sleeping in hotels or guest rooms. *Where do they live?* Terrance wondered. *Do they own apartments? Do they have roommates?* But it was warm, and he was enjoying himself. Then Ricky was sitting on a bale between Sarah and Mark and he turned to the group and said, "Hey, Terrance, tell us a war story."

Everyone went silent. Nobody had brought up the war, yet. It had been avoided as a topic for conversation so that when Ricky said the word "war" he might as well have pointed at Terrance's right leg. But Terrance wasn't fazed.

He kept his legs in front of him, laughed and said, "C'mon, Ricky. Nobody wants to hear that stuff."

"Sure we do." Ricky stood up and moved behind Terrance. "It doesn't have to be depressing or anything. Just a story from the war." His hand clapped Terrance's shoulder and he smiled down at him, eyes wide and gleaming. "Tell us something *crazy* that happened."

"Crazy?" said Terrance, but Mark and Sarah and everyone else in the group were all waiting. Mark sat on the edge of his bale and Jesse, who'd been ignoring him the whole night, had moved to the edge of the group and was tilting his head.

"Okay, something crazy," Terrance said. He laughed and tapped his boot, but the prosthetic grating sound made his mind empty. "Like, *crazy*-crazy? Or just cool-crazy."

"Nah man, nothing heavy," said Ricky. He walked over and stood by Mariana, who was sitting alone to one side. "It doesn't have to be anything heavy. Don't kill the buzz or anything. Just something different. Tell us about something *crazy* that happened."

"Sure," said Terrance, "great." He pinched the hay between his legs, took a gulp of beer and thought first about the homeless boys that would get picked up by older men in cars, only to be returned later in the day. It was something different, something none of them would've heard about, but then he remembered they were at a party, that this was a depressing story and that, really, it wasn't much of a story at all. So, he considered the time that Cinnabon, their SAW gunner, shat himself behind a .50 cal at the firing range. That happened after his second straight meal of seafood kabsa, even though all their COs had warned them about the seafood. But that story would make the girls cringe and civilians didn't laugh about shitting as much. He finally settled on the EFP attack because nobody would know about EFPs and because it was one of the few stories he had where nobody got hurt.

"Okay, I've got one," he said, opening a second beer. It took him a moment because his hand was shaking. "It was right after my platoon switched over to QRF duty—"

"QRF duty?" said Sarah. She was small and pretty and tilted her head when she spoke.

"QRF is short for Quick Reaction Force," said Terrance. Everyone nodded their heads, but their eyes were too wide. "We'd respond to small arms fire or IEDS going off outside of our FOB in Iraq." Now the head nodding had stopped, so he said, "IEDs are Improvised Explosive Devices—bombs—and an FOB is a Forward Operating Base. Our FOB was about a hundred miles south of Baghdad off of MSR Tampa."

Terrance was sweating. He'd lost his train of thought and most everyone had their eyes narrowed or heads tilted to the side. "Basically," he said, and he took a deep breath. "Basically my Humvee—my truck—was leading a patrol through some nearby villages. These were tiny villages, real small, the type where if you got out and talked to the families they'd invite you in for dinner. So there were these kinds of villages and the people were friendly, but all we had to do was drive a kilometer up the road and bullets would start flying."

Ricky laughed at this and when Terrance looked up, he could see the party was congregating around him. "We avoided that area. I don't know why that area was so rough. We called it Hatersville and we'd drive through it just to get them shooting at us."

"You'd go there *because* somebody would shoot at you?" said Mark.

"Sure. That's how we knew who the bad guys were." Terrance felt good about this answer. He took another pull from his drink and smiled. "But we weren't driving through Hatersville that day. We were in a friendly village nearby, and on our drive back we got hit by an EFP. An EFP," he said, "is an explosively formed penetrator. Basically, regular IEDs weren't getting through the armor on our Humvees anymore, so the bad guys designed a copper cone that they'd put in these cylinder tubes packed with explosives. When it went off, the copper melted and shot out like a plasma dart. If they did it right, it could penetrate all of the armor we had."

"No *shit*," said Ricky. His hands were on Mariana's shoulder, but he was leaning forward and his eyes were locked on Terrance. Mariana was locked on Terrance, too. Everybody was locked on Terrance and, as he told the story, Terrance began to feel the story inside of him. He could see it unfolding and he was confident in the way he was telling it. It was a good story and it was the right story for this party.

"We're driving back from this village," he said, shifting to the edge of the bale. "We're about four clicks from the FOB, driving down. I remember we could see Tower Twelve—the northwest tower of our base—and it's this image I'll never forget: that tower and the open road. Because when I try to remember after that, when I try to remember what happened, everything goes black."

"Oh my god," said Sarah. "Is that how—?"

She glanced down and Terrance flinched.

"No," he said, pulling back his leg. "Nobody got hurt that day. Well, my driver's eardrum burst. And this embedded journalist in the backseat started crying." He tried to laugh but his voice cracked, so he talked over it. "But what happened was they set it off too early. The insurgents, whoever set off the bomb, they set it off too early. It entered the wheel hub assembly and exited the top part of our engine block. I remember our truck slowing down. I remember yelling at my driver to keep going—you know, to get clear of the kill zone—I had a new driver who might've froze up, but he told me the truck wouldn't go, that it was disabled. I never bothered with hearing protection, so everything was ringing in a vacuum of noise. I can't remember if I heard him or if I just read his lips. I must've heard something because I remember calling in a status report and hearing my CO call back; I just can't remember what he said. Then we were bailing out of the truck. Everything was on fire—"

"So crazy," said Ricky.

"The EFP had set everything on fire. I told the crew to evacuate, I gave the order. I remember thinking to myself, 'Man, this fire is really spreading.' You know, there are things you'd like to do when you evac your truck. There's a protocol. But all I could do was grab my M4 and this little beanie baby we kept on our hood for good luck. Then I was out, and we began clearing the area.

"But the crazy part," he said, and Terrance could feel the hairs standing on the back of his neck, "the thing that really gives me chills when I think back to it is how when it happened, how right after the bomb went off—"

"Alright everybody, listen up!"

Terrance stopped. Brittany Bloomsbury was standing on a hay bale in the center of the barn and the group surrounding Terrance turned to face her. "I did it," she said, beaming. "I convinced our guests, 'David Sands and the Bourbon Brothers,' to play us a few of their songs!"

Brittany clapped her hands and there was some applause. Most of the people around Terrance began turning in their seats to face the musicians. One of the band members had a guitar and was pulling out a banjo and bongo drum.

"I'm so happy they're going to play!" said Sarah. She and a few others in Terrance's group stood up to move closer. Only Mariana still faced him. Her brown eyes watched him and bore into Terrance to the point that he threw back the rest of his beer and opened another. When he looked again, she was watching Ricky. Ricky was watching Brittany, and Brittany was watching the band. Nobody was watching Terrance anymore, and he was glad for this except for his story. But it was early in the night and it was warm, and he would have plenty of time to finish telling it.

The musician in the tight jeans was the singer. The others tuned their instruments while he cracked a joke about being in "banjo country." His voice was loud and confident, and people laughed when he spoke. He might've been practicing, testing to see which jokes would land in New Orleans, but he finished tuning his guitar in silence. When they were ready, he said, "We're only going to play a few for you guys. We don't want to hog the limelight." There were protests from Brittany and a few others, but Terrance was relieved. "This is a song about a girl I knew in Illinois," said the singer. "I still talk to her, even to this day." He'd started playing guitar so that the words were like a beginning to the song. Then the Bourbon Brothers came in and the music was slow and calm and not too loud.

The song was alright. The lyrics were trying too hard, but the music was alright. Terrance just couldn't place it. Their style wasn't folk, but it had an acoustic twang; it wasn't rock, but it had a pulse to it. He wasn't sure if it sounded more Austin or Nashville, or if that even mattered anymore, but by the end of the song he could tell that the band was alright.

During the next one, their lyrics got drowned out. The band had no microphones and their instruments were louder, and when the tall, skinny one sang he held the notes for a long time without articulating between. During the fourth song, Terrance set the timer on his phone to twenty-four seconds and watched it wind down. It took a long time. David Sands went through a full chorus and Terrance almost finished his beer, but the song went on. Terrance set the timer again, but his mind was on the war and he couldn't stay seated any longer. Everyone else was sitting quiet and listening, but Terrance had finished his beer too quickly and, though he had one amber left at his feet, he decided to stand up and get a beer from the ice chest. He walked across the barn and, after he took out a Michelob Ultra, he let the lid of the ice chest fall. It thudded shut in the middle of a rest and the noise cut into their song. The band played over him, but Brittany Bloomsbury and Sarah and a few others shot him disapproving looks. Brittany even narrowed her eyes, as though he'd done it on purpose. Terrance raised his shoulders with the beer in one hand and shrugged.

When the band finished, everyone clapped. "Alright, that's enough from us," said the singer. He lowered his guitar and appeased the protests by saying that they might play again later, but that it was enough "for now."

Terrance was glad. He went back to his seat on the hay bale where he had been telling his story, but now the group was split and most of the people were talking with members of the band. Terrance sipped his beer and thought that he was comfortable to sit and sip alone, but after a while he felt outcast sitting that far away and by himself so he stood up and found Ricky and Mariana talking with David Sands by the loft.

"Terrance, come here," said Ricky. "Come and meet the band."

Terrance walked up and shook the tall one's hand. "You must be David," he said.

The singer smiled. He had a dark stubble along his jaw that bled into his neck when he spoke. "Call me Dave," he said.

"Okay. Are those your drinking buddies?" Terrance nodded at the two Bourbon Brothers, but nobody laughed.

"Terrance is just back from Iraq," said Ricky.

Dave's eyebrows went up. "When did you get back?"

Terrance shrugged. "A while ago, I guess."

"Well, thank you for your service," said Dave. Then he laughed and said, "I bet it gets old, hearing that."

"Hearing what?"

But Dave was already asking him about Iraq, and what he did there. Then he asked, "Which place is hotter?"

Terrance shook his head. "What do you mean?"

"You know, Louisiana or the Middle East. Because I've been to NOLA during the summer and it's an actual sauna."

Ricky laughed and even Mariana grinned, but Terrance didn't flinch. "Iraq," he said, and the laughter stopped. "Iraq is hotter."

Dave looked at Ricky. "Well," he said, "good to know."

They stood awkwardly for a time. Then Brittany swept in and dragged David Sands away by the arm. "You've *got* to come and meet Sarah. She's been nagging for an introduction all night..."

It was better with just Ricky and Mariana, except that Terrance didn't know what to do if they asked him to finish his story. He could try to gather everyone else first, but then he wasn't sure if he wanted to finish it at all, considering he hadn't really wanted to tell the story in the first place. Ricky had cornered him, and he had been forced to come up with something on the spot. Now Terrance only wanted to finish his story if somebody asked him to.

"Mariana, darling," said Ricky. He kissed his girlfriend on the cheek. "Can you grab me another beer? I just finished mine."

"Of course, *darling*," said Mariana, exaggerating a southern drawl. Then she walked away, and Ricky followed her with his eyes.

"Isn't she great?" he said.

"Sure," said Terrance, but he was thinking about his story. "You think anybody wants to hear the rest of that story I was telling?"

"The rest of it? I'm pretty sure you finished it."

"Yeah. Actually, I never got to the crazy part—"

"Man, if that wasn't the crazy part," said Ricky. "I don't think I can *handle* the crazy part."

Terrance laughed and said, "No, it's not like that. It's not crazy in that way. It's just weird-crazy, because when I got out of the Humvee—all of us, everybody, we were okay—but it was after we got out, that—"

He was about to tell the last part of his story when Ricky held up a hand and said, "You wanna know crazy? You wanna know something *really* crazy?"

Terrance followed Ricky's gaze and saw that he was talking about Mariana. "I mean, other than how gorgeous and smart and exotic she is," said Ricky, twisting the neck of his beer. "No," he said. "You wanna know what really gets me?"

Terrance didn't know. He was confused how they went from his story to talking about Mariana.

"It's how tragic she is."

"Tragic?"

"*Tragic*," said Ricky. "I mean, this girl – she's like a character from a television series. Her dad died when she was little; her mom's an alcoholic; and she told me on our first date that her last boyfriend hit her. Can you believe that?" he said. There was an excited gleam in his eye. "I mean, she left him right afterward. But can you believe that? How tragic is that?"

Terrance had no answer. He shook his head and was silent.

Mariana never came back with Ricky's beer, and after Ricky left to join a different group Terrance began orbiting the party. Conversations washed over him. Some groups welcomed him in, others didn't. At one point he heard the word Iraq and when he turned there was Brittany Bloomsbury, Jesse Kieschnick, and David Sands in a small group. Jesse had just finished talking and now Dave was saying, "Our soldiers in Iraq are just spawning the next generation of extremists. If not for our occupation of the Middle East—" but then Brittany whispered in his ear and they all turned toward Terrance. He knew that they saw him looking, and he heard Dave say, "Ah, shit," but Terrance's face was already red. He thought how angry he should be, but all he wanted to do was leave. Then Brittany was at his arm chattering platitudes and leading him to a group where Sarah and Mark and a few of their ex-classmates were sitting and talking about football. "Here's a spot," she said, and when he sat down her eyes lingered on his ankle where the jeans came up and the fiberglass showed. "You need another beer? I'll get you another beer."

His group was talking about football, but Terrance was too hot, too embarrassed and humiliated, to join their conversation. He sat on the outside of the group thinking about what David Sands had said and about the idea of it, the idea of some band coming to *his* party, uninvited, and throwing their liberal views around. He wanted to get back at them, at Brittany Bloomsbury and Jesse and David Sands, and so he inched himself back into the conversation. Terrance waited for somebody to ask him about his story, to ask him if he would finish it, but they were all too drunk. If he wanted to finish it, he would have to say something himself. And while he hadn't wanted to tell any stories before, now he felt that he had to, that the only way he could take back the party was by finishing his story. He decided to interject the moment the conversation lagged.

"You know what?" he was going to say. He was going to say it the moment there was a pause, but as if he'd thought of it right there on the spot. "You know what?" he'd say. "I never finished that story you guys wanted me to tell." He was going to say it like that, like the thought had just come to him. And when the moment finally came, when the conversation skidded to a halt and nobody was filling the space, Terrance wet his lips and began to speak.

The words caught in his throat. Mark had been mid-thought about LSU's quarterback problem when the music came in. Then he and everybody else in the group turned toward a side of the barn where David Sands, the singer, sat on a chair strumming his guitar. He was playing by himself, with Brittany Bloomsbury and a few others sitting cross-legged before him. The Bourbon Brothers were somewhere else in the barn, probably listening, too, and David Sands

21

was in the middle of a small group playing the guitar by himself. He was playing chords and licks at first, but after everybody got quiet and the whole barn was listening, he wet his lips and began to sing.

His voice was softer now. And even though he didn't have a country voice, the guitar gave him a folksy sound. It was a soothing song, and Terrance listened with reluctance. The words were clearer than before. The guitar by itself was soft and complimented the lyrics. Alone, they went:

"And if the truth were discovered,

who would be better for it?

Not the stars, like chalk dust smeared

across the open sky.

And if the truth were discovered,

what would you want from it?

Not more than peace, for to be alone

is the only real thing."

The lyrics were good. Better than any of their other songs and, as David Sands played the bridge, it occurred to Terrance that the man singing before them might be a good man—that he probably was a good man—and that there might even be a sad truth in what he'd said about Iraq.

The whole party had congregated around the singer and Terrance was left alone with this thought, so he went looking for Ricky Lang. He found him standing on the outside of the group. "This guy," said Terrance.

Ricky's eyes were narrow like he was squinting at a bright light. "He must get so much tang," he said.

"Can you believe him, though?" said Terrance. "Playing music all the time, like we're at one of their gigs."

"Yeah," said Ricky, swaying so that he almost fell over. "But that's kinda the point, id'n it?"

Terrance stiffened. "What do you mean?"

"The whole point of the party," he said. When he saw Terrance was confused, he laughed. "Brittany heard about their show in NOLA and told'em to pass through. Moved her dad's car collection, brought in these hay bales. She even covered the pavement up." He kicked at the ground and exposed the floor underneath. "She planned this thing weeks ago. Been creamin for those guys to come through."

Terrance couldn't speak. He was struggling even to breath, and the sweat was beading down his back in bullets. He tried to be cool, to wait for the end of the song and walk away slowly, but then a Michelob Ultra slipped out of Ricky's hand and fell to the floor. The bottle made a cracking sound when it struck, breaking at the neck. They watched it spill onto the hay-covered concrete. "Oops," said Ricky, and Terrance turned for the door.

Outside the air went deep into his chest. The cold of it was in the pores on his face and in his eyes. The stars came into focus like a thousand nails puncturing oblivion, and guitar chords filtered through the wallboards. Behind him was Mariana, leaning against a side of the barn.

"Looks like you could use one of these," she said, exhaling a stream of smoke. In her hand was a cigarette.

"It's nothing," said Terrance, moving beside her. "You got anything else? I'm trying to quit."

Mariana smiled. Her teeth were straight but stained. "So am I," she said. It took Terrance a moment to recognize the smell, and another to realize it wasn't a cigarette in her hand.

Mariana pulled a second joint out of her pocket. It was in a rolled-up Ziploc bag that she had to open before handing it to him. Then she handed him a lighter. "Ricky doesn't like it."

"There are worse things."

"True," she said. She dropped the butt of her roach and smeared it in the dirt with her shoe. Her trainers were pink and white, and after Terrance looked at them, he saw that she was motioning for the joint. He was still trying to light it. "Let me," she said. "You're going to waste it."

Terrance handed her the joint and the lighter. He'd only smoked weed a handful of times in his life, and that was before the war and generally from a bong. When Mariana took the joint, Terrance watched her take a sharp pull with the flame of the lighter right off the tip. It flared up and she handed it back to him, releasing smoke.

"So, you and Ricky," said Terrance.

"Me and Ricky."

Terrance waited and she said, "I know what you're thinking, but he's not so bad."

"I know," said Terrance. "I think Ricky's great."

"He's not so bad. He's a good guy. It just gets old," she said, "being an expat."

"A what?"

"Expatriate—a foreigner—it gets lonely. Ricky, he can be kind."

Terrance took a pull from the joint. He took a small pull because it had been a while and he didn't want to cough in front of Mariana.

"It's just when we come here," she said, "when we stay with his parents and come to these parties that he turns into a complete asshole."

Terrance was holding the hit, and when he laughed, he coughed as well. "Well," he said, "I guess everybody's an asshole in their hometown."

He'd no idea what he meant by this, but it hung in the air with the smoke and they watched it. Then Mariana took the joint from his hand and said, "What's that make you, then?"

Terrance paused. "I dunno, an expat?" he said. "Either that or an asshole."

They stood against the barn and although the floodlights were above them it was a clear night and they could see the stars. Mariana took a hit from the joint. She let it out slowly so that the smoke mixed with the steam in her breath. Afterward she said, "Your story."

She said this casually and Terrance didn't think he heard her right.

"Your story," she said again. "You never finished it."

Mariana's fingers were long and pinched the back of the joint. Her legs were crossed at the ankles, and even though she was slumped against the barn she was taller than him. The weed was in Terrance's head and he looked at her without turning away. She wasn't the most attractive woman at the party, but now that she was watching him Terrance could see that there was something beautiful about the way in which she stood against the barn in the harsh light.

"You don't want to hear that," he said.

Mariana shrugged. "Not if you don't want to tell me."

Terrance chewed his lip. "It was nothing," he said. "Just a story for a party." He took the joint from her and when she didn't speak, he said, "I don't know. It's just that when the EFP hit—there are radios and they record things; they record everything—but after the bomb went off, there are twenty-four seconds that I can't account for." He pulled from the joint and the smoke tingled in the back of his throat, but he swallowed it down. "There was a half-minute between the EFP and when I gave the orders to evac. Twenty-nine seconds. But in my mind," he said, "in my mind there's only five seconds, maybe less. A few seconds for me to gather my bearings. You know, evaluate the situation, take in my surroundings. A few more to give the command. But the rest of it, the other twenty-four—"

The music inside picked up and a few chords slipped through the wood. "So you blacked out?" said Marianna.

"Well, no," he said. "The radio, they record us. They record everything. And I listened to it later." He paused. "I was there. It's not like I was coherent, but I was talking— chanting, even—just, not giving orders. It was my voice, but it wasn't me."

Mariana shifted beside him. He could feel her eyes on him.

"It's just weird," he said. He was looking at the sky, but he wasn't really looking at anything. "How does that happen? Where did I go?"

Mariana didn't answer. The question hung between them and the spot where his knee met the prosthetic began to tingle. Mariana shifted and Terrance felt her lean into him. He'd left his jacket inside somewhere, but her body was warm where it touched his and their hands brushed. At some point the music stopped and they stayed that way, the joint in Terrance's other hand burning. The smolder of it reached his fingers and he felt himself go stiff. The roach dropped. It bounced off of his boot and sparked like a dying star, shriveled in the cold grass.

RECONCILIATION

We're standing outside of the Kabul International Airport in Afghanistan, a universally recognized "Area of Conflict," but there's little to indicate a war here. Instead, two Afghani bellboys shuffle between the vehicles before us. They're spindly and unarmed—maybe twenty years old—but they're supposed to be escorting us to the Serena Hotel. Our ride is a pair of SUVs that are considerably lighter than the armored HMMWVs I remember from my deployment, and propped against the cars are two poster-board signs that read, "RECCA VI CONFERENCE" in block, sharpied text.

I'm with nine other Americans. We all met at a connection in Dubai, where most of them procured badges with their names and titles. They are correspondents from journals, analysts from investment companies, bureaucratic representatives, academics, historians, economists. It's a muddled bunch, and even the toxic smell of duty-free cologne can't mask the BO trapped beneath our blazers. I'm outcast enough for coming from a small brokerage firm in Minneapolis, but I'm also the only war veteran and now they've got me in the front seat talking to our driver.

"The Serena Hotel is very close to the Ministry of Foreigners," says the driver. He means the Ministry of

Foreign Affairs—where the sixth Regional Economic Cooperation Conference on Afghanistan (RECCA) is being held—but for this weekend, at least, his description is spot on. A maze of barricaded checkpoints litters our drive out of the airport. "We will provide security from hotel to ministry and back. This should not worry you."

Everyone in the back nods along, reassured, but I've got a knot in my gut because a.) there's no .50 cal mounted on our roof, and b.) I'm planning to visit our old terp, Akbar. I hadn't figured out the logistics of that venture, yet, but subverting conference security would be an added hurdle.

"I thought it'd be hotter," says one of the correspondents. Somebody else agrees and they laugh nervously. A whistle of tension leaves the car, and I don't mention that it's September, or that Kabul is 6,000 feet above sea level. Afghanistan in their minds is an extension of Iraq and the Middle East. A giant desert, all scorching, all the time. I wonder what they'd have thought if we arrived in winter, during the rainy season. Water spilling down their backs, rolling their suitcases through ankle-deep puddles of slosh and mud and shit.

They've got their reasons for being here, and I've got mine: nostalgia, my debt to Akbar. I glance into the rearview mirror and catch the Chicago Tribune journalist with his iPhone pressed against the plexiglass. He catches my eye and his face goes red, but he keeps the phone steady, filming the roadside and alleyways of Kabul City in profile, no less. During our two-hour delay in Dubai, I'd overheard him boast about edging out three older journalists for a spot at this conference. I suppose that's abnormal behavior, but I knew guys who chased a year in the Korengal Valley over sunbathing in California. Then, after their tour was done and they'd bitched all the way home, they went back and did it again. Sergeant Strange, Jesse Pink, even Rosco signed up for another tour. And now—after calling them all lunatics—here I am, back again.

The driver turns on his wipers to sweep dust off the windshield. The dry squeaking sound makes my insides curl. A film of dust coats everything here. It leaks through the AC vents, drying the air and carrying me farther away from Minneapolis and the stagnated brokerage firm I'm supposed to be representing. They'd no intention of sending a rep to the RECCA VI—they hadn't even heard of it—but after I confirmed it was on, and after digging up Akbar's contact info in my old war journal, I pitched a load of statistics to my boss about development and investment opportunities that they couldn't ignore. The only problem is, I pitched it too well. See, I really wanted this—I made a PowerPoint for my presentation, referenced peer-reviewed journals, I even brought up my 2005 deployment and a few personal experiences—but in a firm like mine, it's a huge deal to fly someone out to an international conference. Especially when that conference is in Kabul. So my boss, he decided to make a thing of it. He picked a coworker of mine, a kid named Russell, to assess risks and take notes and, more or less, to make sure they got their money's worth.

Russell's the guy who gets nominated for all of the shitty jobs. He smiles and nods during his brief, and even after the shit's over he won't admit how much it sucked. He got his masters from somewhere like Midwestern, and his starting salary was higher than mine after I'd worked for that company ten years. All he knew how to do was work: efficiency, numbers, algorithms. When I heard he was coming, I naturally wanted to cancel. Not because they were sending him to babysit me, but because they were expecting me to babysit him. This was Afghanistan, after all. Russell was possibly the least equipped man they could send, in terms of survivability. But I was well past the point of no return. I'd even reached out to a friend at Immigration for Akbar, and there was our history to think about. I couldn't abandon him again.

My eyes glaze over the brown murk of the Kabul River. It's lined with trash. Across the river, men in robes and women in chadors, firaqs, drift from market to market. They disappear under storefronts and emerge from the next. The buildings are dusky and rundown, temporary looking, like old photographs of the White City from the world's fair but in a desert instead of Chicago. Everything is surprisingly intact.

A guy in the back seat says something to this end, like he's surprised there are buildings at all. Tall and glassy structures loom ahead of us. They're not the skyscrapers of Dubai or Manhattan, but they're modern and frail looking: impractical in a city haunted by shrapnel. Not that everything is clean and modern, but I struggle to recall shimmering glass walls from my tour, 14 years ago. I'd the impression that everything not broken or under construction would resemble a soviet-era bomb shelter more than a commercial-looking business park. A part of me was tempted to measure that as progress, but our FOB had been on the outskirts of the city. The only thing out there were villages and dirt roads, and when we weren't retracing patrol routes we were sitting on our asses looking at the inside of a concrete wall.

The war at that point was a lot like working two fulltime jobs, only the pay was shit and there were mortars. The two "jobs" were Patrol and OP. Patrol consisted of walking or driving around the desert for hours on end, while OP consisted of standing, lying or sitting at an observation post somewhere along the FOBs perimeter. Every now and then we'd get a mission, and this might replace our patrol shift but usually it just ran into our off time.

Granted, we got room and board and all of that cost-of-living shit – but we were sleeping on mats in concrete bunkers with rats and tarantulas for company. The food we ate was the same MRE every goddamn meal until the next bulk shipment came in, and our time off was mostly spent on personal maintenance: clean your kits, call your families, write letters, go to the gym, take a shower, eat food, and then—if there was time—sleep. Hence the Rosco Effect.

Rosco was a grunt in my squad who, during our first month in country, got prescribed Dexedrine for his exhaustion. He was a small guy already, but we gave him so much shit for taking meds that he switched to Monster Energy drinks. Afterward, staying awake became less of a problem for Rosco than falling asleep. By the end of our tour, he was crushing four or five cans before lunchtime. At five bucks a pop, I even wonder if amphetamines would've been cheaper.

We all needed something to keep us going. For me it was nicotine. I went through a pack of Marlboro Reds a night before I met Akbar. It kept me awake during OP, which was clutch because, in the words of Jesse Pink, "If Sergeant Strange catches you asleep on OP, you're more fucked than a pornstar in a gangbang." As part of their "training," Afghani National Army guards were paired with grunts for OP. Most ANAs couldn't speak a lick of English, and a lot of the guys didn't trust them. Like Rosco. The ANAs were harmless, really. Most of them just wanted to work, and while they didn't get paid much through the Afghani Army, they still got paid; which was a lot, considering we came in and blew up most of their jobs and industry.

Akbar was one of those guys. I remember his lanky walk, thinking he was tall for a local. It made him look stretched, like one of the local teenagers, kicking torn-up soccer balls down the street. It didn't help that every time he held a rifle he looked about as uncomfortable as our squad leader, Sergeant Strange, looked holding his six-month-old daughter. But Akbar spoke English well enough, and he was curious.

I don't remember how our talks began—I don't even remember when I could pick out his face in a lineup—but he'd always initiate the conversation with the same two words. "Salaam, Nathan," except he'd accent the second "a" in my name, instead of the first. I can still hear the way he said it, even as we pull into a security checkpoint at the Serena Hotel. "Salaam, Nethaan."

The barrel of a carbine taps against our driver's window. There's a guard in desert camo with a rifle sling around his shoulder. Behind him is a turreted Humvee—a relic from the American withdrawal, no doubt—but at least there's security at this hotel.

We pull through the checkpoint and climb a shaded road to the hotel entrance. Pillars of granite and a pair of brass doors mark the hotel's porte-cochère. Oak trees and looming pines replace the barren twigs that passed for trees along the Airport Highway, and bleached asphalt turns to rich, tropical gardens. Ferns spill onto stone pathways, dripping with mist from the sprinklers.

Our vehicle rocks to a halt and the driver slams his door behind him, jumping out to unload our luggage. We're still lodged in our seats, though. None of us expected the reality of this hotel to match its 5-star brochure. Even I am stunned into silence, gaping at the lavishness of this western palace, hidden within the cracked shell of Kabul.

I climb out with my duffle bag and shift past all the men waiting for the bellboys to unload their rolling wardrobes. The hotel has a massive lobby, and there, standing in the middle of a granite foyer, as if he were my assigned chaperon, stands Russell Corrigan.

"Nathan!" he says, jumping at the sight of me. The soprano pitch of his voice clangs across the foyer as he darts forward. At just 30 years, Russell looks as though he's skipped the filling-out process of adulthood. Almost every time that he joins our team for a drink, he gets ID'd. His small, rounded face is shaven and moisturized, with his hair loosely cropped. The suit jacket around his collar is either a size too large, or else fitted for a larger man. Even his pants are wide, collecting at his feet in a crumple of fabric.

"I'm so glad I caught you," he says, arms wide. I reach out and hesitate, closing his arms in to grab my hand with both of his. "I've been tracking your flight all night. A two-hour delay in Dubai?" he says. "You must be wiped! But there's little time to rest. We've a pre-conference exhibition on regional trade, and nine o'clock kicks off the ministerial meeting in the Grand Hall."

He continues in that tone for a while, rambling about the conference itinerary and pausing only to check on me. My creased slacks and sagging sport coat reek of airport food and a twenty-hour journey. "You might want to change clothes, though," he says. "It's a shame you had to miss our original flight. A family emergency, you said?"—I took a later flight to avoid twenty hours with *him*— "Well, in any case, you'll be able to sleep off the jetlag tonight. I hear they'll be serving lamb curry for dinner. Do you like coffee? Of course you do. Espresso? I'll grab you a double from the bar. You check yourself in, and I'll catch you back here in five."

I manage to lock Russell out of my room and collapse onto the bed a few minutes later, but my head is still clogged. It's too much, too foreign, to be back like this. The coffered ceiling and plush master bed; it's far from the frameless mattresses of Camp Phoenix, the community showers and stifling armor that baked our body odor to a crust. Now I'm in a resort with a jacuzzi and complimentary Wi-Fi. And Russell, waiting in the lobby.

"Let's meet downstairs in—" he'd managed to say before I shut the door on him. He was giddy about forums on economic development and monetizing culture, but with everything strangely unfamiliar, it's Russell's overcaffeinated-jitters that bring me back. He reminds me of Rosco, the way he'd waddle across camp in his oversized Kevlar, the pissed-off look he'd give whenever someone called him Scrappy, or Scrapster, after the wired-up nephew of Scooby-Doo.

Rosco earned that nickname after being held at arm's length by yours truly. He swung his arms and grappled with my wrist to no avail, and to everyone around it looked like Scrappy walking in place, with Scooby's paw on his head.

We had a good-natured relationship, Rosco and I. But there moments when I pushed him too far. Like the time I instigated a "Field Fuck" that left Rosco bruised and bleeding on the ground. See, there was a running joke about my friendship with Akbar—the hypersexual bullshit that accompanies men at war—but Rosco was the only grunt to keep it up by day. "You sore?" he'd ask, swinging his arm to slap my ass. By the way his eyelid twitched, he might've been on his third, maybe fourth, energy drink of the day. "Is that why you ain't with yer butt-buddy?"

"Ew," said a grunt from the side. Even Jesse Pink, our platoon pervert, scrunched up his face.

"Sure, Scrappy," I'd say, and tell him to piss off. He wouldn't, and so I'd antagonize him to the point of breaking. Then, one day, he broke. Rosco moved in for the takedown. He didn't get far, though, as I just about flipped him on his head in the attempt. Our platoon had gathered, laughing at the spectacle, when I reared up and said, "Actually, I could use a good fuck."

What followed was a practice familiar to grunts at war, but it's nothing to be proud of. It began with me pinning Rosco to the ground and holding him there while the platoon dry-humped him into submission. A line of guys formed up behind him and, by the end of it, I almost felt bad. I had to peel Jesse Pink off after he moved up and started pumping the back of Rosco's head, pummeling his face into the dirt. The thing is, everyone knows that the best way out of a field-fuck is to pretend you were getting off to it. You've got to put on a show, to pretend like you're enjoying it more than the guys humping you. But Rosco, he'd squirm and kick until the bitter end. He handled it, though—he was a scrappy grunt, I'll give him that—and the next day he went around asking everybody if they thought Akbar and I used butt-plugs, dildos, or a combination of both.

After the ministerial meeting, we head back to the hotel and send our reports home. Then I'm flipping through the conference itinerary for a gap in tomorrow's schedule.

I'd made a point of getting Akbar's contact info before the end of our tour. I had his PO Box, his email, even his Afghani phone number all written down in the back of a half-empty journal. While there was little hope of reaching him through any of those now, I got what should've been an updated email address from his inactive Facebook page and sent him a note. He replied a few days later. "Salaam, Nathan," was his reply. "Good to hear of you. When are the days of your event?"

There's a break in the itinerary around mid-afternoon tomorrow. Some sideshow, a poster display on the history of the Silk Road that Russell wants to see. After slipping out, I could catch a ride from the hotel to Akbar's—I'd have to hash out a driver with the hotel management, probably lie about an emergency of some kind—but I shoot Akbar an email to fix the time.

Afterward, I'm sprawled out on the bed, sinking into velvet and wondering what he'll be like after all of this time. During the war, he'd been full of energy. He was nineteen when I first met him, a year younger than me, but curious like a kid. When our talks started, they were like interviews. Akbar would press me about my life in America, about our history and politics and TV shows. His English was broken at best, so I did most of the talking. He'd listen, questioning me about expressions or nuances he didn't know, and over time I told him about myself. I didn't mind it so much, then. It passed the time, talking, and I'd never had anybody so curious about my life before. I told him all about California, about my home in Bakersfield with the mountains and the coastline and the politics. I told him about my sisters, how the older one was getting a law degree and the younger was already married. I told him about my mother who was an alcoholic, and my father who'd been a gunny in the Marine Corps. One night, I told him how my father died, just two years before. "Lung cancer," I said. When I told him this, I was taking a drag from my fifth cigarette of the night, but Akbar wasn't the type to point that out. Instead, he said, "Even my father is dead."

I remember it was cloudy, but somehow his eyes were reflecting light. Out of habit, or maybe because I realized how little I knew about the guy, I asked how his father died.

"He was killed," said Akbar. "In the Civil War. We ran a bookstore at the corner of busy intersection." He pointed out at the night like the spot was a few blocks away. "There were many good books. Translations of Western stories, like the *Tom Sawyer*. And there were many famous Russian books that the Soviets left behind. Tolstoy, I remember. And Dostoyevsky." He paused, caught in the remembering. "A scud missile from the Taliban. Building falls and the rubble burns for hours. Books, my father, all gone."

It was our fourth, maybe fifth, shift together, and I still couldn't remember his name. But the bluntness of this—his delivery, and the way he spoke about tragedy like it was just shit that happened and nothing in the world could've changed it—that sparked something in me. Admiration, I think.

It happened gradually. I'd fit questions into our talks. Like, to help me remember, I asked him what his name meant. "To me," he said, "it means 'great man.' It was the name of my grandfather, a famous wrestler. They say his back never touched dirt."

As the months passed, his English improved. One night I asked why he wanted to learn English. "To become an interpreter," he explained. I cringed, because my friend in Intelligence told me how difficult that process was. The loyalty exam checked everything—family relations, education, religion, friends—for links to extremism. If his friend's brother, or the cousin of a parent, was associated with a terrorist group (which was virtually everyone), he'd get rejected. I told him to forget it. "You'd have to go into the field," I told him. "Without a weapon." I told him the terrorists would target his family and friends.

"This even I know," was his reply. "But I must first be an interpreter to live in America."

Akbar wanted a visa to enter the US. His dream was to study classic literature—the kind of shit that's impossible to read, even when English is your first language—but his aim was to return after the war and translate Western classics into Pashtu. He wanted to translate Afghani books to English, as well. "You could sell them on Amazon," I said, but he rejected that. I think underneath it all was the idea of reopening his father's bookstore. "To create a bridge," he'd say, "between your world and mine."

I'd never heard anybody talk like that before. Even with my own enlistment, it's not like I considered what difference I was making in the world, or what the military was trying to accomplish in Afghanistan. I'd signed up after dropping out of community college because it was the best option I had. Meanwhile, here was Akbar who had been beat up, knocked down, and every time came back harder than before.

I started rooting for him. I mean, it made sense to me – connecting people through culture and whatnot. Even as a soldier, I started to give a shit. I'd notice people on the street during OP. I'd look at their faces, their expressions, the way they'd interact with each other. It was all new and weird and at one point, about halfway through our tour, I remember thinking, "These people are hard." Despite sitting at rock bottom, they were trying to get their shit together. And it was my job to help them.

I roll onto my stomach in the Serena Hotel and click refresh on the laptop. There's a knot in my gut as I search for his reply. Nothing, again. After a few fruitless attempts to refresh my email, I distract myself with what he'll be like. I picture him with a Master's degree from NYU or

Princeton, with reading glasses, a bookshelf in the back of his flat long enough to fit in a public library. I'm sure he's been translating, but I wonder if he teaches. Maybe he writes, as well. The bookstore idea always seemed beneath him, but I can imagine him overseeing the business end of it.

What gets me, now—the thing that wrenches my gut each time he slips into my mind—is how he'll react. I have a way to make up for ghosting him like I did, but as I refresh my email again, to no reply, I worry that he might've changed his mind.

I wait another five minutes before I refresh it again, lying on a bed that's too soft for comfort. I almost move to the floor, but it's too early for sleep. To fight the jet lag and distract myself from the glare of my laptop, I head downstairs to the hotel bar.

It's an American crowd. Everyone not staying at the embassy is at the Serena, perhaps as an effort to redeem the hotel from a 2014 attack when a group of teenagers— alleged Taliban—walked in and killed four women and two children. Tonight there's a ridiculous amount of security. A whole platoon occupies the hotel entrance to search guests and vehicles, and the surrounding walls of the hotel are littered with sentries and barricades.

Only the bar is security-free, open to the courtyard. Light pours onto stone walkways and hidden lamps light up trees and vines. Clusters of conference delegates fill the space, sipping French wine, Long Island iced teas and bottled Budweiser. It's the "war tourism" fad, and it's lured most of them here—middle-aged men of upper-middle class—but there are also women in the crowd. Each of them is marked by a pack of fawning bystanders. Everyone should be jetlagged and worn from a day of conference lectures, but sex and the promise of living out some wartime fantasy has drawn them to the wet gleam of the bar.

I maneuver through delegates and order a beer. I haven't even considered the possibility of Russell being there, but he almost cuts me off on my way through. He squeezes himself in so close that I bump against a blazered bub beside me.

"Shit, Russell," I say, taking him in. "What're you doing?"

His hand is clutching a highball glass of Southern Comfort lemonade. The same oversized suit hangs about his neck, his eyelids drooping. "Need to stay awake," he says. "Plus, my room overlooks the courtyard. You?"

I hand the bartender a ten-dollar bill instead of answering, and he motions for more. Eleven dollars for a beer and I'm left wondering whether this is price gouging or profiteering.

"That was some first day!" says Russell. "How about that speech by the Deputy Director General! What was his name, Balagh? His vision for reconciling the economic policies of the East and West by revitalizing the tradition of the Silk Road—"

I can tell by the way Russell's arms flail that he's already half-drunk. He confirms this by stopping mid-sentence and half-yelling at the man beside us, "This isn't his first rodeo in Kabul."

He was pointing at me, and it's enough to prompt the man to look us over. "Is that right?" he says. I twist around and note the plain black V-neck beneath his blazer. He's older, mid-fifties, with a greying stubble around his jaw. "What journal do you work for?"

I shake my head. "We're with a brokerage firm out of Minneapolis."

"Clarkson and Ross," says Russell.

The man cocks his head. "What brought you here? Is one of your clients a sheik?"

It's meant as a joke, but I don't flinch and Russell doesn't get it. "No," I tell him. "I was in the infantry."

His eyebrows shoot up, and that's almost the end of it until Russell says, loud enough for the whole bar to hear, "Fought on the front lines. A true war hero!"

I'm holding beer in my mouth and trying not to cough when he decides to slap me on the back. A pack of delegates look over, and I'm immediately deflecting platitudes. "Thank you for your service," is the line of the night, racking up a half-dozen mutations.

One man steps forward to shake my hand and ask what regiment I was with. He's young and there's a kind of arrogance to him, so I tilt my head and say, "We don't have regiments in the infantry."

I watch the color in his face turn and feel guilty, but I really just wanted to drink my beer in peace. I'm also dreading that some idiot will ask the time-old question of, "Did you kill anyone," but no one does. There's a pair of women at the bar, now. The older one's short with bleached hair, and her colleague's only slightly taller, but with bangs and a business suit. She's leaning down to whisper something into the other's ear, and my eyes fall to the line in her chest.

I don't consider myself a ladies' man. I spend most of my time alone, and I had to end a three-year relationship just months earlier. But it had been a while since I'd been with a woman—in part, because of the anxiety leading up to this conference and my reunion with Akbar—and being a war veteran in a war zone, amongst a bunch of civilians and former embeds, it emboldened me.

"I was in the 4th infantry," I say. "Divisions, they're a lot like regiments." The younger man nods, and somebody follows with the question of when and where. I give my line about FOB Phoenix in '05. "We didn't have all the amenities that grunts did later in the war," I say. "There weren't internet cafes, or recreation centers, or bazaars, or any of the shuttle services they had in oh-nine. Just a bunch of blown-up shelters for barracks."

I settle into a casual spiel about the war. It's a safe one, allowing me to offer up details with few opportunities for follow-up questions. It helps that there aren't other veterans in the crowd. Not that it always turns into a cockfight, but at least I can avoid the passive aggressive exchange of rank, placement, and time served. "Was that before they brought in the CHUs to Phoenix?" Or, "You must've known Sergeant Gutierrez, then."

Nobody interrupts, though. Blazer V-neck guy buys me a lager, and I get another from the kid asking which regiment. It feels good, almost: being back in country, talking about old times. It's a performance; but it's a release, as well. I start to relax and let the moment carry me until I notice one of the women moving for the exit. She leaves her friend, who gives me a sidelong glance that might be an invitation—and it might be a "fuck off" face—but I walk up beside her to find out.

She turns on me with narrowed eyes. "So you're the war veteran," she says. Her name is Penny, and she's a trade representative from the Foreign and Commonwealth Office in London. I read all of that off her nametag, and she smiles with closed lips to say, "try harder."

I start talking about Kabul. I'm not proud of it. I'll say that right off. It's not like I talk about the desert every time I drink. As a kid, I'd listen to my father's friends talk about 'Nam. They'd tell long-winded stories about the jungle, and I'd eat up every word. After the war, though, I found myself emulating my father, his stoic stillness, a quiet kind of strong. But alcohol has the tendency to loosen my tongue, and with the exhaustion and the jet lag and switching to whiskey, I start to feel it slacking.

She asks what it was like. That's a common question, and normally I answer with the truth. "Boring as fuck," I'll say. "99% sitting on your ass, 1% action." But she's been teasing me all night, and I've the urge to change our pace. "It's," I begin, and then start over. "It's impossible to put into words."

"Ineffable," says Russell. He's managed to squeeze in beside us, despite my attempts to shoulder him out. He looks beyond drunk and somehow under the impression that I've been talking to *him* for the past thirty minutes.

And now that the crowd has thinned, he's found a way to weasel into our silences.

Russell and his endless questions carry us deep into the subject of war, and at some point I begin telling the story of the cyclist. To be honest, I'm not even sure how I got started. There're plenty of stories that would've worked better for the context. This one—with its grisly end—I've only voiced twice in my life. But Penny leans forward and once I get going it's impossible to stop. The thing flows out of me.

I start by explaining our OP shifts. "There was a wall, a pile of Hescos," I say, "and our watch post was a few meters above a traffic intersection, outside the wall. In the mornings, there would be all sorts of traffic. Pedestrians, bicycles, cars, all moving in different directions and nobody following the law." Penny nods. She's stopped interrupting me for the first time all night and I can see her weighing up the gravity of what's to come. "Then one day a car, a sedan of some sort." I say, "it clips the back tire of a bicyclist and sends the guy sprawling."

They're both in it now, but I'm not. It's like I've clicked "play" on a projector. "He gets up: the guy on the bike. He's scuffed, but fine. He starts yelling at the driver. He's upset. His bike's been totaled and there's no reliable legal system to set him straight or to make the driver pay him back, so—"

I pause for a sip of whiskey. How cool, how casual it all seems. As if I've told this story a hundred times, instead of on repeat in my head.

"He says something, the bicyclist. I don't know what. My Pashtu, it's poor at best, but it must be bad because," I pause. "Well, because the driver steps out of the car. He gets out from behind the wheel and he pulls a gun from his belt. Two shots. One goes through the kid's neck—"

Penny gasps. Russell, I can see his jaw drop. He's shocked, maybe. I don't notice because I'm not looking at them. I'm above the whole thing, looking down at it. The boy's body falling like a blanket, folding over itself. Not the way I thought that bodies would fall. Not like a tree or like somebody getting knocked over. It was the substance that left him. And what was left of his body just collapsed.

My jaw is locked, and I know I'm not speaking, but somewhere in the back of my mind I can hear command in my ear. "Don't engage," my sergeant says. "It's not our remit." The driver, meanwhile, looks up at me. I have him in my sights. I'm on the radio, but I can't. International law, local police, not my jurisdiction. The guy gets back into his beat-up sedan and drives away. He drives over the bike. Over the body, too.

Russell clears his throat. He and Penny are letting me know of my faux pas, that I've violated something—a cultural norm—by standing there in awkward silence. My head's somewhere else. Outside in the courtyard maybe, or at the city's edge.

"Some of the people," I say, because I have to say something. "The people in other cars, the line of traffic, they get out and move the bike to the side of the road. For a while, the cars drive around the body. Then a guy walks onto the road and grabs the kid by the ankles. Drags him to the curb, out of the way." I cock my head, remembering it.

"When the ANP finally show up—you know, the Afghani Police—they don't interview anybody. They don't even check with our base for descriptions or a statement. Nothing."

I don't know what else to say. Penny reaches out to touch my hand but stops short. Russell says something about the horror of it, the inhumanity. "It's nothing," I say. "Really. Shit like that happened all the time."

I throw back my whiskey. There's not enough to even wet my lips, so I set it on the bar and Russell leans forward. "Nathan," he says, as if there's more to follow. Penny takes my arm. She's pulling me. I can already tell she's the type of pretty that wears off by morning. I might even regret it— this script we've committed to—but for now it's enough that we're on a stage, surrounded by an audience of delegates and bar stools.

Penny lowers her gaze, and that's the moment Russell decides to throw himself between us. "I never knew," he says, swinging an arm. His whiskey lemonade slips from his hand, though, and it spills down the length of Penny's leg. His glass shatters on the floor and we're all left in a puddle of vodka juice.

Penny runs a hand along the fabric clinging to her leg. Her eyes go wide. She takes one step back, and then another. I've peeled Russell off of me, but Penny's already halfway to the exit, her kitten heels crunching glass. "I'm sorry," she says, wiping her pants to press out the wet. "I just… it's all down my leg."

I don't bother going after her. She's grabbed a wad of bar napkins and faded into the courtyard. I wait a few minutes to see if she'll return, but in the end it's just me helping Russell to his room.

My hangover the next morning is of the life-changing variety. I'm all used up, like I just blew two grand on a night in Vegas. But it's worse than that. I wasted a part of myself—a vulnerable part—on someone I'll never see again. And on Russell.

I didn't dream about the cyclist or the man who shot him, but I woke up thinking about Akbar because, in a sense, I'd betrayed him again. And that's likely part of my hangover, because I told the whole story like he hadn't even been there. Like he hadn't been right beside me, screaming at me to do something. After it happened, after the shooter drove off, Akbar got up and left. At the time, I assumed he was going to report it, or to help retrieve the body, but when he came back his eyes were red and swollen.

I didn't know what it meant to him. I still don't. But I know that our talks changed. I know this because I can't remember any of our talks, after that. There were three more weeks before my tour ended and looking back it's all kind of a blur. I remember a vague superstition of dying right before the end of my deployment, during our patrols to transition the replacement squad, but on my last OP shift, the last of our late night talks, I can only remember talking about myself. About what I'd do when I got home. There's hardly even the image of Akbar being there. We finished out the night and I haven't spoken to him since.

I take out my phone and connect with the hotel Wi-Fi. There's no new email, and the fear that Akbar won't reply is in my blood. I try remembering if I'd said anything in those last few weeks, if there was a reason he would flake on me now—other than the obvious—but the weeks surrounding the bicyclist are a blur. I imagine Akbar sending an apology tomorrow, reading it on my flight home: something about their internet failing, a family emergency. It tears me apart, but I force myself to set up the day like he's expecting me. I even dodge Russell in the lobby—waiting for me with an apologetic coffee—and manage to avoid him the whole morning session.

He finds me at lunch and sits down without a word. Together we pick at our plates of chicken and rice. He's embarrassed and probably aching to explain last night, but my mind is on Akbar, on our OPs beneath the stars and the red of his eyes after the bicyclist.

Akbar replies after lunch. His message contains his address and that he's "looking toward" my visit. It's a relief. No, it's more than a relief. It's my redemption. My chance to follow through with my promise to help Akbar reach the United States. A wave of adrenaline jolts me back to life, though, because now I have to follow through. I have to navigate my way across Kabul, outside the security of the conference, and in broad daylight. I manage to shake Russell on our way to the exhibition and get to the hotel concierge with no problem. The manager even accepts a "tip" for his discretion. It's only once I'm sitting on a bench outside the hotel foyer, waiting for my driver, that the whole plan goes to shit.

Russell, in a dark blue sports coat and khaki slacks, charges out of the conference shuttle. He almost runs straight past me, except that I duck into the bench and, in trying to hide, grab his attention.

"Nathan?" he says, skidding to a halt. "What're you doing out here? Penny said you went back."

I groan at the thought of him talking to Penny, but then the shuttle for the conference pulls away and Russell's left making an "oh" face.

"Are you—" he trails off.

"I'm going to meet somebody."

Russell slants an eyebrow. "A ministry official?" he says. "Somebody from the embassy?"

"A friend. From the war."

That last word hangs in the air between us.

"You're... what? Alone? What kind of friend?"

A pale blue sedan pulls up to the hotel's security checkpoint. The driver's pointing in my direction.

"Where? At least tell me *where* you're going."

"South of the river," I say. "To his home."

Russell collapses onto the bench. "Nathan," he starts, "is this about earlier?" I almost laugh, but my car's pulling into the porte-cochère and I have to flag down the driver. Russell goes red. "Look, it's not safe. There have been kidnappings!" he says, loud enough for the hotel bellboys to turn. "I'm serious, Nathan. You can't run off like this. If somebody sees you, if anybody sees you—" I climb into the backseat and look up at him. "Listen," he says, "the Bureau of Consular Affairs just issued a warning to RECCA VI delegates that bounties have been placed on our heads. *Bounties*, Nathan!"

"Don't worry," I say. "I know my way around."

Russell isn't reassured. I watch his world crumbling and wonder if it's cruel of me to leave him there with that look on his face, but I've already handed the driver a slip with the address. "Tashakor," I say, a word I picked up from my talks with Akbar. He shifts the stick into gear and, before he can accelerate or release the clutch, Russell opens the door and dives onto the seat beside me.

The driver's too distracted with security to notice, and I'm too stunned to kick him out. "What the hell're you doing?" I growl, glaring at him. I want to scold him, to tell him he's an idiot and that he should get out of the car, but the expression on his face shows an immense and immediate regret.

"I, well—" he says.

By now we're well on the road and the driver's noticed the extra passenger. He shouts something in Pashtu and, assuming he wants more money, I put a twenty-dollar bill onto the dashboard. When I pull back, Russell's looking at me with his jaw set.

"I can't let you go alone," he says. "Not outside. Not outside of *the wire*."

He says this like a videogame might announce "sudden death." I assume he's heard that phrase on CNN or Fox News, from a segment early in the war. He would've been a teenager, then. Maybe old enough to enlist. I laugh at him and the whole situation, but there's a relief mixed in and we both hear it. He's right that journalists and contractors still go missing in Afghanistan. But it's only ever the ones who leave Kabul's safe zone.

We pull out of the city center toward the Pul-e Khishti Bridge. Pedestrians swarm the bank, shuffling between tents at a trading market. There's a department store to the left and I try reading the board above the entrance, but it's in Arabic script and the sun is a blinding reflection through the aluminum. It's partly cloudy, and a few chunks of road are draped in shade. Everything else looks faded: cars, buildings, even the dust covering it all.

I turn to see if Russell's absorbing any of this, but his eyes are locked on the head cushion in front of him. His legs bounce and his hands, clamped to his knees, go white around the knuckles. He's jittering like Rosco at the end of our tour, squeezed into the middle seat of our Humvee on patrol. Rosco wasn't sleeping by that point. His paranoia woke him up every few minutes at night. Some nights, he'd refuse to sleep altogether. He'd nod off at some point, but if a draft of wind moved the hairs on his leg, he would jump up screaming "RAT!" or "SPIDER!" at the top of his lungs. We often woke up to him stomping or slamming his sleeping bag against the floor. It was the closest behavior to insanity I'd ever witnessed, and still command made him finish his tour. At least Russell, sitting beside me with his vision glazed, is mentally present. Ready to jump out of his skin, sure: but still *there*.

We cross the trash-ridden current of the Cophes. Beyond the river, buildings are falling apart. Plaster replaces stone, and ramps of plywood lead over puddles to apartment doors. The quality of housing, I realize, won't improve the further south we go. Akbar shouldn't be living like this. Not in this poverty. I pull out my phone to track our path on my GPS.

Our blue dot inches past the pin I'd placed in my GPS. The driver isn't taking us to Akbar.

Russell's warning ricochets across my head: "Bounties. Kidnappings." Our driver wears his hair swooped to the side, a black fuzz lining his jaw. The hotel must've conducted a background check on him, especially during a week like this. Besides, what driver would want a lump-sum reward over job security? Unless...

The realization catches in my throat.

Unless it were personal.

My mind churns through the endless incentives a driver could have for turning us over—his family could've been killed by a drone strike; the Taliban are holding his daughter hostage; a terrorist took his place, and the real driver is tucked away in the trunk, bound up or already dead—I'm trying to appear calm, but Russell's watching and can sense my agitation. I go to smile but my face tightens, and I turn to take in air. I wish now that I had kicked him out of the car when I had the chance.

Blood rushes to my head, and I have to lean forward to catch my breath, massaging my temples with two fingers. The fabric of the seat has a kind of plaid design. I focus on lint caught between the threads, little tears in the seam where the cushions end.

The car screeches to a stop.

"Here," says the driver in English.

We remain strapped to our seats.

"Ta poheegee?" he says. "Here. Out."

Russell looks at me and I nod. There's no other option. We're at the drop off. Armed men will surround us at any moment. "Wait for the opening," I think, fighting back the thud in my heart. It's hot in the sun, and the sun is out. There's also no breeze. It's been a long time since the war, but there's a kind of clarity to it all. A puddle in the street glimmers in the sunlight. My pupils contract and we step out of the car. Scraps of paper litter the curb. Tin cans and bits of wood. The building before us is caked with mud. Windows mark four floors, stretching down the block. I scan for movement, a glint of light, the unmistakable sound of an AK 47 snapping rounds into the chamber.

They'd come by car, but the street is empty and between the thud in my ear there's no engine hum, no cars around. The driver shouts at me. I twist around and he says it again, pointing to his watch. I consider taking off at a sprint, or maybe diving in through the window, grabbing his throat, when I notice him making a phone with his thumb and pinky. He holds it up to his face. "Call," he says, and hands me a card with illegible script. Before I can reply, or even cry out, he swerves his car and peels out down the street.

We're in the open. Across the road is a junkyard piled with vehicle shells, microwaves, car parts. The apartment windows are dark and abandoned. It's mid-afternoon and the street is empty. No children running about. All of it adds up to the first lesson you learn in country: ambush.

The shutters of a second-floor window slam shut and I jump. "Move!" I shout, pushing Russell toward the building entrance. We break into the dimness of the complex, panting in the dark cool with my back against the wall.

Inside is dusty and unlit. The hallway leads in two directions. At one end is an open stairwell. We stand that way for a time, waiting for something to happen. Something should've already happened, but that only adds to the confusion. None of it makes sense – the quiet, the stillness, Russell staring calm and confused. My eyes adjust, the adrenaline kicking against the front of my skull, and I watch Russell approach the nearest door.

There's a wooden symbol above the peephole. It's in Arabic script. Russell pulls a pocketbook from his coat and compares the sign with its translation.

"This is room number five," he says, like a tourist reading a map. His voice is too loud. I hiss at him to be quiet, but then it's all I can do to muffle laughter. "Eight," I say, consumed by the absurdity of it all. "He's in room eight."

Russell moves a room over, then turns and goes three rooms in the opposite direction. He glances back at me, warily, before halting at one of the doors. Above the peephole are two dashes that meet in the middle and drop down, like a teepee. Russell's white as sand but nodding me on. The likelihood of this being the wrong "Room 8"—of Russell leading us straight to the Taliban, or Akbar being in on it from the start—is as likely as anything. But I raise my hand to knock anyway. I can't really say why. Partly because we're already in the shit, so there's no point in dragging it out. But mostly because of Russell. The way he's watching me, like I've completely lost my mind. Like I'm some lunatic veteran gone off the deep end.

My knuckles thud against the wood, and an echo sounds down the hall. There's a call from inside. A rustling noise, mattresses creaking. A child wails.

There are no men, shouting. There are no gunshots or insurgents leaping out to zip fabric bags around our heads, zip tie our hands. Instead, the door opens to a silhouette. I hear him before my eyes can adjust.

"Salaam, Nethaan," he says.

An old man stands before us. From his neck hangs a robe, creased on the neck and arms. His hair is thin and pale. Around his face is a beard, whitening in patches at the chin. Kahwah tea has stained his teeth yellow. He recognizes me, but he's too small, too frail. His robes are tinted-brown, shoulders slouching a full head below mine. Behind him, a woman holds a crying baby in her arms. She jostles the infant and shushes in its ear. A child stumbles toward the woman and a third hides behind the man, clinging to his leg.

"As-salamu alaykum," he says, now to both of us. I don't respond. I can't. He adds, "Please, Nethaan. Come in!"

Russell moves first, stepping inside and pulling me in his wake. It's Akbar. The same Akbar who pulled OP shifts with me. The same Akbar who spoke of studying in America, of bridging the gap between the East and the West. Yet, here he is, in the kind of flat we'd search on late night patrols, during a raid.

The flat itself is barren except for a round table by the window and a pair of mattresses in the corner. Half of a wall separates the living room from another space with a sink and toilet. The floor is concrete except for an oval rug at the entrance. Akbar gestures at the rug for us to take off our shoes. I bend down and notice he's barefoot. Dirt has gathered beneath his toenails. The sand on the floor feels like salt on a shuffleboard.

My mind is running to add it all up: the abandoned street, the neighborhood, no children, the destitution: this can't be Akbar's home. Russell digs an elbow into my ribcage. His eyes are pleading, and I realize that everyone seems to be waiting for me. My throat is dry and lined with dust. I dig for something to say.

"Akbar."

The sound of my voice, of his name, comes out flat. The woman coddling her child turns back toward the kitchen, Russell slouches and Akbar, our host, grins. "Akbar," I say again, clearing my throat. I've no idea where to begin. I was relieved to have found him, but still confused and sweating out adrenaline.

"My friend," says Akbar. "Allah smiles upon us. It is a wonderful day that you are come to visit me here."

It's been so long, and his voice is fuller now, patient and spilling with tenderness. I almost tear up at the comfort of it, but there's a switch that's still on and it has me rigid, scanning the room.

I'm forming the question of where we are, why the street's abandoned and why we're in this shack of a home. Is it a neutral location? Somewhere we could meet and maintain his reputation with the community? But Russell clears his throat behind me. "Oh," I say. "This is Russell."

They shake hands. Akbar's fingernails, too, are brown and crusted. "You are welcome in my home," he says. "Come. I wish you to meet my wife, Tahera. Tahera, dalta ra-asha." He leads us to the table. My feet drag across the floor, sand on skin. A pair of chairs line one side of the small table and he returns from the kitchen with a stool. His wife, Tahera, follows. She's wearing a sky-blue dress that sweeps the floor. A baby girl sits in her arm, straddling her waist, and around her head is a white cloth. "As-salamu alaykum," she says. I can tell she wants to say more but is stumped by our blank response. She directs a stream of Pashto at Akbar that I can't follow, but Akbar replies with a calm word. The kettle whistles from the stove, though, and Tahera turns away.

"Forgive her," he says, though I'm still trying to gather my bearings. "The children, they are used to napping at this time of day. My wife is worried they will get dehydrated and not sleep this night."

Sweat spills down my own back. There's only one window and no real cooling system, except for a fan that sits propped against the wall. A bowl of water sits behind it to cool the air. This is Akbar's home. I have to consciously think that, to say it in my head on loop. This is Akbar's home. This is his life. A wave of exhaustion crashes over me. The nausea of last night, the adrenaline of moments before, all of it mixing with the confusion of the war until I'm back carrying Rosco's pack on patrol.

Meanwhile, Akbar's explaining why everyone stays indoors during the afternoon. "The children must sleep to escape the heat," he says. "Here is why there is emptiness outside."

Tahera brings out the kettle and puts a cluster of clay mugs onto the table. She pours without care and tea overflows from one of the cups. When our mugs are full, she walks away, and Akbar watches her go.

"But," he says in silence. "This is still a best time. To avoid the talk." I look up and he explains, "Not that you are in danger. No, it is not so violent in this area. I teach English nearby, and we are favored for this. But, it is easier." He reaches for the tea and Russell does the same. I can only sit there, though, watching. There's more nausea at the thought of tea, of steam striking my face in the heat, so I force myself to speak instead.

"I can see you've been busy," I say, nodding at the kids. "Since the war ended."

It's the kind of thing I'd say to one of my battle buddies in a bar. Not Akbar. Not here. He quirks his head to the side.

"Yes," he replies. "Though I'm not sure when the war ended, or if it has at all."

This strikes me dumb, and I can tell it shows because Akbar adds, "You mean after I left the National Army." I say yes, though I hadn't even considered how he would've continued with the ANA after I left. "Well, that was only two years after you," he says. "I have done many things in this time. Many jobs to bring food to my family." He gestures to the boy in the kitchen. "Today, I teach English for the community."

"Then you did it," I say, taking him for a professor. "You became a terp!"

Akbar smiles at his tea. I can see the sweat collecting at his hairline, but he takes a long sip from his mug all the same. "When I first met you," he says, "I wanted badly to go to America. But even then I knew this was a young man's dream. I never became an interpreter, Nethaan. I remained two years in the ANA for my people and also for the money. But my country did not improve. New American soldiers replace the old and everything starts from beginning." He takes another sip of his tea, straightening on the stool. "The interpreter I was asked to replace," he says. "The Taliban discovered who he was. They tortured him in front of his family. Then they made him watch as they killed his wife and children."

My arm slides off of the table. Russell mutters something beside me, but Akbar is unfazed.

"By then, I was married. Tahera was showing our first child," he gestures to the young boy who'd clung to his leg, "and to take up a position so dangerous—and for a young man's dream—it would have been selfish. Now I teach only at the community center. It is a place for useful learning. I teach both children and adults beginner English," he says. "For reading signs and stories and such things on the internet. It is good."

He lowers his mug to signal that he's finished. There is no reference to opening his father's bookstore, to translating western classics into Pashtu. There are no plans to visit America, to become a scholar or any of the other things I connected with the Akbar of my war. My hands grip the edge of the table to fight the sinking responsibility I feel for him, for his failures. It turns the skin of my knuckles white, but my nausea is replaced by a kind of excitement. I'm excited by the size of what I'm about to reveal, the effect it will have on his life now that I've found him so incomplete.

"Akbar," I say, leaning forward with my elbows on the table. "I want to give you something. But before you go and shake it off," Akbar had already raised his hands in protest, "I want you to hear me out, okay?" I wait for him to nod. "I've been thinking about this a lot the past few months, how I promised to stay in touch, to help you realize your dreams, and then I went twelve years without a single word—"

"Nethaan," he says.

"No, please. Listen. You had a dream to visit the US. It didn't work out, and I'm sorry. I really am. But I want to do something for you." I'm struggling to keep it all in, so it comes spilling out. "I've already got everything lined up. The loose ends are tied. It's a thing I've been working on for a while and, what I'm offering is, I want you to come and visit America."

I let it drop. This is it, my opportunity for reconciliation, for making amends for everything I left behind. I let him protest again before holding up my hand. "We can get you a business visa through my company," I explain. "Plus, I know a guy at Immigration. He's even offered to get your application expedited. We could fly you in next month, if you wanted. Now, we'll have to work it in with your teaching—"

"Nethaan, I can't."

"Sure you can. Look, if it's an issue of money, don't worry. I'll cover it. I'm a working man, I've got plenty saved. I want to do this for you, Akbar. Let me do this for you."

I'm searching him but his gaze is locked on the mug of tea before me. When he looks up, his expression throws me. He's tired—wounded, even—like he's being forced to smile. "Nethaan," he says. "I can't."

"Akbar, I *owe* you this."

"You owe me nothing," he says. There's a sharpness to his tone that cuts through the heat, but he recoils and then looks down at his hands. "You remember, I also wrote your address," he says, quietly now. "I could have emailed you, Nethaan. Even I could have Facebook found you. But this I never did. I am an old man, now. I have a family. I cannot leave them for a young man's journey to America."

"They can come, too—"

"Nethaan, I am sorry, but I am too old for such adventures. Now," he said, gesturing to the mug before me, "let us enjoy the time we have together."

"Akbar," I say, "don't you get it? What I'm offering you?"

"My friend, it is very generous, but I cannot. Now please. Drink your tea." He nudges the mug toward me.

"Forget the tea," I say. I'm close to rage, now, and I've the urge to pick up his clay offering and hurl it against the wall. But there's a pain in his eyes, and I catch Tahera watching from the kitchen. Even Russell's eyes widen.

"I... I'm sorry," I say, wondering how I could've forgotten myself. "I didn't mean... I just want to help."

64

I pull the mug toward me. My vision is blurred, the murk of tea turning hazy before me. It's not steaming anymore, and I raise it to my lips.

The tea was Akbar's gesture of friendship. An Afghan symbol of gratitude and hospitality. My refusing it was a slap to the face. Tea curls into my empty stomach and sweat spills from my temple down. I let it drop onto the table, and when I look up, I'm feeling cooler: cold, even. Like taking a drag from a cigarette on a hot day.

Russell shifts in his seat. Akbar's asking about our work and the conference. "Ah, the Serena," he says to Russell. "A very nice place, I hear."

They go on like this for a time. Eventually Akbar asks how long we've worked for Clarkson and Ross. Russell says something about his time with them. He answers for me, as well, but then he's nudging me. "Akbar asked you something."

"I'm wondering what you did," he says, "in between. After you left Kabul."

There are crinkles in the skin around his eyes from a lifetime of smiling. "After the war?" I say. He nods.

It's all I can do not to bring up the flights that I've already booked, the strings pulled and the back-and-forth with Rick. I swallow it down. The moment's gone. I killed it. Or else it was dead from the start. "I don't know," I say. "This and that. I worked a few jobs, hopping around."

"You got to travel, then," he says. "I am happy to hear of this."

I shrug. He's referring to something I remember saying during our last OP shift. I'd rambled on about plans to backpack Europe, to avoid settling down for a day-job, to do something that mattered. "Like shape policy in the Middle East," I told him. It was all bullshit. Even then I knew it was bullshit. But it was something to say. Something to keep our minds off the image of a body folding over itself.

Akbar asks about girlfriends and marriage, but I shrug him off like my life is some bachelor's paradise. "I keep my options open," I tell him. Russell nods with his mouth ajar. Even Akbar plays along. I start feeling sick again when he asks about Rosco.

"The others?" he says. "The one in your platoon, what was his name? The one they called Scrappy?"

"Rosco," I say. "He's working for an oil company, somewhere off the Gulf of Mexico."

"Do you see him often?"

"Sure," I lie. "Often enough." I try smiling, but I sink into my chair instead. The tea's cold, now. Tahera comes to fill Akbar and Russell's cup, but leaves mine untouched. When I tune back to the conversation, Akbar's bouncing his oldest son on his knee and speaking to Russell.

"How old is this one?" asks Russell.

"He will have ten years in a month," says Akbar. "The others are seven and three."

Russell smiles. "My daughter," he says, "she just turned two."

My eyes go wide. I look at Russell for the first time as a father. I had never asked about his family, or if he had one.

"A precious age," says Akbar. His smile is earnest, remembering his oldest at that time. "You must watch her carefully. They change too fast."

Akbar's laughing, but I can't tear my eyes from Russell. He's talking to the little boy. His tone is childish, and the boy smiles even though he doesn't understand.

"I haven't seen Rosco in years," I say, interrupting Russell. "I don't even know where he is, anymore." It's the beginning of a longer confession, but I stop by grabbing my tea and guzzling it down.

"I'm sorry to hear this," says Akbar. "You were a good friend to him."

I want to deny that and confess to every other lie I've told. I want to lay it all bare and I want to ask forgiveness for the cyclist. I want to ask if he still thinks about it, if the young boy's body crumples as often, as vividly, as it does for me. But Akbar and Russell resume their conversation, and I'm left staring into a well of clay. It's empty and dry but brimming with the image of my return to Kabul, my plans to fly Akbar to the US, and the cyclist on the street. They're all connected somehow, like they're one and the same thing. I want to explain it all, to apologize for the tea again, and my throwing that on him, but there's water building up in my eyes and I've bit it all back before I can even start. It's as if saying it, bringing it up and breaking down before Akbar and his family, would be wrong. That next to everything— Akbar's poverty and the harsh reality of this strange world—my troubles are worthless.

Time passes and the urge simmers out. Conversation straddles family life and I'm left looking in. Tahera returns and Russell drinks down his third cup of tea. Finally, the sun lowers and a cool breeze drifts through their only window.

I break in at some point to say we should leave, that we need to head back before it gets dark. I'm ready to counter Akbar's protest, his invitation to join them for dinner, but he says nothing. "There's a dinner presentation we have to attend," I add, and he nods.

Next is a smattering of thanks and gratitude for their hospitality. There's no talk of staying in touch. No more promises of "next time," or invitations to America.

"It was the greatest pleasure to meet you," says Russell, shaking Akbar's whole body through his hand.

Akbar's laughing. He likes Russell, and when he turns to me his eyes are smiling. We shake hands and say nothing except at the very end, when it seems wrong to let go without a last word. I lean in and with nothing else in mind, I say, "We were warriors."

It sounds ridiculous, those words out loud, but Akbar smiles. It's a sad smile, like when I insisted he visit me in America. He looks up, his brown eyes holding the light. "*You* were," he says.

It isn't until the door's shut and we're out on the street that I realize we need to call our driver. I try my phone, but there's no service this far from the city center. I dread the idea of going back inside and asking Akbar if he has a phone. Not that it'll ruin the closure – I just want it to be over.

"Here, let me try," says Russell. He takes the card from my hand and dials a number into his phone. "I've got international service," he explains. "You know, for the trip."

When our concierge picks up, I take Russell's phone and give Akbar's address. The desk clerk puts us on hold for a minute before assuring that a driver is on the way. I hand the phone back to Russell. Then I take a seat on the curb.

"Do you think," says Russell. "Should we wait inside?"

I shrug. The sun is behind us and shade from the building falls at our feet. Locals are meddling about. A woman unfurls a mat from the second floor of the complex, dust raining onto the pavement. Across the road, a man sifts through the junkyard for usable metal, and a group of boys shout excitedly down the street.

There's no more paranoia about being in the open. It was a farce, really. The whole afternoon—my assumptions about Akbar, about his home and Kabul—but, sitting on the warm pavement, a breeze fingering its way into my jacket, and for the first time in hours I'm able to breathe.

Russell asks again about waiting inside. "Do what you like," I say, staring forward.

He sits down beside me, and it's strange having him there. I'm glad that he's stayed. I'm glad that he came to the conference, that he jumped in the car on my way to Akbar's. And I'm glad that he was in Akbar's home with us, if just to fill the silences.

We sit on the curb and watch a group of boys make their way down the street. They're kicking something—a tattered ball of sorts—and as they close in, we can make out a soccer ball stripped of its covering. It's deflated, caving a little whenever a boy connects with his foot. But as they move beyond us, shouting and laughing in a pack down the street, not one of them pauses to take us in. Two Americans, sweating on a curb at the outskirts of Kabul. They don't even look at us. They just move along, passing their ball with precision, indifferent and laughing along with a world that has given them nothing.

THE TRAVELING VETERAN

He stopped at a Quik Mart outside of Wichita Falls to buy ice. He hadn't bought ice in over a week because it was February in the Texas Panhandle, and the water in his cooler would freeze every night in his trunk. But the last two nights he had slept on a friend's couch in Fort Worth. The trapped heat of the city had melted the ice and the water was beginning to smell.

Ten-pound bags went for $3 at the counter. Mark bought one and broke the ice by dropping it on the pavement outside. His ice chest was in the back of his trunk, and he had to remove a sleeping bag and camping tent to reach it. These he placed on the concrete uphill from the trunk. He removed the ice chest and placed its contents—eggs, milk, bratwursts, and a container of grease—on the concrete as well. Then he poured the water from the ice chest onto the pavement and watched it flow toward a drain at the edge of the parking lot.

Beyond the drain, a man leaned against the corner of the convenience store. He wore a brown coat with a grimy beard, and he began walking toward the car. As he got closer, Mark turned to face him. A wrinkle weighted the man's eyelids and there was no gleam in his eye, even though he faced the sun. There were no other cars at this gas station, and as the man approached, Mark moved his right hand to feel the KA-Bar combat knife he had looped on his belt. He carried the knife with him on the open road because he didn't allow himself to carry a gun.

Mark returned the food items to the ice chest, keeping the man in his field of vision. When the man came to a stop before him, Mark had already opened the bag of ice and emptied it onto the contents of the ice chest.

"Where you headed, boy," the man asked. Mark straightened his back, crumpling the ice bag in his hand.

"Amarillo," he said.

"Amarillo? With all that there?" The man was nodding to Mark's trunk full of camping gear. "Amarillo's not so far a drive for needing all that. Where you comin from?"

"East," he said.

The man flashed a set of teeth that protruded from his lower lip. They were yellow and there was a gap on the left side where his incisor should be.

"G.I., then," he said. Mark didn't reply. "So, you campin?"

Mark nodded.

"Shee-it. In this cold?"

Mark smiled at the man. He wanted him to go away. "At least as far as California."

"And you *campin* all that way?"

Mark began sifting through the ice. He wanted the man to go away, so instead of answering he lifted a cardboard container of eggs. It was soggy and falling apart at the corners, but he had only three eggs left and these were in the center of the carton where it was still intact. When he set it on top of the ice, the cardboard held firm, and he was confident that it would last before the ice melted.

"Iraq or Afghanistan."

"Look," said Mark. He stood straight and loomed over the man talking at him. "I don't have any cash."

The man looked down at his boots. They were frayed along the edges. "Well, that's alright," he said. A faded green uniform curled out behind the man's jacket, and Mark waited. He could tell the man wanted to say more. They always wanted to say more—to compare their war to Iraq and Afghanistan—but this one didn't. Instead, he opened his mouth and closed it. After a moment, he kicked up dust and the tan leather of his cheeks turned crimson.

Mark didn't wait or apologize. He turned away from the man and shoved his ice chest into the back of his trunk, followed by the tent and his sleeping bag. A cardboard box full of camping gear blocked the trunk from closing. The handle of a frying pan was lodged into the trunk's hinges, and Mark had to pull the handle loose to shut the trunk. When he turned back, the man was standing with his hands in his pockets.

"You take care now," said the man.

Mark nodded but climbed into his car without a farewell. Then he pulled onto the faded asphalt of 287 West. On the highway he could see the man in his rearview mirror, fading behind a veil of dust. It was likely the man hadn't wanted money at all, that he'd just wanted to talk and to hear himself talk. Before the war, Mark would've listened to him. He would've clung to the paternal spill of words with a silent veneration for the veteran mystique. But Mark had already venerated his share of father figures: his boot camp drill sergeants, platoon leaders in Iraq, captains and sergeant majors. He didn't have room in his life for anymore.

It was a long drive to Amarillo. The road crossed a series of abandoned towns, one of which slowed Mark down because a police cruiser sat tucked behind a bend in the road. There was a gas station canopy further down, abandoned but for drifting debris and broken glass. An inn right off the highway was collapsed in the center, the rotted wood of its billboard frayed as wool. Afterward, the Texas Panhandle opened up like the pulling of a curtain. Dust and tumbleweeds flew across the road. The wind was so powerful that it shifted Mark's car into the other lane. It gave him the overwhelming urge to speed. He didn't speed, though, because if the adrenaline hit his focus might drift, and even with ten thousand miles between him and the war he might still have blinked and been back in the middle of it.

Mark planned to camp at Palo Duro Canyon, just south of Amarillo, even though his tent probably wouldn't hold up against the panhandle winds. Its cheap, brittle frame was meant for windless summers in the south, ventilated and paper-thin. But by the time he reached the visitor's center of the park, the noon winds had given way to a relative calm.

Mark was eager to stretch his legs. The ranger behind the counter was a middle-aged woman and he spoke with her at length about the canyon and the campgrounds and hikes around the park. They spoke for a long time about the various forms of wildlife, and which trails were the most popular and which campground would provide the most scenic view of the canyon. Mark wasn't interested in the many details the ranger had to share, and he knew there would be little or no time for a hike, but he might not speak to anyone else for at least a day so he asked, "Do you prefer the Lighthouse Trail or the Rock Garden?" And when she said Lighthouse he said, "Is that because of the scenery or the pace of the hike?" Eventually the ranger hinted that he'd better set camp soon or it'll be sundown, because the sun set earlier at the bottom of the canyon. Mark thanked her and took his receipt. He taped it to the inside of his windshield and followed a winding road down.

The canyon was a red gash on the skin of the Panhandle. Crumbling slopes angled down, while others cut jagged walls through layers of red and yellow clay. The wind passed above his car once he was inside the gorge, trees grew above the knee, and a trickling stream—which once had been large enough to carve this patch of earth—now leaked across the road like water from a hose.

Mark's campground was in the center of the park. There was an available site near the Red River stream that was surrounded by mesquite trees and would be sheltered from the wind. All of the sites were available, but Mark chose this one and unloaded the tent from his trunk. Next, he removed the box of camping supplies, the sleeping bag and the ice chest. He rolled out the tent on a flat patch of dirt and slipped the collapsed poles through loops along the tent's edge. Once the tent was standing, he pulled tight the edges and stuck plastic stakes through the loops at the corners of the tarp. The stakes didn't sink into the ground—the dirt was a sheet of baked clay—so Mark found a rock that fit firmly in his hand and he hammered the stakes into the ground. The stakes kicked up dust and threatened to break under the strain of each blow, and as he hammered the crusted dirt around the hole would crumble and cave. When the stake was buried into the ground, Mark could still slide it up and down. When he lifted the edge of the tarp to mimic the wind, the stake slid up again.

"Might as well be drilling concrete," Mark said out loud. His voice sounded strange in the quiet, though, and he decided not to speak to himself again.

It was clear that the stakes would not hold against the wind. There was the canyon and the low mesquite trees to block the stronger gusts, but Mark ended up dragging supplies from his car to weigh down each corner inside of his tent. He put his ice chest in the corner facing the wind, and his box of cooking and camping gear in the corner beside it so that the wind wouldn't collapse its form. Then he left to explore the campground.

Small stones bordered a nearby stream, and a path cut through the mesquite trees toward a canyon wall a hundred meters off. There was an hour or two before dark, so Mark followed a path to the Rock Garden Trail. He chose this trail because it was nearby and elevated and he didn't care too much for long flat trails that didn't loop around. The trail wound through the aftermath of a landslide and was littered with boulders.

Dropping from one rock onto the path, Mark felt a pang in his knees. It was the friction of grating bone, and it came to him after climbing endless fences and landing firm on the ground with 100Ibs of gear, ammo, and his SAW machine gun. Mark continued climbing the boulders, scaling the crumbled wall for a view of the sunset, but his knee continued to hurt and eventually he realized that he was in a canyon and every boulder gave the exact same view. He stopped atop a particularly large rock, folded his legs, and waited for the glaring light to diminish behind the canyon wall.

When the sun fell across the canyon, it was still bright outside because it hadn't set beyond the canyon. It struck Mark that the Ranger would've known this, that she probably hadn't been worried about him setting camp before dark and instead had just been tired of listening to him. Mark dropped down from his boulder to return to camp. His knees ground with a renewed sharpness. The pain colored his vision and he realized that his hands were empty. He reached for his rifle. Panic shot through him at the absence of its strap across his shoulder, the Kevlar around his chest. His vision colored and the glare on the other side of the canyon became red.

Mark fell back against a boulder, grasping until his hand closed around the handle of his knife. His pulse was racing and the muscles in his shoulder contracted. There was no reason for him to be excited other than the pain in his knee and the woman ranger, but his fists were closed and eventually he slammed one against the boulder to calm down. "God damnit," he said. His voice echoed along the canyon walls, chasing the stream around a bend. The sound of it filled him with rage and embarrassment.

Eventually Mark was able to lean against the cold of the rock and let the vividness around him fade to a duller spectrum of light. It wasn't the first time he'd found himself furious or excited for no reason, the adrenaline in his veins. The moment always passed if he waited long enough.

Once Mark caught his breath, he began hiking back to camp. When he returned, there was a car parked several sites away. The campground was flat and dusty, and the only trees were by Mark at the riverside, so he could see clearly the Ford Explorer and the beige tent before it. The car was a faded green, and the tent was larger than Mark's. As he collected a bag of charcoal from his trunk, Mark saw a woman move around the Explorer and toward the tent. She wore a red scarf around her neck and a puffy black jacket. The woman stopped when she saw Mark, maybe to acknowledge him. Then she went back to moving around her car and Mark carried his charcoal to the fire pit.

The bag was almost empty, and he dumped what was left into a ring of sheet metal that lined the fire pit. He arranged the briquettes into a small pyramid and dribbled lighter fluid on top. He needed to collect branches and dried leaves for tinder, so he went searching while the lighter fluid soaked into the coals. In his peripheral vision, he looked for the woman at the other campsite. He saw her once, carrying blankets into the tent, but that was before he'd gathered handfuls of twigs and small branches.

The branches he broke with his hands and set around the pyramid of briquettes. The longer twigs were propped against themselves to form a teepee over the coals, and he stuffed dry leaves into the space between. He used a pair of matches to catch one of the leaves alight. He blew on the receding embers until the lighter fluid beneath the leaves caught and the twigs crackled above the flames.

In his ice chest were the eggs, milk, bratwursts and grease. His hand emerged wet and cold with the container of grease, and he used the same hand to fish out the bratwursts at the bottom of the ice. He cut a slice of the grease with his knife, dropping it onto the pan. Once the coals at the edge of the pyramid were white, he lowered the pan onto the fire and pressed down until there was a plateau of glowing coals. The pan rested steadily on the coals and the grease began to sizzle and pop. He spread the grease around by tilting the handle of the pan. Then he set his last two bratwursts in the pan and left them to cook.

It was twilight now, and as he went to pull a can of baked beans from the cardboard box in his backseat Mark looked across at the neighboring campsite. There was no fire still, and he thought that maybe he could offer to build one for the woman. That would be a smooth move. A harmless, almost natural, introduction. He couldn't know what the woman looked like from such a distance, or how old she might be, but that didn't matter so much. Even if she told him no thanks, that she didn't need a fire, he would feel better just for trying. He wanted to hear the voice of a woman responding to him.

He had to finish cooking the brats and beans, though. Mark returned to the fire and flipped the bratwursts with a plastic fork before dumping the can of beans into the pan. The sizzling ceased, and it took a few moments for the bean-sauce to boil. It did this slowly, and then rapidly in small bubbles. He watched the pan steam above the fire, and finally removed the pan from the coals. He placed the pan on the ground and cut up the brats with his combat knife, licking it clean and then wiping it before tucking it back into its sheath. The sauce got his stomach rumbling. He hadn't been hungry earlier, but once the flavor from the knife hit his lips, he became desperate to eat. He stirred the pan with his fork with the steam coming off, and once the steam lessened, he began eating straight out of the pan.

The first bite burned his tongue. Mark cursed, worrying that the burn would kill the flavor of the rest of the meal. He cooled the next bite on his fork, and when he placed it in his mouth, he moved the food around to make sure he could taste the brats and the beans. He continued eating in that way, letting each bite cool on the fork before placing it in his mouth.

Mark ate until his stomach hurt from eating, and then he ate some more. The coals were still glowing, and he leaned over them. He thought of gathering more tinder to start a fire but remembered a sign at the entrance of the campground that read, "Gathering of Firewood Prohibited." He thought of the woman at the distant campsite. He would gather firewood for her, he thought, even if there was a $500 fine. He would do it if it meant he might talk to her, or maybe share a meal with her. But when he looked over to the neighboring campsite, he saw a flame flickering to life, and by the time he was done eating her fire was a large glare in the dusk. She must've bought firewood from the campground host, Mark thought. But he didn't say it out loud because he didn't want her to hear him talking to himself and he didn't want her to think that he was crazy.

The coals simmered out as he wiped the pan clean with bread. The flavor of the beans and the brats absorbed into the bread and tasted almost better than the meal itself. Meanwhile, the deep blue of twilight receded to night, cold descended on the canyon, and his meal went tepid in his hands. Mark scarfed down the last of his bread and used the water faucet by his car to rinse the pan. The faucet stuck out of a wooden post that came up to his thigh, so he had to stoop to use it. The water turned his fingers to ice and afterward he had to hold his hands over the dying coals for the feeling to return. He prepared to crawl into his tent, grabbing blankets from his car and the electric lantern he used to read by, but first he gave a last glance to the other campsite.

The woman was silhouetted against a dark slope of rock. She sat on a round stone and the edge of her scarf glowed in the firelight. Mark wondered if she was slender and why she was camping in this former Comanche refuge. He wondered why she was camping at all. He thought maybe he would go ask. "Where are you headed?" he would ask. He thought, screw it. What's it to me if she says to get lost? He would ask her what she was doing passing through the Canyon, if she was from Texas or driving west. He would get her talking, and if he could get her talking then she might feel comfortable around him. They could sit before the fire together for a while and hear each other speak. Mark's hands began shaking with nerves. He just had to make a move. He had to get up and walk over there without thinking about it. Mark pushed off his knees and took a deep breath. It came out slow and quivering, steaming the cold air, but he made himself walk toward the fire one foot after the other.

He moved past his own coals, simmering a dull orange, and as he passed the silver outline of his corolla, he caught a glimpse of himself in the glass. Light from the lantern he carried yellowed his teeth and lit up his beard, grimy from another day without showering. Shadows fell across his face from long, tangled hair and made him look mean in the low light. He saw the man who had approached him in the parking lot, the grimy beard and dead eyes. He couldn't go over there, now. The campground was completely abandoned except for the two of them. He would scare her to death.

Mark accepted this, and it relieved him. He wouldn't have to risk being told to get lost; he could just climb into his tent and read a book by the light of his lantern. It was cold in his tent, but he stripped beneath the waist before crawling into his sleeping bag. The book he read was about a road trip across America that his father, who was an English professor at Florida State, had given him to read. Except now he was shivering and couldn't focus on the words. He thought of the woman at the nearby campground, and he thought of his mother who lived alone. White clouds steamed from his mouth and his hands went pale and cold from holding the book. After a while, he packed the book away and pulled the sleeping bag over his head.

His hands and face defrosted in the trapped air, but even after he stopped shivering Mark couldn't sleep. It was 20:00 and he was distracted. Meanwhile, the canyon created a funnel for the Panhandle wind. All of it seemed to pass just overhead, but it wasn't rustling his tent at all. He wondered if he stood on his toes and reached up beyond the tent would he feel the wind in his hand. But he was cold and instead he tangled himself in blankets and listened to the channels of wind howling above. Beside him, the leafless branches of mesquite trees whistled in the stillness.

Mark's mind wandered. He was cold and alone and hyper-aware of his loneliness to the point that he began thinking of how he had no more friends between him and San Diego. Beau Delis had told him he could stay with his parents in Arizona, but Beau was still overseas and Mark didn't want to stay there without him. He also didn't want to answer questions from Beau's parents, to tell them about his time in Afghanistan with their son. They would want to know the things that Beau didn't tell them in his phone calls, like how the "Green Zone" in Afghanistan was nothing like the one in Baghdad, how it was riddled with as many IEDs as it had poppy plants. Mark didn't have the energy or patience to explain these things, even for a warm shower and clean sheets.

There would be sights on the drive west, though; cities and campgrounds that Mark wanted to explore. He planned to pass through the lower Rockies in New Mexico, hike the Grand Canyon in Arizona and gamble in Vegas. He was going to climb the Hoover Dam and pass through Joshua Tree. There were plenty of things to do, and once he got out of Texas the drive would be rolling and scenic.

But he would be alone, and eventually the westward road would end.

When Mark reached the coast, he wouldn't be able to stay with his friends for long. Most of them lived at Camp Pendleton, and the ones who didn't had their own lives. They would grow tired of him crashing on their couch and he would run out of money after a few weeks. Either way, he was bound to grow restless and move on. The question was, "To where?"

Mark saw himself as a train on a pair of tracks, with nowhere to go but forward. He thought of what his father had told him when Mark mentioned the fits of rage he was experiencing. "You're like a cargo train that's been running at full speed," he said. "Now you've come home and you've slammed on the brakes, but you won't just stop. Not all of the sudden. You need to ride out your momentum." What his dad didn't expect was for Mark to take that literally, to drive off and keep driving. What worried him now was that he couldn't feel himself slowing down. He worried that the brakes were broken, or that he was on some frictionless rail and that he might never stop. The old veteran from the Quik Mart crossed his mind. Mark had assumed the man was homeless because of the way there were no cars or other buildings around, but he struggled now to push the man out of his mind. He pictured the coast instead, the violence of the waves and the abrupt cold of the Pacific. He could feel the waves shuddering against the shore, grinding the sand between his toes. Then he stepped out, and the loneliness of the ocean began creeping up his legs. It stung his toes at first, numbing them. Next it lapped at his knees, gently, but gathering all together it slammed against his chest. Mark couldn't move. The weight of the ocean was sitting on him and it constrained his breathing and prevented him from curling or turning onto his side. He was pinned down, and the icy pull of the thing filled his lungs until his breath was so cold that it didn't steam when he tried to breathe.

Outside, the wind was gathering at the edge of the canyon. Mark waited beneath it. He could hear it building and building and then blasting between cliff walls in a howl of dust and dirt. Later, after he was able to roll onto his side, the coyotes began to cry out with loneliness. Their song would travel in a pitch that rode the wind, echoing the contorted screams of a thousand Comanche horses, only there would be no terror in it—no paralyzing fear or vocalized pain—just a muffled sense of urgency.

In the morning, Mark relieved himself to the glow of dawn. He returned to his tent parched, but the water in his water bottle was frozen. He was also cold, so he pulled on his jeans and, bent over in the short tent, rolled up his sleeping bag. When everything was packed, he loaded up his car. He removed the stakes of his tent, collapsed the poles, and folded the flattened tarp three times before rolling it into a fat cylinder that would fit inside of its case. He packed the trunk full, and when he was done with this his blood felt warmer than when he'd started.

With a Tupperware container, he mixed milk that had crystalized from the cold with old cereal. He ate that breakfast in the Corolla, letting his breath steam up the windows. Afterward, he rinsed out his Tupperware at the faucet, climbed back into his car, and keyed the ignition.

The red Explorer was still parked by the larger tent. It would have better insulation, despite its size, but as Mark shifted his car into gear, he watched the tent's flap unzip. A man stepped out, middle aged and shirtless. Right afterward, Mark noticed the sticker on the back of their Explorer. It had black text beside a red and gold emblem. Mark knew what the sticker read before passing. "The Proud Mom of a U.S. Marine."

They would've embraced him, had he approached the night before. They would've asked questions about his parents, about his transition home, and then, combing his hair with her fingers, the woman would've looked down at him and said, "You're just like my son."

Mark drove past the car and the man waved. Mark didn't wave back. He kept driving and didn't look back. He felt rested, and as he wound his way up the canyon walls he thought only fleetingly about the day before, and less about the days before that. Instead, he planned out his drive for that afternoon. He would camp at Capulin Volcano in the Northeast corner of New Mexico. It was a national monument, and there were always good facilities at national monuments. He would have to stop for gas before the border, but by dusk the wasteland of north Texas would fade from his rearview mirror as completely as the homeless veteran from the day before, and the barrenness of the Panhandle—all nine hours of it—would be forgotten.

STEPPING STONES

She found his eyes the most attractive. They were large and black and glimmered in each picture of him smiling. It was as though some deeper secret forced those lips open, wide and relaxed and always on the brink of laughter. His photos were casual, too—not the pseudo-glamour shots of the other men who had messaged her—and while the description on his profile read age thirty-three, there was a youthfulness to his expression that made him look younger.

"Get a drink with him," said Katherine, her head nurse at the VA's Internal Medicine ward. "Worst case scenario is that he's a creep and you have to beat the shit out of him."

Katherine was one of Beth's few non-military friends. She was under the impression that every female veteran, even ex-helicopter pilots like Beth, had the Amazonian qualities of Wonder Woman. But Katherine had been instrumental in navigating the dating website that Beth used. It had been her idea, really, and in the end she had commandeered Beth's profile altogether, discarding the various photographs Beth had chosen for her cover image: the one with her dad and his new family, another of her mother's dog, and the one in her flight suit beside the medevac helicopter she'd flown in Iraq. "No, no, *no*,"

Katherine had said, pointing out the last picture. "This kind of shit intimidates men. You need to make them feel empowered. Besides, you're not showing enough cleavage." Beth had allowed Katherine to adjust the profile to her standards, and overnight a flood of messages poured in. The quantity alone prompted Beth to turn off her availability.

Beth didn't consider herself a particularly beautiful woman. She was tall, but not lean. The curve of her waist had flattened over the course of her tour in Iraq, burgeoned by nine years in the Navy, and again during her two years of schooling to become a physician's assistant. Now, a web of wrinkles was spreading out from the corners of her eyes.

This was one of the reasons Beth had chosen James. His apparent vivaciousness promised to counterbalance the exhaustion Beth felt every night after returning from the hospital. It was also nearing Christmas. She'd bought a fake Christmas tree for a corner of her apartment, but last weekend Beth woke to the realization that it had been a year since Chandler left her to travel across Asia. She didn't want to spend another Christmas alone.

Beth responded to James's introductory message—the one-word comment, "hey," suspended above white space—and after a few nights of conversation, she accepted his friend request on Facebook. She spent her nights afterward blinking awake to the glow of her computer screen, scrolling through James's friends and photos until she was able to convince herself that he wasn't "catfishing" her. ("That only happens to men," Katherine had said. "And desperate men, besides.") And yet, despite a conditioned skepticism of harmless-looking men— "They're the most dangerous ones," she'd told Katherine— Beth conceded to a drink. "Just one," she answered, and when she set down the phone, she was surprised to feel her lips part. She was smiling.

Beth wasn't a prude. She'd slept with men during her time at the Naval Academy, and a few more in the Navy before she'd met Chandler. Her three years with him—a rescue-swimmer who crewed search and rescue missions in Guam—had been the most adventurous of her life; but they hadn't made her soft. Nine years in the navy introduced Beth to the harsher realities of living in a man's world. "And make no mistake," she told Katherine over lunch, "the Navy is no more owned and operated by men than this very hospital." She'd managed to adopt survival techniques, though: don't stay out late at foreign ports; don't set down your drink (ever); alternate gin and tonics with club soda; and avoid speaking to men outside of your squadron. Even though she was out of the Navy now, Beth had no intention of meeting a stranger from the Internet without taking proper precautions. She told Katherine where she'd be going—the Marina Laguna, a chain bar close to the VA hospital in Houston—and at what time. Then she messaged, half-jokingly, "If you don't hear from me in an hour, sound the alarm."

Now that James was standing before her, though, Beth doubted the necessity of her safeguard. He was as harmless as his pictures suggested: smiling excessively and receiving her as if any sudden movements might scare her off. Still, there was a dissonance that Beth couldn't pin. His skin, for instance, was more pallid than in the pictures. Frown lines split his eyebrows, and while his eyes were still big and black there seemed to be less depth, less mystery. Their gleam was dimmer than in the photographs.

James led her to a table behind the bar. It was empty in the back, and their distance from the entrance made it warm. Beth had hoped the temperature would be cold enough to leave her jacket on. She'd worn a pea coat with a ribbon belt, and when she tied the ribbon it suggested a deeper curve to her wrist. But it wasn't her figure that worried Beth the most. It was her skin. The first cold front of the season had arrived, and even in Texas the cold was enough to suck the moisture from her limbs. Patches of childhood eczema surfaced—a condition that had all but disappeared before entering PA school in Galveston—and ever since Chandler had left, her skin had become irritated in places she'd never experienced before: along her forearm, below the curve where her thumb and forefinger met, on the top of her calves. She'd progressed to using steroid creams, but with the dry and the cold her eczema was beginning to fight back.

Beth adjusted her blouse without raising her hands above the table. The patch on her wrist was raised and red, contrasting against her arm like blood on the hem of flight pants. She resisted the urge to scratch it by exaggerating her interest in their conversation. "So you've seen all of the superhero shows. What else are you into?" James answered all of her queries with noncommittal smiles and laughter. He felt that *The Sopranos* had dragged on and "just kind of faded out," but when Beth told him that it was her favorite show he shrugged. "Maybe it went over my head," he said. *Game of Thrones* was a classic, even though branching beyond the books was a mistake. "It oversimplified the

Stephen J. O'Shea

plot." Beth nodded despite never watching *Game of Thrones*. She didn't want to kill the conversation, and, ever since ten-hour flight patterns had become routine, it was the silences that made her anxious.

They'd already blundered through the icebreaker phase— "Can you believe how cold it is?" "Global warming, amiright"— to their current analysis of television; but when James finally left to order drinks at the bar, Beth couldn't help acknowledging that his online profile had been a misrepresentation. She didn't suspect him of foul play or Photoshop. He wouldn't have manipulated his photos. He might've added a filter or two, the kind you could find on any smartphone, but it was more likely that his pictures had been from a few years ago. A reflection of physical insecurity, Beth thought. That was normal enough—misrepresenting yourself to get a foot in the door—it was perfectly normal. After all, Beth had allowed Katherine to manipulate her own profile. What struck her now was that James might be equally critical of *her* not being the same as the image he'd built in his head. Perhaps it disappointed him that her breasts didn't "pop" like in the selfies Katherine taught her to take: slipping one arm underneath her chest, lifting her phone to capture the image from above. "It's all about the framing," Katherine had said. "Now try again but open your eyes wider."

James smiled enough, though, and when the barmaid arrived with their drinks, he laughed at himself for ordering a vodka cranberry. It was a loud, confident laugh. The kind of laugh that only a white, middle-class man could belt out in public without so much as a blush. It made the barmaid flinch and attracted the attention of two couples on the opposite side of the bar, but Beth couldn't help admiring his indifference to them. She even laughed along. It was as though, after three years of sleeping with a man who only drank Jack Daniel's on the rocks, it came as a kind of relief to sit across from someone who was confident enough to order a drink one ingredient short of a cosmopolitan.

It comforted Beth that he was flawed, that he accepted it, and that he could laugh at himself. After hearing about his work as a turbine engineer, his years studying at Arkansas State and the past decade of his life in Houston, she even began to feel lucky. Not because he was some sort of catch—she found his job and life in general to be boring—but because he was normal. He wasn't a creep. She wouldn't have to finger the plastic of her mace spray on the stairs to her third-floor apartment, or "beat the shit out of him" for following her home. The Internet, as bizarre and misleading as it could be, had connected two relatively normal people in a Houston bar for a relatively normal date.

Beth was thinking about this when James admitted to not studying hard enough in college. "I was too distracted by girls," he said, following the neckline of her blouse. Beth brought a hand to her neck.

"So," she said. "Have you done this before?"

"Done what? Gone on a date?"

He was joking, but there was a defensiveness to his tone that surprised her. "No," she laughed. "I mean through the internet. You know, 'online' dating."

"Right," he said. "Honestly? You're my first."

Beth blushed, but began wafting air at her face in a mock-dramatic display. "Oh my," she said, exaggerating a southern drawl.

James laughed—a loud, obnoxious laugh that turned the barmaid's head—and a tension released in Beth's lower back. "Same," she said, holding his eyes.

His laugh faded out, leaving an expression that resembled the suspended grin of a confused child. "Actually, he said, lifting a hand to his chin." It's a funny story." Facial hair lined his face and neck in a week-old scruff to sharpen the diminished line of his jaw. He scratched at it, and a sandy powder crumbled onto the black of his button-down shirt. "Because I did meet my ex-girlfriend on Tinder." Beth's stomach clenched. "That was a fluke, though."

"Oh?"

"I mean we had mutual friends. You know, in the 'real world'."

"Oh."

"We just started dating through Tinder. We'd met before."

"Well," said Beth. "That's alright, I guess."

Except that it wasn't alright. Not by a mile, because if he'd met his ex-girlfriend on Tinder, then how many other girls had he met online? How many other times had he had this exact date? Repeated these exact lines? Spewed that same scripted charm, riddled with his obnoxious laughter? Beth's lips tightened around her teeth, and James—noticing the shift—began to ramble. He explained how he'd broken up with his ex-girlfriend after she'd accepted a job on the opposite side of town. Beth waited, so he added that the distance was too difficult, that he couldn't handle the "strain of it." He paused only to brush the dandruff off his chest.

Beth decided to let it go. After all, it wasn't like he had lied to her. He had only misspoken, and Beth attributed that to his nerves. He didn't seem nervous—the way he sat reclined in the stool with his arm draped around the back—but he smiled less as he spoke, admitting in the end that the breakup had been his fault. "I had been selfish for wanting her to live so close," he said, "for not wanting to drive an hour after work to see her. It would've ended eventually. I just didn't want to drag out the painful part."

Beth nodded along. She admired how James could recount his entire relationship history to a stranger, even if it was painfully one-sided. He was trying to be upfront, and, ever since she had stumbled upon a video of Chandler kissing a girl in Thailand before he could "untag" himself, honesty had become very important to her. It reassured her that James was confident and upfront, that he wasn't afraid to talk about past relationships; but a tremor shot down her spine at the realization that he hadn't asked a single question about her background. It landed at their feet like a grenade. They were strangers, completely foreign to each other. Even his honesty couldn't compensate for how little she knew about him, or that he knew nothing about her. He wouldn't even know that she'd served in the Navy, or that she'd been to Iraq.

Beth found herself visiting her gin and tonic more frequently, in bigger sips. Her wrist itched as well. She'd catch herself scratching it in her lap, fighting the urge to relieve the itch with her saliva. The barmaid walked past, and Beth ordered another round of drinks. James struggled to gulp down his vodka cranberry through the straw and had to break from his screed to finish the first drink before the next arrived. Afterward, he leaned back in his seat, stretched, and said, "You're a Physician's Assistant at the VA."

Beth nodded. "Only for the past few months, though." She said this too loudly.

"Oh. Okay. Were you in private practice before that?"

"No," said Beth, fingering the rash on her wrist. "I graduated from PA school three months ago. Before that I was in the Navy."

"Whoa," said James. His eyebrows shot up and a web of wrinkles spread across his forehead. "And what was that like?"

What was it *like*? "It was alright," she said. James blinked in response, and Beth panicked. She never wanted to talk about her service—even with her family and closest friends—but it was bound to come up, and she thought it was better to get it over with. "I flew helicopters. Search and rescue missions, mostly. In Iraq, I flew medevacs."

She felt that she'd been talking for ages. Her mouth was dry, her eyes unfocused like the end of a ten-hour shift at the hospital. James nodded across from her, but his smile was gone.

"And you went straight into PA school afterward? That's just two years, right?"

"Yup," said Beth. She glanced down at her lap. Her left hand was scratching the eczema on her right. She pulled them back, stuffing both into her pockets.

"That's pretty impressive," said James. He smiled again, scratching his chin. Beth marveled at that, how they were both scratching. She wondered if he was nervous, if he scratched his face only when he felt anxious. Perhaps that's what all people did when they were uncomfortable around somebody else—tore at their skin, the barrier separating them from everybody else—stripping away flesh until finally they broke through and blood smeared and the brilliance of it, the vibrancy of its color, shocked them into stopping.

"Why the VA?" he said. "Isn't that place supposed to suck?"

Beth frowned. "It isn't the best place to work."

She wanted to stop there. She wanted to move away from this talk about work and her life in the Navy, but the fear of him interpreting her motives as failure—that he might assume her grades weren't high enough to get into private practice, or that she didn't fly commercially because her wings had been stripped—egged her on. Releasing the straw between her lips, she spoke.

"When I was in Iraq," said Beth, "we picked up a wounded marine from a hot LZ. He'd lost a leg from an IED and bled out before we could get him to the hospital in Baghdad. Ever since that moment, I've wondered what might've happened. You know, if I had been the one in the back of the bird—the one administering first aid instead of flying—if I'd taken the crewman pipeline instead of becoming a pilot. Because, if I had, then maybe I could've saved him."

James sat with his arms dangling by his side. His expression could've been awe or fascination, but his eyes were unblinking. Beth had let her guts run onto the table and now they were both siting there, staring at it. The worst part, though, was that she couldn't remember why she'd said all of that in the first place. She hadn't even told her parents about that marine. The only person she *had* told besides her team in Iraq was Chandler, and that after two years of being together. Yet here she was, spewing it up like a plotline for the next "Avengers" film.

Beth picked at the skin of her wrist. It stung to think that the barmaid would've overheard her, that she was watching them still. The empty tables and bar top closed in around her: shimmering mahogany, the glinting of light off pint glasses. Mariah Carey's "All I Want For Christmas" echoed from a speaker somewhere and reverberated across the bar. It was a song that Beth had belted across the empty space of her apartment last winter, believing that Chandler was only a few months away: that they would be living together soon. Now the song made her nauseous.

James shifted in his seat. He moved his arm to the middle of the table and looked at the floor. His eyes only flicked up to glimpse the barmaid as she walked past. Beth wondered why she had told him that. What had compelled her to? Pride? Was she simply repaying him for the line about his ex-girlfriend? She at least hadn't told him about the paramedics, how they had sprinted from the hanger with an empty stretcher, bent beneath the rotor blades, only for Petty Officer Bannon to step out and say, "He's dead."

She hadn't mentioned the blood, how it covered the floor of the helicopter, staining her boots and the hem of her pants so that when she stepped out onto the concrete it left tracks. She had stayed behind to help maintenance clean the bird, scrubbing blood from stainless steel in the sweltering heat. But then she hadn't told anyone this. Not even Chandler. He didn't believe in talking about those sorts of things. He'd say, "Come on, baby. What good does it do to bring that up now?" Or, "Just don't think about it." And Beth would listen. She always did. She hadn't thought about that incident in years, and even now she was trying to suck it all back into her mouth with the gin and tonic.

An awkward silence followed. It might've lasted five minutes or no time at all, but Beth had to remind herself twice that she was in the Marina Laguna by the VA, that the man sitting across from her was a stranger she'd met on the Internet. Meanwhile, James thumbed the rim of his Collins glass, brushing dandruff from his shirt. "So," he said at last. "I bet you get some weirdos at the VA."

Beth waited to see if he'd more to say, if he would elaborate or clarify what that even meant, but eventually it occurred to her that he was just uncomfortable. He was squirming to fill the silence. She had led them into an area of conversation that was foreign to him, and Katherine's words hung in the air around her: *he needs to feel empowered.* Beth leaned forward. Without a second glance, she pushed herself from the stool and stood. "I'm sorry," she said. James touched her wrist with his hand and Beth flushed. "I just need to use the restroom."

Once Beth could inspect herself in the mirror to confirm that she hadn't been drugged—that, in fact, she was tipsy at best—she began to accept that everything she'd said was of her own free will. It was funny how that could happen, exposing herself to an internet date in the middle of the Marina Laguna. "Funny." The word filled her mind like a dose of James's laughter.

He would think she was crazy, now. All of those nights sweating over a keyboard about what to say—the days spent contemplating what to wear for this exact moment, the hour she'd spent on her make-up alone—all of it thrown to the wind because she had over-shared like a fool. Leaning over the sink of the empty women's restroom, Beth realized how pathetic it all was: the amount of effort she had put into impressing a stranger. She imagined herself returning to the table. James would be gone and the whole bar would be empty except for the barmaid. The barmaid: blonde and pretty and shrugging. Maybe James would've gotten her number before leaving. She pictured him laughing about how internet dates never end well, laughing like he had when the barmaid gave him a vodka cranberry.

Beth had bent over her purse and was sifting for lotion when the screen of her phone lit up. It was eight o'clock. Barely evening. Beth let out a sigh, remembering that it had been her plan to meet so early, but at least now the whole night wouldn't be ruined. She could go home and pick up ice cream from Trader Joe's, stream another documentary on Netflix.

Her phone buzzed again, and Beth skimmed the series of messages from Katherine. "How's it going?" read the first, followed by, "Are you alive???" and "Text back 'I'm fine' if you've been kidnapped."

Beth smiled. It was a welcome distraction to have Katherine worrying over her, and she allowed herself to escape by swiping open the messages. "I'm fine," she wrote back, but realized too late that she had accidentally cued Katherine to sound the alarm. She began typing out a second message when, to her relief, Katherine's call interrupted her.

"Oh, thank God."

"I'm fine. I'm fine," said Beth.

"You're *fine?*"

"I mean I'm good," she said. "I'm okay. Please don't call the police."

Katherine laughed. "Fuck's sake, I wasn't going to do that. If anything, I would've driven down there to watch! That guy would have to be on steroids to carry *you* off."

Beth rolled her eyes. "Well that's flattering."

"So, what's he like? Are you gonna bang him?"

"What?!" said Beth. "Christ, Katherine. I mean, he's not terrible. He's nice. A little self-absorbed…"

"Typical."

"But I'm not going to 'bang' him. I thought you knew me better than that."

"Consider it a trial run," said Katherine. There was a muffled crunching sound between her words, like she was chewing popcorn. "Like a foothold, you know, to get back in the game."

"Katherine."

"Look, do what you like! I'm just trying to help."

Beth waited. She had the phone wedged between her chin and shoulder, lotioning the eczema on her hand. "Not like it matters," she said, capping the bottle. "Pretty sure I just blew it."

"Don't be ridiculous," said Katherine. "This guy found *you*. He messaged you and he's taking you out for drinks. Besides, he's registered on Cupid. He'd probably fuck a goat."

Beth set down her purse. "You sure know how to get a girl excited."

"Now get back out there and give him what the Honey Badger doesn't."

"A fuck?" said Beth, but it took her too long to connect the dots. Her phone returned to a half-written text message, and she was left gazing into the blank white of her screen.

She supposed that Katherine was right, in a way. That it was practice. That she could finish out the date with James and learn from it, move on to the next guy and the next. She was done sitting around at home watching Netflix, clinging to Instagram posts of Chandler sprawled out on tropical beaches, surrounded by sluts in string bikinis. "Sluts." That's the word she had used a week before, spitting at the screen of her phone in the middle of a hospital Starbucks. She'd regretted it immediately, and not just because of the way an elderly woman snapped her head around in condemnation, but because those girls were probably just trying to enjoy their lives. They were kids on a weekend vacation from university or part-time work. They didn't know that when Chandler left her for India, he promised to be back by the time Beth graduated PA school. They didn't know that in the beginning he had messaged her twice a day, sent her postcards from every country he visited, and made time to Skype each week. They didn't know that gradually, almost imperceptibly, Beth had dissolved out of his life and into the routine of the VA, the hollowness of her tiny corner in Houston. Beth didn't want to hate those girls: she used to *be* them. She also didn't want to become the caricature of a bitter, middle-aged woman who spoke to her pets more than other humans. She wanted to go out on dates, to drink and meet men. She wanted to enjoy her life.

Beth snapped her purse shut and glanced in the mirror. Her eye shadow was a subtle gradient that blended into her skin, and the foundation she'd used accented the careful shifts of her features with such mastery that even the pretty blonde barmaid would be impressed if she saw her in this light. Beth had put effort into this date, and the determination with which she tossed her hair and walked out of the ladies' room surprised even her.

James was facing the entrance, but he twisted back at the sound of the restroom door and offered a smile that was one part relief and two parts encouragement. He was still there. He hadn't ditched her. And on the other side of the bar, Beth could make out a line of patrons trickling in. Talk and laughter mixed with the overbearing Christmas music, and the bartenders were making drinks instead of eavesdropping on their conversation.

"So. What were we talking about?" she said, pulling up a stool. "The VA?"

James, startled by the new pep in her voice, bobbed his head twice. "Sure," he said. He took a sip of his drink and Beth heard the slurping as he finished. The barmaid was approaching with another.

"I'll take a club soda with lime," she said, pushing her drink to the side.

"Aren't you going to finish that?" said James.

"Sure," she said.

His eyes narrowed on the drink, a smile plastering his face like wet gauze. Once it became clear that his stare wasn't going to lift from her glass, Beth began to speak. "The VA," she said. "To be honest, it's not really that different from your average hospital. The biggest difference is that most of my patients are overweight, white males."

James laughed generously.

"We get a fair amount of creeps. And a lot of belligerent older men. We had to throw one guy out last week after he went on a rampage over his Norco prescription—"

"Norco?"

"Yeah, it's a hydrocodone," said Beth. "A really addictive pain killer. Anyway, we were weaning him onto this non-opioid called Tramadol when he completely lost his shit."

She stifled a laugh because it had been Katherine who threw him out. Katherine: a, caffeine-fueled rabbit of a woman, backing an NFL-sized man across the waiting area into the elevator. She'd done it entirely by herself, and before security arrived. Beth was going to describe the incident—how, if the man had simply fallen forward or tripped, he would've squished Katherine flat—if only as a distraction from her slip about the marine dying. But before she could start, James shook his head and said, "My ex-girlfriend took medication for a while. She was depressed."

Beth stopped. She was leaning over the table, her mouth open with the first words of her anecdote in the bottom of her throat, but now her jaw swung loose. She failed to connect an opioid-enraged patient with an ex-girlfriend on anti-depressants, and by the time she'd given up trying James was halfway through a tangent about his ex's therapy. He had tried to help her, apparently, but had only made things worse. "She doesn't even talk to her parents anymore," he said, staring at the double doors to the bar.

Their third round of drinks arrived, and the barmaid left Beth's half-finished gin and tonic behind, despite it resting at the edge of the table. James stared at the drink even as she took a pull from her club soda. She didn't want more alcohol to leave her blabbering about the Navy again, but as James went on about his ex-girlfriend Beth found herself tempted to throw back the rest of the drink. Something stopped her. Habit, she supposed. *Don't set down your drink, ever; alternate gin and tonics with club soda.* But now that she was swallowing club soda, it refused to go down smoothly. In fact, the last club soda she has was three months ago, on the night she graduated from PA school. Beth had expected to hear from Chandler then—a "congratulations" call, or just a text message—and so she'd remained sober throughout the night. He never called. He didn't even "like" the photo she'd posted to Facebook.

"Let's get out of here," said Beth. The suddenness of her voice surprised her almost as much as James—she had interrupted another one of his ramblings—but the bar was getting crowded and soon it would be full. James's laughter would attract attention and eventually the whole bar would suspect them of being on a first date. Besides, Beth had the circadian urge to go home and watch *Narcos*, to drink hot chocolate with her Trader Joes ice cream for the contrast of temperatures, and to run away from the bland taste of her club soda and half-finished G&T.

However, it dawned on Beth —based on the way James's face brightened—that she had said the wrong thing: that her words had come out in the wrong order, or perhaps had been the wrong words altogether. She might as well have said "Netflix and Chill" the way his forehead jumped. The words "let's get out of here" led him to swallow the rest of his vodka cranberry in a single pull. He even came around the table, helping her into her jacket, while Beth blanked on how to go about clarifying that she hadn't necessarily meant "together."

Beth walked outside with James guiding her by the small of her back. She went pale as they exited the bar, and when James finally noticed the discomfort on her face he winced. His arm dropped from her back and he stepped toward the curb, shoulders hunched to hide the heat in his face. She caught a glimpse of subverted complexity; even his eyes glimmered like a dark well. It was one of the rare moments in Beth's life when she looked at a person and suddenly felt that she knew them; that—if she could paint or sculpt or write—she would be able to capture exactly what it was that made them pulse with life. James stood apart from her, glancing down both ends of the street, and after breathing out steam he turned back and said, "Should we split a cab?"

The collar of his jacket was propped against the wind, black textile speckled with white dandruff, and his hands were stuffed into his jacket pockets: the same hands that brushed her wrist as she moved for the restroom, that had rested on Beth's back as they left the bar. Beth screened him—a sad smile on his face, eyes shimmering in the lamplight—and in that moment she didn't see James as he was, but as his online profile had been. She saw a photograph of a younger man, with glimmering eyes, and it struck her how handsome he was.

Beth shivered. She couldn't know whether it was the cold or the echo of Christmas music that reinforced the weight of her own loneliness, but when she finally met the glow of his eyes, she found herself smiling. "I'm just around the corner," she said.

They called a cab because "just around the corner" still meant a five-minute drive in Houston. Beth sat pressed against the window of the taxi. She didn't say a word the entire drive, and for the first time all night, neither did James. He might've been reminding himself to smile at the doorman, or to keep his head down in the lobby, before killing her in cold blood. But Beth hardly noticed his silence. She was preoccupied with the realization that she'd invited a stranger to her apartment: inadvertently at first, but then as a conscious decision. Her thoughts turned to Katherine, how she was Beth's only civilian connection. Katherine had been her coach for the online dating site, her instructor for merging back into the confines of civilian life, and now—ushering James into the living area of her apartment— Beth wondered if it was her own hand opening the lock, or if Katherine was there guiding her.

James took his time orienting himself. He was Beth's first guest since she'd moved into the apartment. Even her parents hadn't dropped by to visit: her father with his new wife and son; her mother, alone. Glancing around the living area, with James in the middle of it, Beth had a new impression of how empty it was. She'd been living there for six months, and while most of her life took place at the VA and gym, she had yet to hang so much as a poster on the wall. There were no pictures or paintings outlined by a frame. The only decorations were a Christmas tree, naked and crammed into a corner, her fish tank that she regretted buying, and a postcard tree displaying all of the letters she had received from Chandler during the beginning of his trip. There was one from Dubai, another from New Delhi and the beginning of his Southeast Asia trek: Laos, Cambodia, Vietnam. The letters had stopped before Thailand, and by the time he reached Malaysia she was more or less forgotten. Beth displayed the ornament on her dresser, primarily because it was the only piece of furniture she had brought with her from Galveston. The way it was situated before the mirror allowed Beth to read the messages on the back of each card, inverted and scribbled by Chandler's pen.

James's gaze lingered there the longest, but he didn't lean close or ask who they were from. "It's nice," he said of the apartment. "Very clean."

Beth could tell that by "clean" he meant empty. Her prepared defense was military conditioning. She'd grown up in a military family—her father being a Captain in the Navy, retired now—and during her enlistment she had spent four nine-month-long deployments at sea, crammed into a bedroom the size of her walk-in closet. In Baghdad she had lived in a tent for a year, sleeping in a grave. James might've understood some of this, vaguely, through images he had seen online or in movies about war. Most people could grasp the minimalistic idea that accompanies military life, even if it had never been forced upon them. But what they couldn't know was that the only time Beth had ever allowed herself to settle down was during the tail-end of her time on Guam, when she had all but moved in with Chandler and set to work on their house. "It needs a woman's touch," he'd said. Now he was touching twenty-year-old girls on a beach in northern Australia while she was treating obese veterans at the Houston VA.

It was a rare occasion when Beth felt nostalgia for her childhood home in Georgia, but standing in her empty apartment with a strange man she felt a sudden longing for the east coast. It wasn't a specific house or town that she missed—her parents had divorced years ago, selling the house she grew up in before Beth left for the Naval Academy—it was more the shallow shores of the coastline; the sand descending gradually enough that she could walk the length of a football field before the water reached her shoulders. It was a continental shelf in stark contrast to

Guam (where there was none) and Japan (where it dropped off like a mountainside). Even Galveston's shores had been riddled with seaweed and polluted foam, the surf dropping after a few meters.

"Do you live alone?" said James.

There was a calculated hesitation between each word, but Beth nodded anyway.

"Me too," he said. "Well, I live with my brother, but he spends most of the week at his girlfriend's." He let this linger as if it were important. "This your fish?" he said, moving onto the arm of her couch. He leaned over the meter-long tank, peering through an algae-stained lid.

"Yup," said Beth, wondering why else he might think she kept a hundred-dollar fish tank in her apartment. "His name is Zodiac."

James laughed. "Amazing."

"Yeah," said Beth. "I bought him so my other fish could have a boyfriend. Then he killed her."

Her mother had given her a goldfish in a bowl as a house-warming present, even though she knew that fish depressed her. "Consider it a stepping stone," her mom had said, "to getting a cat or a dog." Her mom had wanted Beth to get a dog ever since their German shepherd died, but instead Beth had bought a bigger fish tank and another fish. She didn't know that the second fish was a Betta fish, or that Betta fish were territorial. She had picked it because of the vibrant colors and because she remembered hearing that fish were like peacocks: that the men were supposed to be the more beautiful. "Of *course* something that pretty and delicate would be lethal," she'd told Katherine when, two days later, she had found her goldfish bloated and upside down. Now every morning when she left for work, Beth leaned over the tank and begrudgingly scraped flakes of food into the water. "That's what happens in a man's world," she'd say to her fish and to no one. "Beautiful men thrive, and the women get flushed down the drain."

Beth didn't tell James any of this. Instead, she glanced toward the kitchen. "Want some wine?"

James settled onto the couch while Beth went into the kitchen. Red wine would've been ideal. It had a sensory weight to it. "Aphrodisiac," she had read somewhere, rolling the word across her tongue. Despite buying a case of Merlot from Trader Joes two weeks ago, though, she couldn't dig up a single bottle. This only mildly surprised her, as Beth did all of her drinking at home. Caffeine was her drug of choice, but returning from a ten-hour shift at the hospital she would pour two glasses of wine so that, once she turned on the television, she wouldn't have to get up for a refill.

Beth managed to dig a bottle of Sauvignon Blanc out of the fridge. It was open from two nights ago, when she had erased Chandler from her Instagram. It was less than half full now that she was holding it up to the light, but it was the extra-large kind and she guessed there was enough for three or four glasses.

Her view of the living room through the doorframe included the edge of the couch. However, Beth couldn't see James there. His elbow should have been propped onto the arm rest, or his body leaning into the corner. Beth wondered if he was on the couch at all and became struck by the premonition that he would be crouched on the other side of the doorframe. She saw herself passing into the room

Stephen J. O'Shea

right before he threw a string around her neck, or stuffed her face with a pillow, pushing and squeezing until she suffocated. Beth considered how he had stared at her unfinished drink after she returned from the restroom, how he'd laughed at her fish's namesake. His own name—James—was suspiciously unsuspicious: harmless in the way that only a maniac would seem harmless. Beth tried to shake the feeling but slipped the wine glasses upside down with the stems between her fingers, like she'd seen waitresses carrying them. She'd be able to move her arm more quickly that way. She even wrapped her other hand around the neck of the wine bottle, grasping it so that she could swing the heavier end like a club.

Rounding the corner, Beth found James. He was sitting on the couch with his hands opened. He had moved away from the fish tank and the armrest, toward the middle. Beth measured this for maliciousness but, moving toward him, recognized it as the childish ploy it was. He had positioned himself where she would have to sit beside him, rather than at the opposite end of the couch.

"I've only got white," she said, measuring her breath.

"Perfect," said James. "White's my favorite."

Beth set down the wine glasses and poured them both a glass. James was leaning forward, the bottom of his hands reflected in the glass of the table. Beth's hands were shaking. She sat down beside him and the two of them stared at the black screen of the TV. Beth could hear her heart pounding, but she didn't know how to slow it down. She didn't want to take deep breaths and freak James out—he would've thought her crazy enough—because, even though

111

she had no idea why she'd invited him back in the first place, now that he was here she didn't want him to leave.

"Is everything okay?" he said, reaching for his wine.

"Yeah, sure," said Beth.

"You know," he said, "it's been a long time for me as well—"

"No, no. It's not that. I just remembered something. I don't know."

"Mmm." He took a sip from his wine, measuring the taste. "It's good," he said. "The wine. Where'd you get it?"

Beth didn't respond. She had closed her eyes and was focused on her breathing. In and out, she thought. In – and out. "What's that?" she said, after he asked again. "Oh. Walmart, I think."

James adjusted on the couch. He put his arm behind her and then lowered it back to his side. His eyes were scanning her living room. The light on her DVR blinked green from the night before when she had fallen asleep, depressed, after watching a documentary about the psychology of happiness. It was only nine in the evening now, and she could easily reach for the remote and put on a movie, but the idea of turning on the TV, of staring into its LED light for another two hours of her life, made Beth even more unsettled than the silence. She took a last breath in, then turned to James. He was yawning.

"Who are the postcards from," he asked.

Beth had just reached for her wine and she took a very, very long sip. She wanted to be fair. He had been blunt with her about his ex-girlfriend, and now she wanted to be blunt with him. She leaned back—felt James's arm around the back of the couch again—and said, "My ex-boyfriend. He sent them after starting a trip around the world."

Beth waited for the questions. Where had he been? Why did they break up? Why did she still display his letters on her shelf? But it took a long time for James to say anything. He drank from his wine glass twice, and when at last he spoke it was to say, "Long distance can be hard."

Beth's stomach clenched. On her dresser was a dreamscape of mountainous jungles, immaculate temples and crystalline shores, propped and promulgated by an aluminum web that she'd found on Pinterest. It *was* hard. To live in this concrete landscape so far from home and yet not nearly far enough, returning from the hospital every day to a display of tantalizing pictures that reminded her of a life she had turned down. For the first time since she'd moved to Houston, her response of "what else would I put there?" wasn't enough. Beth set down her wine, stood, and without show or dramatic flair lowered the postcard stand onto its face.

Settling back down, James lowered his arm between them and drank the rest of his wine. He leaned forward, emptied the rest of the bottle into his glass, and sighed. "You know, my ex-girlfriend," he said. "The one that I broke up with because she moved to the other side of town—"

"The one you met on Tinder."

"Right," said James. "I didn't meet her on Tinder. I didn't meet her at all."

Beth scratched at her wrist. "What do you mean?" she said.

"I mean that I made her up. She doesn't exist."

James leaned forward, elbows on his legs, and rubbed his face. Dandruff sunk into the wooden floor like snowflakes. His silence somehow lessening the lie. Of course she didn't exist. She had never existed, and Beth felt as if she'd known this all along.

"My real ex-girlfriend," he said, speaking through his hands, "she was depressed. *She* was real. We dated for two years and we loved each other. I mean, I've never loved a woman as much as I loved her." He stared at the screen of the television, but his smile was gone. His knees bobbed up and down so that he had to rest his glass of wine on the armrest. "We were happy together for years. Then, out of nowhere, she just stopped wanting me. Like she stopped being attracted to me."

Beth listened to this. She looked at James: this man she had met online. It amazed her that he was telling her this, even though he had lied to her and that he might be lying to her now. Beth pictured him lying to his brother, to his hairdresser. He might've lied to everyone in his life, but it didn't matter. Everybody lies, thought Beth. What mattered was the quiver in his voice, the blank stare of his eyes when he spoke.

"I think she was depressed, but I don't really know," he said. "Things had been great. She was finishing up her anthropology degree. I'd gotten promoted from fieldwork. We kept trying, you know, but one night she pushed me away and said that she hadn't orgasmed in a year."

James was moving his hands. He was talking to her, but his hands were talking to the wall. "We'd been together that whole year," he said, "having sex like that for a year, and in all of that time she hadn't orgasmed once." His head was still, eyes squinted. "We tried therapy after that. I even went with her to the first session, but the therapist wanted to work with her alone. Not that it changed anything. The therapy, I mean. She never came home after with a sudden desire for me. If anything, she'd come home feeling more depressed, like the therapy was making it worse."

They sat in silence. Beth doubted that he wanted her to speak. She didn't know what she'd say even if he did. James met her gaze for a moment, but then turned away.

"We broke up, eventually," he said. "Of course we did. I mean, how can you stay with someone that doesn't want to even touch you? I still loved her, and she still loved me. I believe that. I believe that much. It's not like she was cheating on me. I would've known if she had been cheating on me." He was speaking faster, his knees bobbing. "It's just," he said, "it's been over a year since we broke up, and in all of that time I haven't 'been' with anyone else. I haven't had sex in over a *year*."

His hands opened to the wall, and Beth understood now that he was finished. This is what had been eating at him all night long, the reason he'd circled back to his ex-girlfriends again and again. She leaned back with her eyes wide, wondering if she was his first real date in over a year. She hoped that she wasn't, despite him being her first date since Chandler. She even found herself wishing that his make-believe Tinder girlfriend had been real, that they had met and broken up because of distance like he'd said.

James inhaled beside her, hands open. Then he swept his wine off the table and finished it all, half of a glass, in a single gulp. When he leaned back beside her, their arms were touching. "I'm sorry," he said. "Nobody wants to hear any of that crap."

He shuddered, swallowing a belch, and Beth realized that he was drunk. The three vodka cranberries at the bar and two full glasses of wine had done him in. His shoulders expanded beside her, rhythmically pressing against the couch. Beth considered why he had told her all of that, if it was because he was drunk or because he trusted her, but then she remembered her own moment at the bar—when she'd told him about the marine dying in her helicopter— and an enormous sympathy welled up inside of her. She felt the warmth of his shoulder against her own, the weight of his body as he exhaled onto his chest. Beth faced him, lightly touched his arm, and said, "That must've been rough."

It was an empty statement. Beth knew that much. But she spoke it in a way that reflected the tragedy of her own life. She sympathized with this man, with his loss and sense of rejection, and after hearing her words his shoulders caved into themselves. His head curled forward, and for a moment Beth thought that he was going to cry. She didn't know what she would do if he started crying. She'd only seen men cry in Iraq and as a teenager, when her mother drove away and left Beth's dad in the kitchen with a printout of the emails he'd sent to their au pair. But James didn't cry. Instead, he placed his empty wine glass on the table and, as if on cue, leaned against Beth and rested his head on her shoulder.

Beth didn't have a particularly comfortable shoulder. Her bone jutted out at an awkward angle and already she could feel it digging into James's temple and, after he adjusted, his jaw. Meanwhile, her glass of wine had been in the hand that his head was pinning down. She had to cross her other arm over—slowly, to not disturb him—in order to relieve her immobilized hand. And after draining the glass she had to hold on to it, pressed against the couch, for fear it would fall and break.

James shifted, allowing Beth to glimpse the back of his head. She had no desire to sleep with him, now. She couldn't remember a moment when she *had* wanted to sleep with him, even once he was in her apartment. Still, there was something delicate about the way he had laid himself bare, exposing himself to her. Even the act of placing his head on her shoulder moved Beth, and she felt responsible for him in the way that she might feel responsible for a child curled up in her arms. It was as if a tiny thread connected their bodies at the wrist, thin as silk, and invisible if she didn't look for it. But Beth was looking. Even with dandruff speckling the short brown of his hair, his scalp, Beth felt an affection for the head on her shoulder.

Straining not to move, and taking shallow breaths, Beth sat as still as she could. There was a tension in James, an inconsistency to his breathing that suggested he was waiting for something. It occurred to Beth that him telling her his story—and her telling him about the marine in Iraq—could have been normal. That this is what happens when you spend too much time alone: the details of your day, of your life, build up inside of you until finally it all comes spilling forward.

"I had this patient the other day," she said. The sound of her voice surprised her, like she hadn't meant to say it out loud. "Thursday. A marine. A double-amputee." James nodded, encouraging her. "He'd stepped on an IED in Iraq and lost both of his legs above the knee. But after hearing that I had been a pilot in Iraq, he told me about being medevac-d to the hospital in Baghdad."

Beth didn't know what direction she was taking them or how it would end, but she knew that, whatever it was, it had been lurking in the back of her mind all week. She had seen the marine everywhere since that Thursday appointment: in the faces of men on the street, in her patients at the hospital. Even her dreams were tainted by the blood on her boots, the tracks that it left on the pavement of their hangar. "He didn't remember much of the flight," Beth said. "He would've been in shock. But he told me he remembered arriving at the hospital. He remembered asking the doctor there, begging her, to kill him. He even remembered her name. That's how lucid his memory was."

Beth licked the rash on her wrist. "Anyway, she didn't kill him. The doctor, I mean. She saved his life because that's what you do. Then, six months later," said Beth, "there he is in my clinic, more grateful than any human I've ever met just to be *alive*."

She waited, trying to feel out the core of what she was getting at. "The thing that eats at me, though," she said. "What I keep coming back to—"

James stiffened. He didn't interrupt her. He didn't ask, "What?" or encourage her on. He just lifted his head and looked at her with those big, black eyes. Beth didn't look back. She was eyeing her wrist. The rash was facing upward, exposed to them both. For the first time all night it didn't itch.

"I should've been inspired, you know? Reassured, maybe, about my decision to pursue medicine. I mean here he was, like a second chance at the marine who died in my helicopter, and I was helping him. I know that. I know that's how I should've felt. But it's funny, because the only real thing I felt in that moment was envy," she said. "You know, for this man—this boy, really—who'd been in the wrong place at the wrong time and lost both of his legs. I was jealous of his optimism. Jealous that he'd lost a part of himself, but still had more motivation and appreciation for his life than I've ever known."

The words felt like the wind getting knocked out of her. She fell backwards, and James was left studying her face, the curve of her nose and lips. She met his gaze this time, and found that his eyes were as black as the TV before them, absorbing the light of the room but none of what Beth said. There was no glow to them. Their gleam in the photographs on his profile, Beth realized, would've been a reflection of the flash. Even outside the bar, when he'd asked if they should "split a cab," there had been the lamplights, the brightness of the bar front shining down. Beth watched him through the reflection of the TV screen, and when he leaned forward to put his head in her lap it seemed the most natural thing in the world.

They sat like that for an hour. Neither of them spoke, and for a long time Beth didn't move. Then she began stroking his hair. She ran her fingers along his head, against his flaking scalp. She combed around his ear and felt the sand in his hair, beneath her fingernails. He nuzzled into her thighs in response, and eventually he fell asleep. Beth knew he was asleep because of the drool that seeped through her jeans. But, even then, she didn't move out from under him. She didn't replace her lap with a pillow, and she didn't stop stroking his hair. She was content to hold his head in her lap like that, like he was a child, and leaning over him she saw how beautiful it was. Not James—not his face or position, the awkward bend of his body in the short space of the couch—but the way that he was lying in her lap, still and vulnerable. An image crossed her mind, flickering like the shadow of a rotor blade. She wondered if this is what it would've been like, crammed into the back of her helicopter with the dying marine in her lap. She imagined cradling his head against her chest, her tears absorbing into the Kevlar of his armor as he bled onto the floor, whispering to him that if he only survived, if he only lasted until they reached the hospital, that he could go on to live his life and to live it with more gratitude, with more gravity, than everyone else in the entire world.

FROM THE LAND OF GENESIS

Part I: Texas

He returned from the war in the Spring. His division was stationed out of Fort Carson, Colorado, and they returned to the base in late April. Since this was early in the war, civilians were still excited about troops returning from Iraq and there was a parade. It was cloudy and cold, but the wind was calm and the chill was an echo of winter. Large crowds of civilians came. Lots of old men. Some with wives; some with wrinkled uniforms curling out from beneath their jackets. Lots of families and children and little hand-held American flags with red, white, and blue confetti and signs that read "Welcome Home" or "Thank You for Your Sacrifice" or "Iraq's Heroes." The low light of sundown glinted off of glitter and danced on the pavement like shattered glass.

Families were waiting afterward but they had to wait much longer since the entire company had two weeks of mandatory decompression before they were formally discharged. Ryan wanted to stay in Colorado Springs, though, even after he got released—to "get laid and blow cash" with his battle buddies—so his mother and younger brother and sister went back to Fort Worth and left him his brother's Ford Fusion to drive home when he was ready. It took only a week of alcohol and strippers for Ryan to spend most of his money. Then he checked out of his hotel, threw his pack into the trunk of his brother's sedan and drove home.

Home was in Fort Worth, Texas. He came through the plains of Colorado and the panhandle with the dry landscapes crumbling around him. Dust blew across the road from gusts of wind and filtered through the AC like in Iraq, and he found himself studying the shrunken trees with their dendrite canopies, waiting for water to pass between. Then he reached the suburbs, and when he pulled into his old neighborhood it was the same as he remembered. The lawns and trees and the driveway curling behind his home had not changed since he left two years before. The grass was still short and green; the people all wore ties and slacks and drove sleek, colorless cars; the gas stations and Whataburgers and HEBs were all right where they had been, all bustling with people living the same little lives as when he had left. His dad still owned the Ford Dealership off 35W, and his mom still hid in her office downstairs, sending emails and running PTO meetings at the local high school.

Then there was his room, which was the same. Ryan's mom had gone great lengths to keep it that way for when he got back. The only addition was a framed picture of his platoon graduating boot camp. Proud, ignorant smiles plastered their faces, and Ryan put the photo face down on his bedside table. His bedspread was the Dallas Cowboys logo. Muscle-car posters lined the wall, and a bulletin board with photos of friends from high school and prom and the football team hung on a wall above his desk.

His sister, who had been young when he left, was now a sophomore in high school, dressing and talking twice her age. His brother looked the same but was at SMU and not at home. He was more distant than before the war, when they had been close and he'd looked up to Ryan. Now he wouldn't return Ryan's phone calls. There was also the family dog—a now 11-year-old lab—who had become old.

These were only minor differences, and Ryan managed to settle into a rhythm during his first weeks back. He'd get up late, rarely before noon; spend time around the house getting ready; shower, maybe; eat half a box of Eggo Waffles; and then, most days, he'd drive into town. He never had errands to run or people to meet, but he made them up as he went or wandered outlet malls or parks or nice neighborhoods. He called his mom for a grocery list once, and she asked him to pick up hamburger meat at the Central Market for grilling on the 4th of July. He found it in the refrigerated section. Each package crawled with pink maggots, everything squirming beneath the plastic. He felt hot, then, and the tile beneath his feet shifted and the fluorescent lights above him turned into glaring light. But the freezers of the store were cool, and after burying his face in the coolness he was able to buy the meat and leave.

After that, Ryan would only run errands if his mom needed him to. But it wasn't the errands that got him out. It was his truck. He loved climbing into his truck and sitting on the hot fabric of his seat, baked from the sun. He loved rolling down the windows until the AC was cool and then blasting the cold air on his face with the heat all around him.

His father, who had never fought in a war, wrote Ryan while he was in Iraq to say that he had sold his old Jeep. "It was just layin around, son," his dad wrote. "More of a hassle than it was worth." Then, when Ryan spent his entire first week at home sleeping and playing video games, his dad pulled up one day with a new F-150. Ryan tried to look more confused than excited, but his dad put a different pair of keys in his hand. "Here, son," he said, giving Ryan his old truck. "I got the new one for myself."

But that was alright, because Ryan didn't really care for new cars. They felt cheap, like they cost more than they were worth. But his dad's old truck—a '98 F-Series—was reliable and tough, and Ryan felt like the biggest thing on the highways when he drove around. It was big and loud, and Ryan drove comfortably into Fort Worth because he didn't have to worry about IEDs or snipers or rockets or any of the crap that he had worried about while driving around in Baghdad. He still drove in the middle of one-lane highways, and in the left lane everywhere else. And sometimes he felt a rush of adrenaline at the sight of a bag of trash on the side of the road or passing through the historic downtown where tall buildings lined the streets in a colonial wall. Sometimes he imagined men with RPGs popping out of windows and rooftops. He knew he wasn't in Iraq and there weren't hajis getting ready to blow him to shit, but for some reason the rush always came. It always came and he had to let it pass by breathing deep and staring at the simmering concrete before him. It excited him, though. And sometimes it reminded him of the war and that stole him away from the monotony of civilian life.

Ryan also loved working on the truck. It was several years old and had some wear from commutes to work. Nothing serious, but he would spend hours in the garage, trapped in a sauna of heat, tweaking away at the engine and gears. Those had been his favorite parts of the war, working in the safety of the Motor Pool. Like when an RPG clipped his vehicle and blew off the rear bumper and mangled the back half of it. After the shock passed and the dust settled and they escaped the bursts of small arms fire and the clustered streets of Baghdad, Ryan got excited because it meant a week of repairing the damage. A week in the motor pool, away from the heat and the small-arms fire and IEDs and the sniper that got Terry on a patrol through town.

Ryan worked often in his garage at home and he liked driving the truck around his neighborhood, past the elementary school and community swimming pool and high school. He liked seeing kids playing soccer no more happy or sad than the homeless kids laughing in the alleys and streets of Habbaniyah. He liked looking at women, too. And he could do that a lot from his truck and with his sunglasses on. He tried not to do it in a creepy way, and he never hit on them or approached them or even let them know he was looking. He just liked watching them. He would watch them walk across the shopping district in their short summer shorts and skirts, tight t-shirts and spaghetti strap dresses and round hats with big round sunglasses. He loved Texas women. He loved them more than any other women in the world, although he hadn't seen many other types of women. In Iraq, the only part of a woman he saw were the eyes. And those might have been beautiful, but they never held his gaze.

Ryan loved Texas women, and at times wished that he could have one. But he didn't know where to start. His mother had friends with daughters. And there were Facebook friends and old high school friends and random friends of friends, but they were in college or professional school or working and they didn't have time to show Ryan around, to introduce him to their circles, or to make him feel that the war had been good.

Occasionally, he'd catch up with others: high school friends he'd known several years ago, or friends of his other battle buddies. They'd go out for a beer. But even with the alcohol in him, the only women that Ryan approached were bartenders. They always talked back and seemed to like him, and he didn't feel guilty or embarrassed about bothering them because they liked it and it was their job. He'd talk to them all night, buying drink after drink and round after round and leaving big fat tips. The next day he'd wish he hadn't gone out at all because of the money he spent and the depression that it left him with, but then a few weeks would pass and he'd do it again.

He started going alone because of the questions his friends would all ask. Like, "What comes next?" Once they learned that he wasn't going to school or back overseas, they'd lose interest. They were especially condescending when he didn't give a specific enough response. "Take your time," they'd say. "You've earned it." Or, "I'm sure you'll figure it out soon." They'd also probe him about the war, trying to gauge how much action he saw or how fucked up he was. But they didn't want to hear real stories. They wanted to hear about the dirt, about something sensational like the April 28th Massacre or whether or not he'd killed anyone. They didn't care about the daily shit that fucked with his head. The constant threat, patrolling every day on the streets of Fallujah, Baghdad, hoping for an attack so that they could just *find* the enemy.

One time Ryan caved and gave his friends what they wanted. He told them about the kid they played soccer with on the FOB. His name was Rahim and he was 12 years old, but he was quick and smart and fun to talk to. The grunts all showered him with gifts, and he became the platoon mascot. Then one day they found Rahim stuffed in a rice bag at an entrance to the base. His body was dismembered. Sand mixed with the blood and covered his pale skin. Terry was with them screaming at everybody to clean him off, to rinse the sand off of his limbs because it was eating away what was left of him. But nobody moved until Terry started trying to do it himself.

Ryan told this to his friends, and they went quiet and looked at him strangely. It was what they'd wanted to hear, but after hearing it they stopped calling him back. Still, he had his mom and his sister, and they didn't mind having him as long as he got out of the house every now and then. And he had Vixen, his dog, who he took on long walks in a country park every day, not because he liked walking but because he could see the excitement in Vixen every time he helped her into the bed of his truck. The future was far away, and the present was the summer and it felt like the old days, like summers in grade school before his first job. And that helped him forget things.

All that changed when Vixen died. Ryan had been trying to get her back into shape. Vixen was a chocolate lab, and she'd been healthy when Ryan left but now she was slow and lazy and wheezed when she got tired. Ryan blamed his mother for not walking her while he was gone and he decided to get her back into shape. For a while, he convinced himself that she was getting better. Then her wheezing got worse and her larynx began to collapse. Ryan had to stop walking her, but the wheezing continued until she couldn't walk to the mailbox without an attack and so his mother decided to put her down.

She did this without telling Ryan. It was a humid day, even for July, and by the time Ryan woke up he was sticky with sweat. His mom had already been to the vet and back, but it took him an hour to realize that Vixen was gone. "She must've got out!" he said, excited because it meant there was still life in her somewhere. But then his mother sat him down and she picked up his hand with her eyes watering. Ryan cursed before she could even explain.

She said she did it because she thought it would be easier that way, but also because Ryan had said that he wanted to pull the trigger. Ryan had told her that he wanted to be the one that put her down. There was no sense in paying some veterinarian a thousand dollars for something that he could do at home and with a single bullet. He'd told this to his mother multiple times. But now Vixen was dead, and all Ryan had left was her ashes.

That afternoon he went to an indoor firing range and went through a hundred rounds before the panic attack hit, and then he had to sit down and hide because he was ashamed. When he left the range, he didn't bother collecting his paper targets, each of them tattered where the "x" and the 9's were. Instead, he paid his fee and climbed into his truck to drive home.

The next few days Ryan spent in his room or in front of the TV. He slept and lounged until he'd almost forgotten what he was upset about. He was tired and bitter all the same, to the point that he wouldn't leave the house even to drive. His mother worried about him, and Rachel, his 16-year-old sister, worried as well. They tried getting him out of the house—tried getting his brother, who was at SMU, to come home even though he had finals and didn't look up to Ryan like he used to—but it ate away at his mother until one morning she woke Ryan around noon with a plan of her own.

"I made breakfast, honey," she said from outside of his room. "Come downstairs."

"Be down in a sec."

He stayed in bed and almost fell back asleep, but the smell of waffles hit his stomach and he dressed and walked into the kitchen.

"Here you go," said his mother, placing a plate of waffles before him. The syrup and peanut butter were already on the table.

"Chocolate Chip?" he asked, feeling lazy and tired like you do after sleeping too much.

"Your favorite," his mother smiled. She sat in front of him. He noticed his sister, Rachel, was there. And his brother.

"Hey Kev," he said. "When'd you get in?"

"This morning. Can't stay, though – exams next week."

Ryan grabbed a knife and spread thick peanut butter over his waffles. "Oh. Well that's no good."

They watched Ryan finish with the peanut butter and then watched as he poured on syrup, cutting the waffle into quadrants to keep the other quarters from getting soggy. He was heavier than before the war, and as he cut off a piece of his waffle and put it in his mouth, he felt his stomach clench.

"Ryan," his mother said. He put another piece of waffle into his mouth. Melted chocolate oozed onto the plate. "You remember Sally, Rachel's friend?" She nodded at Ryan's sister. "Well, she says her older brother is in town. You remember Louis?"

Ryan chewed and didn't look up. "Yeah, I remember him."

"Well…"

"Mom thinks y'all should hang out," said his sister.

"Oh yeah?"

"Yes, honey," said his mom. "I think you would have fun with him."

"He was a year younger than me, ma. I hardly knew the kid."

"I know," she said. "I know it's hard, honey. But Louis is home for the summer and just dropped out of school, and Sally's mother and I were talking and, well, I guess…"

"They think you might be able to help each other out," said Ryan's brother. He didn't veil his disgust.

"Huh." It struck him, then, that nobody was eating with him.

"Listen, honey. He's going through a rough time, too. And his mother thinks he should start looking for work and I just thought that the two of you..."

"That's it?" Ryan asked. He was angry but kept his tone flat for his sister and brother. "Ma, if you want me to move out just say it. Don't go killing my dog and hooking me up with your friend's kid just to get me out of the house."

The corner of her eyes became wet, and when Ryan went to cut his waffles he did it harshly, so that the fork and knife scrapped against the porcelain of the plate.

"We just want you to be happy," said his sister. "You know, have some fun. Hang out with people."

"I thought maybe you could go *dancing*," his mother blurted.

She was crying now, and Ryan felt angry but also guilty so he lowered his head and shoveled forkfuls of waffle into his mouth.

"Look," said his brother. His voice was deep. "No one's trying to rush you. We know you took Vixen's death hard. But it was cruel to keep her alive any longer." When Ryan didn't reply, Kevin said, "I don't know, maybe you and Louis could pick each other up or something."

Ryan stopped eating his waffles. His mother's sadness had tapered and the time between her sniffles shortened.

"Come on, Rye," said his sister. "Mom already set the whole thing up. Louis said he knows a few girls that'll come with y'all so you'd have people to dance and have fun with."

Ryan swallowed back the last bite of his waffle with difficulty. The peanut butter had dried his mouth, and he drank down his glass of orange juice.

"I thought maybe you'd meet a girl," his mother sniffled. "Someone you could date and start a life with, get a good job or go back to school, and maybe one day…"

"Uuuhhgg," Ryan groaned, rolling his eyes. "Ma, come on."

But this only hurt her more and her eyes spilled over and she pushed back her chair to be excused. Ryan felt the glares of his brother and his sister as he watched her go to the sink. She ran the water but didn't move any of the dishes. Her hand went to her forehead and stayed there, so Ryan called her back and apologized.

"Look, ma. I'll do it. I'll go hang out with Louis or whoever. Just don't expect me to come home with a goddamn wife."

And that was that. His mom told him they were to go dancing that night, that Louis had already said he'd do it and they were to meet with the girls at Billy Bob's around nine in the evening. Then Ryan's brother got up and drove to SMU and Ryan's sister hugged him and said that she loved him and was proud of him.

Several hours later Ryan threw on a shirt and jeans and his boots without showering and went down to drive his truck to the Stockyards. His mom suggested they carpool, but Ryan wanted the opportunity to bail if things got weird. He considered not going at all as he drove there—leaving Louis out to dry—but he figured that Louis would tell his mother, and then she would tell Ryan's mother, and then he felt like he was in grade school all over again.

He pulled into Billy Bob's and was stopped by a vaguely familiar face as he walked up. It was Louis. He'd recognized

Ryan right off, which was good because Ryan no longer had a cell phone. He had been outside smoking a cigarette and he motioned Ryan over with a wave.

"Louis?" he said, walking up.

"Yeah, but don't call me that. Lou is fine."

"Alright."

They walked inside and flashed their IDs. There was a ten-dollar cover. Ryan could have got out of it by showing his military ID, but he didn't want to risk the embarrassment of being shrugged off by the bouncer and still having to pay. Ryan didn't mind. He was more relieved that Lou was a smoker. That meant he wouldn't care if Ryan smoked. He lit up a cigarette and they grabbed two whiskey-cokes from the bar and found a few stools by the pool tables.

"You been here before?" Lou asked.

"Yeah," lied Ryan. But he'd heard enough to feel safe lying about it.

"Cool," said Lou. "You as fuckin sick of your parents as I am?"

Ryan laughed. "Yeah," he said.

"Good. I'm getting the fuck out of town soon as I get enough money to ride out. Goin to Austin, probably. Or San Diego, if I can save enough."

Ryan didn't ask what for, because he didn't want Lou to ask him where he was going and why. Lou didn't ask, and he liked that. Lou didn't ask about the war, either, which Ryan liked even more. They talked about casual things, like women and pool and drinking. Lou knew a lot about drinking, and Ryan felt a little behind for living dry for so long, but Lou didn't test him or anything and Ryan figured he could learn a few things by listening a bit. They played some pool and ordered another round of drinks. Doubles this time. Waiting for the girls, Ryan thought. But he didn't ask Lou about the girls because he didn't want to ruin the idea of their coming.

A round or two of pool later they were feeling pretty good. They got another double and Lou won a match when Ryan scratched on the eight ball. This made him angry, but Lou didn't seem to care either way and the place was getting crowded and they were eying the girls, laughing and pointing out the girls that were uptight or too loose or underage.

Ryan was feeling good. He loved looking at women in boots and short jean shorts and button-down flannels that parted at the breast from the tension. They went another round in and he started feeling pretty restless, except then Lou went and asked a girl to dance and they walked off and started dancing. Ryan watched and laughed for a little while, returning a thumbs-up and goofy looks with Lou as he twirled his girl around. He was impressed with Lou's skill at twirling and two-stepping. Ryan didn't know how to two-step, really, and wondered where Lou had learned how to dance that well. Probably school, he decided. At the community college where he danced too much or flirted with girls too much and had to drop out.

Ryan wasn't laughing anymore. He watched Lou and his girl dance another song and she was smiling. Then Ryan started to think that it was a pretty messed up thing for a guy to go out there and leave his friend hanging like that,

that it was pretty messed up to leave him alone just for a dance. Ryan felt uncomfortable now, and Lou disappeared in the massive dance floor and he was alone and without a cellphone. He looked around at their unfinished game of pool. A few couples and groups of friends hung around the table in circles. His eyes locked on a pack of women by the bar. They looked nice but one of them met his eyes and he turned away in embarrassment. He thought he heard them giggle but he didn't look and started to feel embarrassed.

He decided to go to the bar and order another drink from the bartender. He liked her cowgirl hat and skinny, long boots. She had smiled and held his gaze while he ordered before. Maybe now he could find a stool and talk with her a bit, at least until Lou finished his dance. That made him feel better. That calmed him down. He found a stool by the pool tables and dragged it to a gap at the bar. The bartender came right over, and after she brought him a double-whiskey and coke he tipped her ten dollars.

Part II: Colorado

Ryan was watching Mariana get ready at the mirror in his bedroom. Mariana had bought the mirror on craigslist, and asked Ryan to place it above the dresser so that she could sit and apply her makeup in his room. Now she sat in tight jean shorts and tall boots, wearing a sky-blue bra with no shirt as she put on blush and eyeliner. Her hair was bound above her in a loose tangle. Ryan followed the locks of interwoven gold down to the sharp angle of her waist, her tense back to the curve of her legs. He liked that she was in his chair. He liked that he lived in Colorado Springs now instead of Texas, and that Mariana was sitting in his chair in his apartment and at his dresser. He'd left Fort Worth at the end of summer, after school had started and the vacations and shopping ended, and everything was dead in the August heat. His friend Jace, a battle buddy from the war, had gotten him a job with a mechanic in Colorado Springs. It was tough work and he wasn't paid much at first, but he worked hard and he met Mariana and now he was thinking that he wanted to keep her here in his room and at his dresser.

On most nights, Mariana would come back from the bar where they met and crawl into bed with him, even though her hair smelt of smoke and he usually didn't see her until the morning when she was asleep. But he was watching her now and thinking of how much better he was doing since his return to Colorado Springs; how the war seemed long ago now that he had Mariana at his dresser talking to him.

"I think I should get bangs," she said. "Bangs would look good. Ryan?" she said, glancing at him through the mirror. "What do you think?"

Ryan was lying on his bed. "I don't know. I like your hair the way it is." He was imagining her long hair draped across her back and over her shoulders, the way it had been on the night they met.

"Everyone used to love my bangs. I think I look good with them."

"Okay. But I like your hair the way it is."

"Well, you didn't know me back then. I got great tips when I had bangs. Besides, it's time for a change."

"Well then you should get bangs," said Ryan. He was following her fingers as they drew a careful outline around her eye.

"Maybe. Or maybe I could just cut it short. Do you think I would look good with short hair?"

"I think you'd look good no matter what," he said, though he was beginning to question how he felt about losing her long hair, the feel of it in his face.

"Maybe I could cut it short. Like one of those twenties girls. What did they call them?"

Ryan pulled himself away to remember. "Flappers," he said.

"Yeah, that's right," said Mariana. "Do you really think I'd look good with short hair?"

"Sure. I think you'd look good no matter what you do."

He saw her eyes roll in the mirror. "Oh, whatever," she said. "I don't know why I even bother. It's not like you care."

Ryan pushed himself off of the bed. "You know I care," he said, walking over to the mirror. He put his hands on her shoulders and felt the softness of her skin. It amazed Ryan how bare her body was before him. "You know I love everything you do." Her skin was warm, and her hair brushed against his hand and he looked at her beautiful, painted face. He was massaging her shoulders and looking down at her chest through the bra and feeling really, very lucky with how far he'd come since the war.

She smiled and met his eyes in the mirror. Her eyes were deep and brown. Dark like her mother's, Ryan thought. Her mother was Mexican and that's where Ryan assumed she got her brown eyes and straight teeth, but she stayed out of the sun to keep her skin light, and she died her hair.

"Really?" she said, pausing to look him in the eye. "You'd love me even if I cut off all my hair?"

"Of course I would." But Ryan wasn't thinking about her with short hair anymore. He was admiring her skin and her hair all wound up and the loose strands soft against his hands. He knelt down behind her and kissed her neck. Mariana closed her eyes and pulled her arm up to his face in response. Then she straightened out and reached for her mascara.

"Thanks, baby. I don't think I'll cut it short. But I do need to dye my hair – the roots are starting to show."

She went on talking that way, but Ryan wasn't paying attention anymore. He was kissing her back and feeling her waist and arms and breasts through her laced bra, thinking about how lucky he was, how far he had come from the stale abstinence of the war and the coal-black burkas of the women who never held his gaze. He had come a long way since then, and now he was with a girl he could have whenever he wanted.

While Mariana spoke, Ryan decided that's exactly what he wanted. Right then. He wanted to take her and lay her in his bed and kiss her beautiful, made up face before she went off to work and came home smelling like smoke. He started running his hands over her body and her legs, working his kisses up to the small of her neck.

"Ryan!" she said, smiling, but still brushing her eyelashes with the mascara comb.

Ryan pulled out the band trapping her hair and watched it fall down her fair, soft back. It shimmered in the light of his bedroom and he held her, nuzzling his way through her hair.

"I want you," he whispered in her ear. He kissed her neck and then her cheek, turning her around to kiss her lips.

"Wait, I just put on lipstick!" Mariana pushed him away with a twist of her waist. "And you messed up my blush." Her voice was shrill, and it made Ryan cringe. She turned back to her makeup and pulled up her hair to repaint her face. "I'm sorry, baby," she said. "I just don't want to be late again."

Ryan sighed and looked at her for a moment before returning to his bed. He rolled onto his back and watched the ceiling fan spin. The crusted film of Mariana's blush ground between his fingers and, with the rotors churning above, Ryan felt the grains crumble off of his hand, hurtling across the room in rippled waves of sand.

Mariana finished her makeup and pulled down her hair. She brushed it quickly and threw on a plaid button-down shirt. Then she leaned over Ryan and let her curtain of hair drape around them.

"We can play when I get home," she said, grazing his cheek with a brush of her lips.

But her hair would reek of smoke when she got off work, and she wouldn't be home until three in the morning since it was a Thursday. Ryan would have to wake at seven for work, she would sleep until much later, and then he might not see her before she left for her shift on Friday.

"Okay," Mariana said, straightening her shirt. She grabbed her keys and let the door close behind her. Ryan sat up a moment later and twisted around in the bed, fixing the pillows so that he could sit and watch TV.

Ryan thought about staying awake for her, but he was tired. Maybe tomorrow, he thought. They could Febreze her hair to get rid of the smoke. They did that sometimes, even though it only worked when he was drunk. Maybe he would get drunk tomorrow. He could work late and drop by the bar to check on her. Then he could stay awake until she got home.

Part III: Montana

Ryan listened to his wife breathing beside him. He'd spent the afternoon in downtown Colorado Springs, and now he was struggling to fall sleep. He often struggled to sleep, but on this night, he wasn't going to try. Instead, he waited for his wife to fall asleep and when he peeled back the covers to leave the bed, he made sure that she didn't wake up.

On sleepless nights, Ryan would usually work in the garage. He'd work on his '98 Ford until he got tired or until morning came, and when he set down his tools he would do so carefully, so that the metal didn't clang against the concrete. His torque wrenches were the hardest because they were pure metal and had no rubber handles. Whenever he used a torque wrench, he would grab a towel from the kitchen and set it on the concrete to put the wrenches on. That way he wouldn't have to worry about waking up Carly.

But Ryan no longer had a car to work on because he sold his old Ford a few months ago to buy a new F-150. It was a 2016 model and didn't need as much work as the '98. Since he had just cleaned it yesterday, Ryan had nothing to do but lift the garage door and, as quietly as he could, drive out of their cul-de-sac home.

Theirs was a nice house in a neighborhood of nice houses. Ryan had been promoted to manager at the mechanic shop several years ago, and after he began dating Carly—who he met when she was clerking for a downtown towing company—he started saving money to place a down payment on a house. This past year, there had been talk between Ryan and Jim, the shop owner, about opening a second location; Carly's Christmas bonus had been double what it was the year before; and as the market in Colorado Springs grew the value of their house rose. They had appraised it four months before and found it worth about thirty percent more than they had bought it for.

With all of this adding up, Carly decided that Ryan should buy a 2014 F-150. She was secretly embarrassed riding in Ryan's old '98 Ford, and she thought that a new truck might pull Ryan out of the garage and into the house more. The new car had leather seats and an automatic transmission that hummed as he drove out of town. Its air-conditioning could hold comfortable temperatures and the

V8 engine was enough to press him against the back of his seat whenever he accelerated onto a highway ramp. He was accelerating onto I-25 just now, heading north, and because he hadn't slept for two nights and was slightly delirious he didn't think much about where he was going until he reached the outskirts of Denver.

Ryan went driving to calm his nerves. He almost never left town, but he had a half-tank of gas and his conversation in the recruitment office the day before was still running through his head. There were mountains to the left and empty plains to the right, so Ryan cut west onto 470 away from downtown.

He'd always liked the mountains. When Ryan was a boy, a truck came to their house in Dallas and unloaded a bed of bricks for their garden onto the driveway. They piled into a heap and, to Ryan—who'd grown up in the Panhandle—that was as close to a mountain as he'd seen. He climbed it straight away. When his parents told that story, they said he was naked and that he cut himself on the way down. They also said that he pushed his younger brother off when he tried to follow. Ryan didn't remember this, but he'd laugh when they told it. He'd also laugh when they told the story of him biting Kevin on the back. Kevin had finished his first puzzle, and everyone was clapping and so Ryan bit him. "Jealous of the attention," they used to say, and Ryan would laugh because it was funny but also because he felt bad.

Ryan was skirting Denver when he got the urge to call his brother. He wanted to ask him about his work and to laugh about the old times. It was nearly midnight in Dallas, and hour ahead, but Ryan suspected that his brother would be at work. He didn't know exactly what kind of work Kevin did, but he knew that the law firm he worked for in Dallas was famous and dealt with corporations.

Ryan scrolled through his phone and used his Bluetooth to call Kevin. He heard the ringing around him as he drove with his hands on the steering wheel. The phone rang four times and then it went to voicemail. "Hello, you've reached Kevin McDermott, attorney at law. I'm unable—" Ryan hung up the phone and called again. This time it rang twice before the answering machine picked up. "He's probably trying to sleep," Ryan thought, and as the recording rolled he tried to think up a message to leave. "Hey little brother," he wanted to say. "Just calling to check up on you." But it sounded weird in his head because he hadn't called to check up on his brother maybe ever, and the last time they had talked, Kevin had asked the "checking-in" questions. Then Ryan remembered that he hadn't called his brother since he heard that Kevin was to be made partner. His mother had told him over the phone, and while Ryan had meant to call and congratulate his brother, he had forgotten and never did.

The Bluetooth bleeped off and, as the silence set in, Ryan saw that he was passing through Boulder, Colorado. The drive became steep after the university, winding in a series of switchbacks up the mountainside. It was dark, but the moon was out, and Ryan could see the glow of Denver and the barren line of the plains beyond. Snow on the road was being wisped by the wind, and as Ryan climbed higher he started worrying about ice, but it was the end of May and the snowplows would've been through for Memorial Day.

143

By the time Ryan reached Estes Park he could feel the altitude. He had lived in Colorado for fifteen years, now, but the mountain air still felt thin. He had to take deep breaths to get oxygen into his chest, all while he sat without moving in his truck. The strain reminded him of a time that he hyperventilated during a snowball fight with his brother. Afterward, his father had placed a paper bag around his head to steady his breathing.

Ryan pulled into the Beaver Meadows entrance at Rocky Mountain National Park a half-hour later. There were five kiosks at this entrance, but only one of them was open at 3am on a Wednesday. When Ryan rolled down the window, he felt how much colder it was than in Colorado Springs. The Park Ranger took Ryan's pass and held it close to his face.

"What brings you out, this time'a night?"

The ranger was friendly. When he smiled, the skin around his eyes pulled back and crinkles formed along the corner of his face.

"Stargazing," said Ryan. They both knew this wasn't true, but it didn't matter.

"Couldn't get away for Memorial Day?" said the ranger. Ryan held his gaze without answering. "Moon'll set in a few hours. You might catch a few constellations 'fore dawn, but it's not the best night for visibility."

The man's face was tan and weathered. His skin scrunched together, measuring Ryan up as he glanced into the bed of his truck. It was a new truck and the bed was clean. When he looked back at Ryan, he raised the gate.

"Trail Ridge Road is open," he said, handing over the pass. "Just be careful drivin it. Sure to be icy this time a'night."

The ranger was right. There were several patches of ice along the road, and Ryan had to drive slowly to avoid fishtailing. Walls of snow lined both sides of the road except along the switchbacks, where the edge was sharp and exposed and carved its way into the mountain. After each of these, Ryan would rev his engine to get the truck moving again. It was a heavy truck, with a V8 engine that rumbled every time he accelerated up a switchback.

Ryan knew there were beautiful views at each of these turnouts, but even with the moon he couldn't see beyond the glare of his headlights. They reflected back at him and kept his eyes dilated so that at one point he became frustrated and pulled into a scenic turnout. He idled for a moment and turned off his headlights. Then he stepped out of the truck. The cold was enough that he could see it coming out of his mouth. There was no wind, and the steam collected in the air with each breath. After his eyes adjusted, he could see the mountains outlined by moonlight, the pavement glow behind him.

He got back into his truck and drove for a while with the lights off. He could see the snow and the road clear enough in the moonlight, but before he could reach another switchback, he switched the lights back on. "Can't be doing that," he heard himself say. "You're too old for that, now."

When he turned the lights back on, he noticed the fuel gauge on his dashboard. The needle hung just below the letter "E." Ryan flicked the glass with his finger. When he'd hit Denver just a hundred miles back, it had read a half tank. But it was a new truck and Ryan had not anticipated how his V8 engine would handle the steepening slope of the mountains.

He'd also no way of knowing how far he had driven down Trail Ridge Road. His phone had no service and there were no mile-markers above the snow to mark the nearest park exit. Ryan decided that he would drive into the next campsite, instead, and try to find a park ranger. But as he drove with his foot lightly on the pedal, he began to realize that he might not make it to the next campground.

When his truck finally sputtered to a stop, Ryan was on a slope with very narrow lanes, but he managed to coast to the crest of a short hill. Going with his foot on the brake and both hands gripping the steering wheel, Ryan guided the car toward a switchback at the bottom of the slope. It was hard to control the truck with the engine off. Ryan had to wedge his shoulders against the seat and push his whole weight against the brake for the wheels to slow. Then he tucked the car into a small turnoff where it would be safe from traffic and falling rocks.

Ryan still had no service on his phone, but he knew that if he found a ranger soon and got some gas into his truck, he might be able to get home before Carly woke up. Or else he could drive to an area with reception and call so that she wouldn't be worried sick. He could even make it to work on time and go on pretending like he'd never gone into that recruiting office the day before.

But he didn't go looking for a campsite to find a ranger. He didn't even get out of his car. He sat there in his seat until the warmth was gone and the battery died, and when he noticed the trailhead sign before him it was already four in the morning. It was the cold that finally pushed him out of his car. The snow beneath his sneakers broke as he stepped out. In his backseat was a jacket that said Jim's Motor Repair. It had oil stains on the sleeves, but Ryan put it over his coat as an extra layer. Then he put on his boots and a pair of work gloves and walked over to the trailhead sign.

The sign was a triangular slate on a wooden post. Ryan pointed an LED keychain light at it, but the lettering was so worn that he couldn't make out anything except for a ponderosa pine and below it a word that might've read "Campground." Ryan zipped up his jacket. He would hike the trail to the campground and find the park ranger there. He imagined himself hiking through the woods in the mountains and driving home to the sunrise. He walked for a long time. His feet moved beneath him, and his breath came out in spurts from the altitude. Mountains shimmered in the moonlight and a river trickled somewhere far away.

Ryan had enlisted over a decade ago because he wanted to fight in Afghanistan. "Kabul," his recruiter told him. "If you go anywhere, you'll go to Kabul." He told Ryan about Kabul. He told Ryan that it was a city surrounded by mountains, that it was higher in elevation than Denver and that it wasn't hot there like people thought it was. He told Ryan about the food and the culture and the vibrant colored robes that the women wore, and he told Ryan about how the people would view him, an American soldier. He told Ryan that he would be their liberator. This gave Ryan an image of himself as a field soldier. This image was shattered the night that George W. Bush appeared on live television and told the world that there were weapons of mass destruction in Iraq. Two months later, Ryan was driving a truck across the desert to Baghdad.

It took two hours for Ryan to find a sign that read "Colorado River Trail." By that time, he was thirsty and faint from the walking. He'd reached the ruins of an old ghost town and knew now that the trail would not lead to any campgrounds or park rangers, but he wasn't concerned about reaching home in time for work anymore. Ryan had forgotten to pack any water.

It took a long time for the thirst to kick in. Cold and exhaustion kept his mind distracted, and when he'd left his home in Colorado Springs six hours before, he hadn't even thought to bring a bottle of water. Now the river was a taunting trickle in the darkness and Ryan's throat hurt.

Ruined foundations from an old ghost town scattered an opening before him. A post in the middle read "Lulu City," and beyond that was a riverside beach where the water became wide and shallow. A stream trickled over stones, pushing against the pebbly shore. Ryan's boots were waterproof, but he was tired and thirsty and not thinking of the cold, so he underestimated the river's depth. When he took a step in, the river came past his ankle. It flooded his boots and soaked his socks. Ryan didn't notice this until after he'd scooped the water with his hands and drank from it. Then his hands and his lips and his feet were cold. He kept drinking until he felt the cold inside of him, and even though he was thirsty he stopped drinking because now he was shivering.

Ryan took a few steps back and sat down on the shore. He stayed like that, hugging his knees to fight the convulsions of his body, but the cold was in his gut and in his lungs and on the rocks beneath him. There was another hour before sunrise, and several more before the air would become warm. He had no food or gas. He wasn't even sure anymore if he knew which direction his car was. Breathing became difficult and his vision blurred. Above him the night was pale, and the stars became a shower of light.

Then there was mortar.

The shrieking of it fell around him and Ryan began to gasp. His heart shuddered with every concussion. There was an explosion ahead of him and he was on his back, panting for air but there was nothing to breathe. He felt a pain in his side and thought he might be hit, that his lung had collapsed. Ryan's vision cut out. There was a man carrying firewood. Trees fell and Ryan was shaking, curled up on the rocks. His chest was moving too fast. A man leaned over him, young but weathered. Heat from the blast steamed from his face.

When Ryan woke up, he was lying on the ground before a fire. There was dirt in his hair and on his lips. His elbow throbbed and he could tell that he had been dropped there. His eyes adjusted past the glare to find that they were bordered by the remnants of a ruined log cabin. Behind Ryan the wall was two or three logs high. The other side had no walls. There was a fire, a tent, and a man. The man was young, and he was preparing a kettle. Ryan could smell coffee.

"You hyperventilated," said the man.

Ryan tried to sit but his head was ringing. "Jesus," he said.

The man placed a flimsy grill over the fire, pinning it into the dirt. "The altitude. Plus, you were hypothermic."

He had a full voice and long beard, but the hair at his cheek was longer than on his chin and the hair on his head was matted down. He wore jeans that had patches at the knee, and his coat had fur on the inside.

Beside Ryan were his boots, drying by the fire. His socks had been draped across them and his feet were bare. His work jacket, which was across him like a blanket, was beginning to slip from around his shoulders.

"How long was I out?" said Ryan.

"Fifteen minutes. Not long."

Ryan felt his toes. They were still cold. "You carried me here? Made a fire—"

"I was already making a fire."

Ryan watched him place the kettle onto his makeshift grill.

"That's how I found you," he said. "I was gathering wood for the fire."

"Oh," said Ryan.

The younger man poked at the fire with a stick and glowing flakes shot up. Above them, the night peeled back into a violet haze. To the east was a line of orange, broken by the ridgeline. Carly would be awake, soon.

"You're a veteran," said the man.

Ryan nodded. "How'd you know?"

"Your driver's license." Ryan reached for his wallet and the man said, "I didn't take your money."

Ryan's hand fell back to his side. He looked at the young man across from him. His boots were Army. There was a bayonet looped onto his belt, as well. An army combat knife.

"Iraq," said Ryan. "The invasion. You?"

"Afghanistan."

Ryan nodded. He wanted to ask when but supposed it must've been recent. He looked about mid-twenties, when you took away the beard and the firelight.

"What's your name?" asked Ryan.

"Doesn't matter."

"No, I suppose it doesn't," he said. "But it's something to call you. Something besides 'Kid.'"

"It's Mark."

Ryan nodded. "Okay," he said. "I'm Ryan."

The coffee percolated and Mark used a rag to grab its handle. "I only have one mug," he said. He poured half of the coffee into his mug and the rest into a bowl. He handed the bowl to Ryan. He didn't apologize for the bowl or offer him the cup. Instead, he moved with his mug and sat down across from Ryan. The hairs of Mark's moustache grated against the cup when he sipped.

"I don't suppose you have any sugar," said Ryan, pulling his legs beneath him. His body was stiff, and he couldn't remember the last time he'd sat cross-legged.

Mark didn't answer. Instead he said, "You're from Colorado Springs. Why were you out hiking in the middle of the night?"

"I was driving. Ran out of gas a few miles back."

"Driving here, in the middle of the night?"

"I couldn't sleep."

Mark pulled out a pan from his backpack. It was dirty and charred on the bottom. He placed it over the grill and took out a plastic Tupperware. He used his combat knife to carve a glob of grease from the container. It sizzled when it hit the pan.

"Not a lot of people drive through the mountains when they're trying to fall asleep."

"That's true," said Ryan. He stared into the brown murk of his coffee, let the warmth of it wash over him. "But I went to a recruitment office, yesterday."

Mark's face tightened. "What the fuck'd you do that for?"

Ryan was silent. The answer now was the same as it had been two days earlier, at the Memorial Day barbeque. It was because of Terry, his gunner, who had slumped to the floor of their Humvee with a bullet in his eye, but it was also because of the smoke pits, early mornings in the chow hall and afternoons at the motor pool. Ryan thought about New Years, when Marty snuck a case of Bud Light into the FOB and spewed all over his boots after his third can. The four of them sat in the dirt afterward, already drunk when the flare went up. All of Iraq turned red for five, maybe ten seconds. Ryan thought about that flare and how simple the world had been then, but that story was too hard to tell so when he looked at Mark he said, "Near the end of our tour we got stationed at an outpost on the road to Basra. It was a pile of rocks, really. Hesco walls, tents for sleeping. In the morning I'd wake up to the sunrise and make coffee with my sergeant over a fire." Ryan watched the flames as he spoke. "I guess you just miss it, sometimes."

While Ryan spoke, Mark cracked a pair of eggs over the pan and had to lift it off of the grill to stop the grease from popping. When Ryan was finished, he contorted his lips into a grimace.

"You think that," said Ryan, the bowl of coffee steaming over him. "But wait until you have a 9-to-5."

"Fuck that. I don't need a desk job and I ain't going back to that shithole."

"I said the same thing ten years ago."

Mark was breaking the yolk with his spatula on the pan. "Yeah," he said. "But you went to Iraq. You were part of the invasion." Mark said this like it was a privilege. "Take it from me. There ain't nothin left in Afghanistan worth fighting for."

Ryan thought about this. The coffee in his bowl was cool enough to sip now, but he held it before his face without drinking. "I guess it doesn't matter," he said. "The recruiter from yesterday, the one at the office I went to, he said that it was their busiest time of the year." Ryan looked up. "He said they'd already met their quota. That I was too old."

The spatula halted and, for a moment, Mark held it above the pan in perfect stillness.

"I've always wanted to go to Kabul," said Ryan. "But it doesn't matter. Iraq, Afghanistan. Maybe I was lucky."

Mark looked like he might say something, like it was on the tip of his tongue if he could only find the words. Then he shook his head and said, "Fuck it." He turned back to his food. "There ain't nothin back there for me."

Mark took the pan off the fire and put it on a stone in the ground. He used the spatula to pick up an egg and balanced it there with the steam coming off it.

They sat in silence for a while. Ryan sipped from his bowl. The coffee was bitter and burnt, but the warmth and the smell of it gave him chills. It felt odd that just moments before he had hyperventilated and might've died of hypothermia. The thought was uncomfortable, so he looked across at Mark and said, "What about you. What're you running from?" He gestured to the ruins around them. Etched into one of the logs was the phrase, "Fuck the police," and half-buried next to him was a crushed can of Coca-Cola.

"Running?" said Mark. "Who said I was running?" Ryan didn't reply, and Mark shook his head. "I ain't running, man."

"Okay," said Ryan. "Then why are you here."

Mark didn't flinch. "That's a long story."

Ryan opened his arms. "Well," he said. "Nobody's making you tell it. But I'm in no rush to get back to my truck."

Mark sighed. "Sure, but it's not like I'm gonna walk you there." He said this and then rolled his eyes. "Look, I took off on this road trip from Florida. Working as I went, camping to save money. I hit the west coast and was gonna go all the way to Alaska..."

He trailed off and Ryan waited. "What happened?" he said.

154

Mark shifted. The spatula was in his hand, and it moved with the egg still steaming. "My buddy killed himself."

Ryan absorbed the blow without flinching. He waited for Mark to say more but the younger man only leaned forward, blowing at his egg to cool it.

"Shit," said Ryan. "I'm sorry."

Mark took a long time to reply. His jaw was clenched. Then he shrugged and said, "It happens."

They sat that way with Ryan lost for words and Mark cooling his egg. Then Mark looked up and said, "Anyway, I'm not planning to go out like that."

Ryan pushed at the dirt with his foot. He wanted to ask Mark what that meant, whether he was inclined toward a "blaze of glory" type ending, but Mark didn't strike Ryan as the type. In fact, he came off more stable than most of the guys that Ryan worked with in the shop.

"So, what comes next," asked Ryan.

"I'm gonna keep riding it out," said Mark. "Gotta go until I can't go any further. That's the idea—why I'm here—I'm gonna take the Colorado down to Mexico." He glanced at the river where he'd found Ryan. "All of the way to Baja California."

"You've got a car around here?" said Ryan, craning his neck to look.

"Na," he said. "Had to sell that for a plane ticket to my buddy's funeral."

"So you're on foot?" said Ryan.

"Sure, that's right."

"You're gonna hike to Mexico."

"I'll raft once the river gets deep enough," said Mark, his shoulders tensing. "Fish for food, camp the riverbanks. Not like I'm the first to do it."

"And the Grand Canyon?" said Ryan. "The Hoover Dam? What're you gonna do there?"

"Keep goin, I reckon."

Ryan laughed. He liked Mark. He liked Mark and he liked his spirit. He made Ryan think about his old plans for after the war. This made him quiet, but after a while the smell of fried egg taunted his stomach and he had to ask Mark for a bite. Mark gave him a whole egg. It was still in the pan and he had no utensils, so Ryan had to wait until it was cool enough for him to eat it with his fingers.

"I'm just a few miles down the trail," said Ryan. "Let's get me some gas and then I'll take you into town, buy you some gear. I'll drive you all of the way to Grand Junction, if you want."

Mark took a bite of his egg from the spatula. He had to breathe in and out to cool the egg. "Nah," he said. "That'd defeat the point."

Ryan was surprised. He wanted to ask Mark what the point was, or how else he could repay him, but Mark was busy eating and Ryan's own egg was steaming in the pan before him.

"What about you," said Mark. "What're you gonna do, now that you can't reenlist?"

Ryan shrugged. He knew the answer was to go home, to open up a second repair shop and start a family. But he couldn't say that. Not here. Not eating eggs with his bare hands and the mountains all around. "Montana," he said.

"That right?"

Ryan pinched the egg with his fingers. It was dirty from the grease in the pan, and the yoke wasn't fully cooked through. "Upper Rockies," he said, biting it at the edge. "Cabin in the woods. Maybe I'll do some mechanical work on the side. You know, small-time stuff for the locals." He said this, and after he said it, he could see himself there. The vision was so real it was like he could pull it out of the earth and hold it there with the grease in his hands.

Above them the sky was white. A yellow dawn had pulled back the curtain of twilight and now the sun was about to breach the mountains. It would've already risen on the other side of that ridgeline, but as Ryan waited for it to come over the mountains, he thought of how it would be higher in the north, in Montana. The sun would be well above the Atlantic, meanwhile—Europe, as well—and a few hours before dusk in Iraq. Ryan thought about how the sun set in the States at the same time that it rose in Iraq. "The Land of Genesis," he said out loud. He pulled his knees up and felt the dirt on his feet. His toes ground together with the sand between them, digging into the earth. He took another bite of his egg. Yolk broke from the core and dribbled onto his chin, the pan.

"Here," said Mark.

He handed Ryan a slice of bread from his pack and took another for himself. Ryan used it to wipe his face. There was dirt on the bread from his face, and then from the pan, but he ate it anyway. Across from him, Mark was wiping his spatula with the bread. He tore a piece with his teeth, and together they ate the bread in the sunlight, savoring the rich flavors of grease and yolk.

ON LONELINESS

After the meal is eaten and the bottles of Priorat wine removed from the table, a round of drinks is brought over to the couples. Peter orders a Johnny Walker straight, while Alan takes his on the rocks. The waiter gives a mocha to Helen and then a stemmed glass of Amontillado to Sheryl. Peter is still breathing in the fumes of his whiskey when Sheryl excuses herself for the ladies' room. "I'll join you," says Helen.

Alan pivots to admire the swish of Sheryl's dress as they walk away. "She's a nice piece," he says.

Peter studies Alan's expression for irony. He finds none and says, "Helen's been trying to set her up for months."

Wine is buzzing in his ear and he can see that Alan is smiling too broadly and that his eyelids are sagging over the blue of his eyes. Alan is relatively new to their law firm in downtown Seattle. Peter knows little about him, other than his being much younger than the rest of them. His face is handsome and bronze, with a dark stubble defining his jawline. Peter once overheard him telling a secretary in their office that she had "toned calves."

"You think she's too old for me?" he says.

Peter stretches out on the booth. The leather is plush and feels cool against the back of his neck and hands. "I think *she* might think that," he says. The leather of the booth is a deep shade of red, like burgundy. "But she doesn't look too old for you."

"I think she's too old for me," says Alan. "I can't read older women."

Peter lets his head lean forward. A recorded saxophone blends with the hushed tones of love-speak from a table diagonal to their booth and Alan yawns. "Age makes you better at hiding things," Peter says. "But it's not a real thing. Age is the kind of thing that gets dissolved by conversation."

"Conversation is dull," says Alan. His head lolls to the side and his bangs fall into his line of vision.

"Age isn't such a thing," says Peter again. "People don't change so much with age. They learn things. They adapt to the world and become desensitized to things. But they don't change, really." Peter looks at Alan until the younger man is looking back. "You know, ninety percent of your personality is established before you're five years old. Did you know that?"

Alan laughs, the ice in his glass rattling.

"The last ten percent is set by twenty-three. Things like emotional stability, how happy you'll be, whether you'll lead a life of scholarship or labor or laziness—"

The women return. Peter shifts into the corner and Helen slides in next to him. Her bleached hair falls across one shoulder and she smiles at Alan so that the skin around her eyes becomes crinkled. Sheryl sits across from them.

She's a physician with Helen at the hospital. They are of a similar age, but Sheryl's brown hair and eyes glow with the suggestion of youth. Her laugh is similarly vivacious, though she hasn't laughed since Alan got drunk halfway through the night.

"You're saying that I'm the exact person I was ten years ago," says Alan, as if the women never left. "But that's impossible. Ten years ago, I despised the taste of scotch. Now I can't imagine my life without it."

"No, no," says Peter. "You're missing the point. Acquired tastes don't apply. It's more about your persona." Nobody seems to understand him, so he adds, "Picture a finished mold of yourself—like Plato's theory, you know the one—only, that mold of you isn't somewhere up in the sky, it's somewhere in time."

"Plato's *Republic* meets *Interstellar*," says Sheryl.

Helen laughs. "I swear," she says. "We leave them alone for two minutes."

Peter curls scotch around his tongue, following the sting of it to the Spanish wine in his head. "It's like this," he says. "After the age of twenty-three, neurons in the frontal lobe of your brain—the area of your brain that deals with personality—they stabilize. They get locked in. That's how your personality comes to be, the person you are today."

"Really," says Helen, "at twenty-three? God, that time was such a blur."

"I was finishing a degree in Literature," laughs Sheryl.

"I had a roundabout path to medicine," she tells Peter. "Maybe if my personality had developed earlier."

"Maybe," says Peter. "The problem, though, is that twenty-three is also when our brain cells start dying off faster than they can reproduce. Unused dopamine receptors wilt away. Neurons shrivel up. The whole brain starts rotting to zilch so that—"

"Now isn't that a pleasant thought," says Alan.

"So that who we are now, Alan, isn't who we were at the age of twenty-three, after all. In fact, it's *less* of who we were, making the experiences we have today like shadows of what we used to feel. Ecstasy back then is now closer to glee. Pain doesn't hurt as much. And love consumes less of our world than it ever did before."

Peter finishes and sets down his drink. Notes from a Kenny G album drift between them and laughter echoes from a nearby table. "I remember reading about this," says Alan. His eyes roll behind his upturned scotch glass. "Yes, I remember now. The immensely reputable *Buzzfeed* featured this in a blog post the other day."

Peter flushes. "I'll have you know," he says, "I took a number of psychology courses after my tour. And besides, there's a documentary on Netflix—"

The group's laughter drowns out his defense. "Ah, where would we be without Netflix," says Sheryl.

"It's not so terrible," says Peter, his eyes following the gleam of Sheryl's hair. "Some of their documentaries are educational enough."

"Peter binge-watches documentaries like they're *Game of Thrones*," says Helen. She slips her arm about his and Peter has to stiffen to keep his scotch from spilling.

"They're not so terrible."

"How is it we got onto this subject, anyhow?

"And what subject is that?"

Helen smiles. "The subject of love."

Peter frowns. "I'm not sure," he says. "In fact, I'm not sure we're talking about love at all."

"Sure we are," says Alan. "Graced by the company of these two beauties, how could we avoid it?" He looks at Sheryl, who becomes absorbed in the workings of her fingernails.

'No, I don't think so."

"You said," Helen says, jostling his arm. "You said that love consumes *less* of our lives than it did when we were younger. I just can't bring myself to believe that."

"Well it isn't *me* saying that. It's basic neurology."

Helen releases his arm. "Sheryl, have you ever dated a lawyer?" But before she can answer, Helen says, "You learn quickly how *not* to win arguments."

"This isn't an argument. It's a discussion."

"Naturally."

Peter looks at Alan. "Helen wouldn't know a discussion if it hit her in the face. Our dinner conversations always turn into a monologue about her trip to the dry cleaners. This is a discussion," Peter says, turning to his flushed wife. "And it's a discussion about the human condition."

The Kenny G album comes to an end in the background, and when the music returns it's a song they heard at the beginning of the night. Alan breaks the stillness and says, "Love and the human condition. Is the one not a result of the other?"

"Exactly," says Helen.

"Well, I suppose that might be the case if our capacity to love was the distinguishing quality of humanity," says Peter. "But is our ability to love the main thing that separates us from animals?"

"Yes," says Helen. "It must be."

"But in what way?"

"Well," she says, the spoon of her latte rattling on the plate, "the love that I have for you…"

Her voice fades out and Peter says, "But what you're talking about is romantic love. Let's look at romantic love. Are there no animals that demonstrate romantic love?"

"Penguins!" says Sheryl. Then, less excitedly, "Penguins. The males have this whole ritual where they spend days sifting through stones, trying to find the perfect one to give to their mate."

"There you go," says Peter. "Penguins. And what about swans? Or wolves? Don't they all mate for life?" Helen rolls her eyes. "Most *humans* don't even mate for life. So, if we're going to talk about a thing that distinguishes men from animals, I'd hardly say that the thing is love."

"Then what *would* you say?" asks Helen. She's crossed her legs and is leaning back against the booth.

"I think," he says to Sheryl, "personally, I mean – I think it's our imagination."

"Is that right?" says Sheryl. She's working her fingernails again, but her eyes are on Peter.

"Imagination," says Peter, skimming the gleam of Sheryl's hair, "is our ability as humans to wonder. To question abstract concepts and reach a kind of self-consciousness, an understanding of our place in the universe."

"UW's next director of Philosophy," says Alan.

Helen leans forward. "You'll have to excuse my husband," she says. "He gets philosophical after a few drinks." Peter looks at Helen. "What?" she says. "It's true. You know it's true. Remember our first New Years together?"

"You know I don't. And I don't believe one word of your story."

"Marty was there! He saw the whole thing."

Sheryl straightens. "What about Marty?" she says.

"Martin's an orthopedic surgeon at our hospital," Helen explains to Alan. "And Peter got so hammered at his house one New Years—"

"Do we really have to do this?"

Helen continues over him. "It was the beginning of my residency, and Peter was just starting at UW Law. Only, he got so hammered that I ended up taking care of him the whole night! He was stumbling about, vomiting on the carpet; I had to put him in Marty's bathtub, it got so bad. Then he got real dramatic, sitting in the bathtub with his head lolling about, and he started saying things like, 'Time is relative!' and, 'The universe doesn't exist!'"

"Slanderous hearsay—"

Helen extends her arms, crying out to the restaurant, "Time doesn't exist!"

165

Their whole booth is laughing. Even Peter stifles a grin. "No wonder you keep talking about the Human Condition," says Sheryl. Her eyes shine as she sips her sherry, pinching the stem of her glass.

"Sure," says Peter, but he's smiling, and his eyes drop to Sheryl's neckline. "But I'm not the one who brought it up. You two brought us here with your talk of love." Sheryl shrugs. "Here, let's try this. Let's try talking about an emotion that's innately human; something that anybody can relate to." He looks down at the glass in his hands. "If we're going to try that," he says, "if we're going to try talking about a thing that people can relate to at all times, then love is hardly the thing. Let's try this. Helen, sweetheart. Tell us how you feel when I say the word 'loneliness.'"

Helen is still thinking about their New Years at Marty's house, and looks surprised when everyone goes silent waiting for her response. "I don't know," she says. She glances across at Sheryl and the two share a smile.

"Alright, can you knock it off?" Peter snaps, but he flinches at his own harshness and then places a hand on Helen's knee. "I'm sure you know," he says. "Just tell us what you feel when I say that. When I say the word 'loneliness.' What do you *feel*?"

Helen studies the funneled glass of her Mocha, the crusted foam around its edge. "I don't know. I feel... I feel sad, I guess."

"Exactly!" Peter beams. "But what kind of sad?"

"What kind of sad? What do you mean, 'what kind of sad'?"

"I mean what *kind* of sad." He lifts his hand from Helen's knee to face the group. "Is it the fleeting kind of sad, like when you heard that a hundred thousand civilians lost their homes during the Second Battle of Fallujah? Or is it something else, something deeper—"

"Peter," says Helen. Alan and Sheryl cringe at the mention of war. "I felt more than a *fleeting* sadness for those people, and you of all people know how I feel for you and everyone who had to fight in that war."

"Well I was in Afghanistan, but sure," says Peter, shrugging. "It was a terrible thing. And the reality of that much destruction is so much more than we could ever hope to grasp. But you'll have forgotten all about that in five minutes. And if I said it again and again out loud—that 100,000 civilians lost their homes, and countless others died—you might listen to me and you might feel something, but gradually that statistic would lose its weight. It's the same with a word like love. Semantic satiation, that's the term," he tells Alan. "But loneliness—"

"Pete," says Helen, touching his hand. "Pete, honey, I think you've had too much to drink."

"Oh, come on! Can we cut the shit? Can we all just cut the shit already? Or will you keep trying to undermine my whole point."

Helen flashes an apology to Sheryl but finds Alan instead. Sheryl is staring wide-eyed at Peter.

"Can I go on?" asks Peter. "I'm sorry, Helen dear. I didn't mean to yell at you. But can I go on? Can I go on without you undermining my whole point?"

Helen wafts a hand through the air. "Go ahead," she says. "Blow us away with your whole *point.*"

"Good. Now, what was I saying?"

"Something about loneliness—"

"Right! Thank you, Sheryl. Now Sheryl, you're a woman that understands—a woman that appreciates a good discussion—I can see it in your eyes. You've very intelligent eyes."

"Digression," Alan says, wagging a finger.

"Okay, okay. What I was saying about loneliness: it's a word like that—left out on its own like that—it's the kind of thing that strikes a chord with people. With all kinds of people. It makes you *feel* something. Right, sweetheart?"

Helen doesn't reply.

"It makes us feel it deep down, the gutted feeling of it—the loneliness of our whole existence—it all comes back to our imagination and our awareness of mankind's place in the universe, but we feel it with a word like loneliness and it hits us deep down like a blow to the balls."

"Lovely," says Sheryl. Helen laughs abruptly.

"What? You feel it," says Peter. "You can deny that you feel it, but you do. And I think we feel that gut-wrenching feeling of it because it's the only thing that's inherent in all of us. Happiness, hate, despair: those are all just fleeting. But Loneliness – loneliness is our natural state. It's where we return each night before we go to sleep, and it's how we start every day. Now Alan, you and Helen would argue that the human condition is more about love. But the kind of love that you're referring to is the transient kind. Romantic love: it's an illusion. That's Thomas Moore speaking, not me. True love is unintelligible."

"We're back to love, then," says Alan, sliding his arm up the booth behind Sheryl.

Sheryl leans forward. "Who was it that said love is being stupid together," she asks Peter. "It was a French philosopher—"

"Well it doesn't matter because it's true, isn't it? Love *is* stupid."

"Woody Allen has some great quotes about love," says Helen, rousing. "What's the one about love and suffering? To love is to suffer, but not loving is just as bad?"

"I know that one," says Alan, raising his chin. "To love is—"

"Of course you do," says Peter. "And that's love. It's unpredictable, irrational, inconsistent, whatever you want to call it. And it's like that because even in love we feel the ache of loneliness, how every time you hold a woman in your arms you want to squeeze her into you." He pauses to stare at the golden blend in his glass. "That's what it is," he says. "It's the anticipation. The anticipation of being apart. Of that togetherness ending. And our awareness of that is the only thing that heightens with age. The realization that—regardless of happiness, longevity, prosperity—we will, each of us, inevitably die alone."

The table goes silent. In the restaurant, the music has been turned off and beside them a young man helps his date into her jacket. They leave and a busboy swoops in to clear the table behind them. He places dishes onto a plastic tray before wiping the glass with a sponge. The glassware rattles on the tray as he lifts it.

"There was a Spanish girl that I loved, sometime after my deployment," says Peter. He eyes the maroon leather of the booth, his empty glass cupped in one hand. "I was in London at the time, studying politics on a year abroad. She was younger than me, but she had an intelligent look. You know, a troubled look that complemented her features. And big, sad eyes—"

"This was before we met," says Helen.

Her face is pale and Peter turns to her as if those were the first words she'd spoken all night. "It was," he says. "It was also before I moved to Seattle, a few years after Afghanistan. And here was this Spanish girl. She was lonely, you see. We were both lonely, stuck in the middle of London. I mean, there we were in London, one of the biggest cities in the world, and we were completely alone. But we found each other at a party and—nonsensically, as is the nature of love—we were drawn together. Drawn from the moment we met."

Peter sets down his scotch and stares at Sheryl's wrist. "I was only twenty-five at the time—she'd just turned twenty—and while I'd seen too much of the world, she still wanted to change it. She was dramatic and passionate and there was something in her that just spilled with sentiment. Like how infants feel so much of the world that they have to become numb just to cope with it, except that she was still *feeling* everything."

His gaze drifts off in the telling. "She used to nuzzle into my neck when I held her at night, her whole body convulsing. I'd feel her face move against mine so that the hairs on my chin bristled her cheek. When we slept together, it was like our conscious minds were released somehow. Like we were inside of ourselves, but with no control over what we were doing."

A waiter passes the table for the fourth time and Helen gives him a nod for the check. "Whenever you get the chance," she says.

"The first time we kissed, I felt her shaking in my arms. I thought she was cold because it was winter in London and my hand was on her neck, but she explained in broken English that she was scared. 'I can't help it,' she told me. She just felt so much.

"She was that way about everything. She'd cry just reading the news. An idealist, you know, but she had a certain purity that was everything I wanted after the war. I'd wake in the middle of the night to her moving blankets around the bed and I'd ask her what she was doing. 'Your arm was cold,' she'd tell me. She slept like shit every night I stayed over because she'd worry about how I was sleeping. And we could only watch romantic comedies together because they were the only thing that wouldn't break her. The one time I forced her to watch a serious film—Pan's Labyrinth, I remember—she cried for an hour and then slipped into depression for the next week.

"And I can't really tell you why, but I fell madly in love with that girl. It was nonsensical, but it was real. I don't expect you to understand, and I've no idea how it happened. Christ, we hardly even spoke. She'd stare into my eyes without saying a word all because she was embarrassed of how it would sound in English. One night she spoke at me in Spanish for a minute straight. At the end of it, she collapsed into my arms and slept like a child. She thought I understood, you see? Not the words so much as on a deeper level."

The waiter returns with the bill. Helen fishes for a credit card from her purse and passes it along. "I'm so sorry," she tells him. Across the hall, servers flip chairs onto tables and a busboy sweeps the back of the restaurant. The lights are on.

"It got to the point that I wanted to tell her everything," Peter says. "About the war, I mean. I started with simple stories—funny ones, nice ones—and she'd listen because she grew up reading romance novels on the Second World War and recognized war as a thing with a happy ending. Then she'd run her hands through my hair and say all of the clichés I'd never heard from a woman. Eventually, I worked my way up to telling her about Branson."

"Peter," Helen says. The waiter returned with the receipt and she's signing it. "Peter, the restaurant's all but abandoned. Let's grab a cab before it's too late."

Peter stares into the booth.

"I think that might be a good idea," says Alan. "Sheryl?"

Sheryl reaches for the stem of her glass. "Well, I've hardly touched my sherry."

Peter smiles. "Sheryl, you gorgeous bird," he says. "You have the most beautiful eyes. Do you know that?" Alan looks across Helen, who looks away. "Anyway, I'm almost to the point. Now here was this Spanish girl that I wanted to tell everything, and one day I muster up the strength to talk about Branson. This was my first tour, and I'm all over it now but what happened was this kid in my platoon committed suicide."

"Jesus," says Sheryl. "That's terrible!"

Peter nods. "Shot himself in the head. I'm over it now, but back then... Well, she's the first person I'm telling this to, and it all comes out jumbled and broken and I break down crying before I've even started. She has no idea what's going on. Even when I try again the next day—to tell her, I mean—it's a lost cause. She tries to listen, but there's the language barrier and the brokenness and I don't even know it but I'm not telling her about Branson just because I want to get the thing off of my chest. I'm doing it because I want to *show* her something. And what I'm trying to show her is the whole bigger picture of what I'd learned of life up to that point, about loneliness and how it's the root of everything and the reason that Branson killed himself. Only, by the fourth or fifth time of telling it, she stops even listening. Because this isn't a romantic story, see? The kid shot himself in a latrine. We found him curled up on the floorboards, soaked in shit and blood. But she's Spanish-Catholic, saying things like, 'I'll pray for his soul,' while I'm getting frustrated because I don't care about his soul—that wasn't why I'd told her—and after talking all that time, I'd have to start all over again.

"It killed her, I think, to disappoint me," says Peter after a pause. "But I was obsessing over it and I wanted to make her see it so that by the end of the term, the night before she left for Spain, she refused to even say goodbye. I sat there banging on her door with her flatmates all around and everybody telling me to leave. She couldn't look me in the eyes. Like it would hurt so much that, physically, she couldn't even do it. Can you imagine that? I mean, just looking at me. It's like just looking at me would've killed her."

The empty glass quivers in Peter's hand. "But that's just how it goes," he says. His mouth opens to say more, but then he closes it and bites back the words.

Sheryl exhales from across the booth. "Peter," she says, softly enough for Helen to look up. "You must've been crushed."

"I guess I was, in a way," he says, setting down his glass. "I often think of how I failed her. And I think I failed because of love." Helen coughs and covers her mouth. "You know, because I wanted her to understand what happened to Branson, the loneliness of what happened to him, but I was in love and in denial of my own loneliness so that, even as the whole point of it was eating out of me through Branson and the way that he died, I still couldn't get it across."

"And what *was* the point," says Helen.

"Well, the point—I guess—is that you can be in the middle of a thing as big as a war, surrounded by people every single day who would lay down their lives for you, and still the loneliness of it can crush you. That's what happened to Branson. The weight of his loneliness killed him."

Peter lowers his glass. He sags against the booth as if he's finished a task, and only Sheryl is still watching him. Alan's looking down, and Helen, shaking her head, follows the waiters as they lift the glass tabletops to remove the cloth underneath.

After a time, Alan attempts to fill the void of Peter's silence by remarking on Sheryl's Amontillado, but Helen interrupts him. "The restaurant's closed," she says, reaching for her jacket.

They follow Helen through a maze of abandoned tables to the exit. Outside, mist dampens their faces. Alan flags down a pair of taxis and the two couples stand across from each other. Alan watches Sheryl watching Peter. Sheryl flushes, the wine rising into her face. "Really," she says, "it was a wonderful dinner. Thank you for inviting me."

Peter begins to reply but feels the cold of Helen's hand on his arm. "Of course," says Helen. "We should do it again."

Sheryl looks at Helen and then Peter. Her fingers work the buttons on her coat. "Well, goodbye, Peter," she says. She kisses him on the cheek and Peter rests his hand on her waist. His eyes linger as she backs away.

"I'll see you on Monday," says Helen.

Peter turns to Alan. "Should we get another cab?"

"I don't know," says Alan. "Sheryl, where do you live?"

"By the university."

"We could share, if it's not too much of an inconvenience. I'm right off of Sand Point."

Sheryl seems to nod as she steps in after him. Peter has hardly registered their agreement before Alan lowers himself into the backseat of the car.

"Lovely to meet you," Helen says. Alan smiles back with a bewildered satisfaction.

"Goodnight, Helen," he says.

"You two be good, now," says Peter.

"Goodbye."

"So long."

"See you on Monday."

"Goodnight."

Their taxi sets off down Market Street and Peter watches it fade into the haze. He wonders what drew Sheryl and Alan together like that, right at the end of the night, and feels a small ache in his chest. When he turns, Helen is sliding into the backseat of another cab. They pull away and Peter watches her withdraw to the far window. He touches her arm. "Are you alright, sweetheart?"

Helen nods, facing the bay. Her gentle profile darkens as they accelerate. "In the restroom," she says. "Sheryl told me not to let her go home with him."

"You never know with people," says Peter. Outside, the rain collects in puddles and around drains. The cab slows through a flooded curb and water sprays up around them. "She must've been lonely."

Helen doesn't respond and Peter turns to face Seattle glowing through the rain mist. He pictures Sheryl's hair and remembers himself in London so many years ago. Then he's remembering the war and how much he felt during that period of his life. It's nostalgia and it warms his chest in the stale cold of the cab, radiating into the space around him. The warmth of it reaches his head and Peter feels an echo of passion. He remembers how passionate his Spanish girl had been, how passionate he had been with her. Though now, sitting in the warmth of the cab, he struggles to remember her name.

They near their flat and Peter turns to his wife. She's staring out of the window, her slender waist cutting an angle in her form. Peter has the sudden urge to take her. He would do it now if he could, but he decides to follow her into the bathroom and take her there. He would press her against the counter while she was at the mirror undoing her hair. He could picture it now, the passion of it warming his head, the feel of her loose hair.

Their building has an open foyer with a desk clerk and a crystal chandelier. Peter follows Helen past the clerk to the elevator. Their footsteps echo off of marble tiles and Peter wonders how late it must be. They arrive at the twelfth floor and, inside of their flat, Helen hangs her coat by the door. It falls, and Peter picks it up. The silky cloth feels cool against his hand as he hangs it with his own. Helen passes through the living room, their black couch filling the space with a scent of leather. In the kitchen, Helen moves to the fridge, pressing a small glass against the filtered water faucet. Her figure reflects off of the mirrored metal and Peter watches her. He imagines the cool feel of the stainless steel, the trickle of running water like the mist outside of the restaurant. But he waits until she's in the bathroom.

Peter takes off his shoes at the edge of their room and goes to wash his hands. The water is soft and warm, like air against his skin. After another moment of waiting in the bathroom, he goes into the bedroom. He looks for Helen by the dresser, then in the kitchen. He wonders if he should call for her. He tries the laundry and then their room again. He's about to phone the lobby desk clerk to see if she went back down when at last he spots her curled up on her side of the bed. She lies fully clothed on top of the sheets, facing away from him in the dark. Her shoes are still on.

Peter looks at her delicate form, lying there in all of her clothes. He studies the dip of her waist, where the left side of her body molds to the mattress. He imagines her thinking about loneliness. He imagines her thinking about what he'd said that night about loneliness and the human condition. Then he's climbing over the bed, lying down behind her and wrapping his arm around her waist, across her chest.

Helen doesn't move. She lies rigid, and when Peter lifts his hand to her cheek he feels the damp cold of a tear.

"Sweetheart," he says. "What's the matter?"

Peter's stomach clenches. Helen, his Helen, is crying in a curl on their mattress.

"Tell me," he says to her. "You can tell me." Excitement burns in his chest and he lifts his head, resting it on her cheek to kiss the wet beneath her eyes. "What is it?"

Helen sniffs for a long time. Then she breathes out twice.

"I didn't know you still loved her," she says.

Peter stops. He lifts his head from her cheek and for a long while he's unable to move. They lie together, two stones in the cold sand. Beyond them the wall is a window to the harbor. City lights reflect off of Elliot Bay like flares flickering under water, and the warmth in Peter's chest rises up to his face. He pictures Sheryl with Alan, their toned bodies blending; then Branson, curled up on the latrine floor. Helen is asleep beside him. Her breathing lessens to a shallow hum and Peter rolls away from her onto his back, his right arm extending off the edge of the bed.

THE PARTS

The first time that I told the story of David Jenson, I was in a high school gymnasium. Massive lights hung from the ceiling like exhaust cones and the four of us sat in a circle. It was a group therapy, and when I finally spoke the fluorescent lighting weighed onto my shoulders like a tactical assault pack.

I hadn't spoken about David Jenson before this, so I didn't really tell it right. I didn't tell the story right because the whole thing wasn't really there yet. Four years after Iraq, and I still hadn't realized it. I hadn't formulated it. I hadn't pieced together all of the little things that are necessary and that you can see when you're standing on the outside of a thing but miss when you're right there in the middle of it.

It's a simple story, really. Four men in Mosul. All of them are near the end of their tour, stop-lossed so many times they can't believe they're headed to the airfield on leave. Only, they have to take a civilian bus because all of the Humvees and armored vehicles are on patrol or QRF duty. They make it halfway out of the city when an IED detonates beneath them and they're dead.

I wasn't there for that part. I was on a patrol through downtown Mosul when the boom set in. My platoon saw the dust and smoke rising over building rooftops like it was any other blast, like it could've been a team of Iraqi Security as easily as a platoon from the 23rd Infantry Division. I didn't know that it was David Jenson who got blown to bits. I didn't even know it was our own guys until we got briefed on the scene. So when I told the story of David Jenson for the first time, I stuck to what I knew.

Our whole therapy group went tense as I told them how when we arrived there was a pinkish spray of blood across the pavement. I told them how when the sun broke through the clouds and shone on the dark and dried-up puddles it made them shimmer. I told them how there was a crust of bone in some of the spray like grains of sand; how blood covered bloodstains in the filth-stained streets of Iraq; and how all of it was centered around a wreck of metal, torn to shreds.

I went with one of the other veterans to a Manhattan sake bar after our first session. This was about a month before I'd opened up about David Jenson and the word "therapy" still made my jaw clench and the heat rise into my face. I was outside for a smoke when one of the guys walked up to me. "It's Zac, right?" he said. His name was Martinez, and before I could answer he said, "Let's get a drink."

I agreed because the buzz from my pre-therapy six-pack was starting to wear off. He hadn't said a word the entire session, and neither had I. But when we had pints of Asahi in hand, at a bar off 93rd and Amsterdam Ave, I started to talk.

I told him about my work as a desk clerk at an apartment complex in the financial district. I described the yuppies and Wall Street traders who dropped a hundred thousand a year on rent just so they could walk to work. My aunt, I explained, was letting me crash on her couch in the upper east side—she shopped at Whole Foods, lived the upper-class life—but only after getting a settlement from some dietary supplement that destroyed her liver.

"She's the reason I'm here," I told him, and my voice dropped a pitch. "A few weeks ago, we were barbequing on the roof of her apartment building when I passed out," I told him. It happened just like that. Boom. My aunt brought me to the hospital afterward, but when the doc learned I was a veteran and suggested therapy, my aunt said I had to go. Said I couldn't stay on her couch anymore unless I "gave it a try." Martinez listened without really backchanneling. He'd been forced into therapy as well; the difference being his leg was blown off above the knee.

Outside a group of millennials stumbled past the entrance in Santa outfits. It was early for a Manhattan night, but there was an event going on called Santacon: like Halloween in December, a winter drinking fest. The shouting and stumbling of passersby distracted us from our drinks, but the rest of the bar was quiet. The other patrons whispered in softer tongues and Martinez and I turned back to the bar.

Martinez wasn't going to talk about stepping on an IED during a routine patrol, and I wasn't going to ask; instead he told me about how he failed a mental health exam after checking yes to a bunch of questions that everyone else knew not to check yes. We talked about the VA for a while and then, somewhere into our second pint, Martinez brought up this sergeant he knew from the Iraq invasion.

"It was right at the start of the war," he told me. "Infantry were pushing into Baghdad and there was a squad pressing down the streets, clearing buildings. They took small arms fire from windows, the roofs of buildings, but marines had taken the brunt of it so really they were just dealing with stragglers who'd no chance and knew it. They'd pop up and spurt a few rounds until our boys pinned 'em down and an Apache flew in to clear 'em out. They're still high-strung cause it's the invasion and first contact and these guys are right out of basic, but they're trained for this. They keep their shit together and advance steady, responding to movements and sweeping the street for muj. That's what it's all about at that point."

He said all this like he'd been there, but after a minute he paused, and I followed his gaze to a crowd of kids crossing the street. The guys wore mall-style Santa suits, from beard and boots. The girls had on high heels and red stockings with low-cut fur jackets. Martinez's eyes lingered, and I tried not to glance at his prosthetic shin. Laughter rang through the glass and echoed in our heads like a memory we should've had.

"Anyway, these guys," he said, turning back to his pint, "they're strung up and tense. The sarge is out front pressed to a side of the street when a door beside him swings open. He senses the movement, silhouette to the side, and fires a three round burst. Only it's a small girl," he said. "I don't know, six years old?"

I realized by this point that I'd heard this story before. That I'd read about it in the Times or an IVAW pamphlet.

But Martinez didn't flinch. He was watching beads of condensation spill down the glass of his pint glass.

"Two to the chest, one to the head," he said. "The sergeant breaks down. Who wouldn't? Their platoon needs to push forward—that's what you do, you can't just stop—but the grunts, just fucking kids, they've no idea what to do. They're half as shook up as he is. And the LT, he tries to console the guy, but the sergeant won't move. He tries forcing him on, telling him it's okay and that shit happens, but the sergeant won't even budge." Martinez shrugs. "Eventually they have to call in a medevac, just to get him out of the way. He's shipped back to Kuwait and they give him some time to recover, whatever that means."

Martinez laughed a short, barking laugh. Then he went rigid, propped on the stool and screwing his pint into the bar. When he turned to look at me, it was as if he wanted to tell me something but didn't know how. Like he wanted me to *feel* it.

"That's the story we know," he said, "the story that we can tell, and that the media's beat to death, because it's the one that makes sense. But it can't be the real story, because how could anything like that ever make sense?" An Asian couple beside us got up and moved to a booth across the bar, but Martinez didn't notice. "That moment," he said, "whatever that sergeant experienced, goes beyond the words we'd use to describe it. Imagine it, man! That would've been hell and it would've been the lowest shit possible and it would've been beyond whatever anyone else has ever processed, what any one person could ever process, but you won't hear *that* in the New York Times. You can't write the truth if it undermines the whole fucking story. Because even in a journal article the story must come back 'around' somehow. So they cut it down to something people can relate it to. A sergeant doing what he was trained to do; what anybody would've done."

The bartender took my glass and I motioned for another. He might have been listening in, but probably wasn't. Martinez didn't care. He was staring at his hand and he said, "But, for some reason, I just can't. I keep putting myself in his shoes, that sergeant. I keep trying to get away from the story and to imagine what he saw, to picture that little girl's face. It would've been every girl's face, right? Her eyes would've been full of life, the same as all of the ones we saw in Iraq. But then the color would've drained from her eyes, and her cheeks, and her black hair in the dirt would be like roots drinking up the blood around her—" His fingers open, release the glass. "But that's just another lie," he said. "Get it? Because her face wouldn't have even been there. Because her face would've been a gaping hole. And if one of her eyes was left it would've been hollowed and bloodshot and not a thing you could stare at for long or even wrap your fucking mind around except, maybe, to think something empty like, 'Oh.'"

He shook his head. I sat stunned beside him, glancing around at the other patrons and worrying we might get thrown out. "I know," he said. "I know. It's a bunch of bullshit," he said. "All this 'therapy' talk, getting to my head." He forced a laugh. "But sometimes there's just nothing else to say about the war, other than it's not something you 'recover' from."

I let him know I agreed, and we sat that way for a long time. Martinez slumped like he was finished, and me with nothing to add. I bought us another round of sake, even though I had work in the morning. It was mindless work—servile pleasantries, holding the door for yuppies—but Martinez was unemployed, so we finished our shots before walking into the night. A swarm of Santa suits separated us at a crossing, and I watched him stumble toward the "R" line, breathing fumes. I took Broadway to 66th Street and cut across central park. Tossed Santa beards littered the street like so many dead animals.

My therapy was a group thing. There were four of us: Aaron, a tattooed country-boy from Tennessee; Matthews, a born-again Christian; Martinez; and me. All of us were veterans from Iraq or Afghanistan. We met in a high school gym next to the hospital because there were no rooms available at the Brooklyn VA and our psychiatrist's office was the size of a custodian's closet. We gathered in a circle beside the tip-off point each time, perched awkwardly in classroom desk-chairs, and our shrink would talk. "They've proven it," she'd tell us. "That words have the capacity to heal."

Her name was Alison. She had short black hair and wore business-like skirts with low heels to our sessions. She was young and always coming back to this idea about words. It was a spiel she'd given maybe a dozen times before and it had to do with the power of words, how just talking about our experiences could help us like it was some goddamn magical spell. She wanted desperately for us to speak, to open up about our experiences, but she was a woman and a shrink, and it was an uphill battle besides. Whenever she felt outnumbered, like the time Martinez called her a civilian, she'd use big words to build herself up. She'd often have to sit in silence to make any one of us talk, and that took a toll on her, I think.

What she never said about words, though, is how they can hurt as often as heal; how they can cement a thing, give it shape; and how they can make real what, only moments before, was a shadow on the wall. "Words," she never said, "create structure." It's a frail structure, and it's artificial. But if we think them enough—if we write them down or say them enough out loud—that structure becomes stronger. The shapeless mass takes form. A wrangled bus becomes Jenson, spilt into puddles on the street.

The first time that I told the story of David Jenson, I found it lacking. I was a month into therapy, several weeks after my night at the sake bar, and since Martinez had skipped out after a smoke break, I was left with our therapist and the two other guys. Both Aaron and Matthews had already spoken out, so there was a pressure for me to speak. I was pissed that Martinez had left, that he hadn't told me he'd be skipping out. I kept twisting my fingers in my lap. The fluorescent lights hurt in the silence until, finally, Alison looked at me and said, "Zac? Is there anything you want to share with us?"

David Jenson's name was halfway out of my mouth before I even looked up. I hadn't been thinking about him then—not in the concrete sense—and I hadn't spoken his name in years. Yet, there it was. "David Jenson," I said. But the rest of it, everything else that came out of my mouth, sounded foreign; like I was making it up. "Blood on the street," I said, like I didn't know what blood looked like.

I took the subway to Hoboken after each session, but that night I got off before the Brooklyn Bridge and walked. The suspension cables collapsed around me and every time I went to breathe it felt like the air was catching in my throat. I crossed the East River sweating bullets, and by the time I reached the green line it was midnight. I was drunk again and had work at four in the morning, but the moment I laid down on my Aunt's couch I was filled with a restless compulsion to connect the gaps. I needed to make the story real. I owed him that much.

Google helped. I organized events online and chronicled the dates of IED attacks. Then I found a Tribune post about a civilian bus targeted on the outskirts of Mosul. A week later, with the help of a friend in Public Affairs, I got a copy of the press release. It was a photo of the computer screen, really—blurred and taken from a smartphone—and there was a glare that blocked some of the address in the top left corner. The rest of the release was legible, though. It read:

MOSUL, Iraq (April 3rd, 2008) – Explosives experts have determined that insurgents deliberately attacked an Afghan civilian bus on Wednesday in Nineveh Provence, killing four members of the US infantry and six civilians while wounding ten other bystanders.

The Parts

The device used in the explosion was a victim-triggered mechanism of pressure plate configuration.

US Infantry were the first to respond to the explosion in northern Mosul, providing security, medical evacuation for the victims, and forensic detail. KIA military personnel include:

Private First Class Jay Williams, 19, from Detroit, MI.

Sergeant Migel Segoviano, 23, from Santa Fe, NM.

Specialist Austin Thomas, 20, from Dallas, TX.

Sergeant David Jenson, 24, from Concord, CA.

No further injuries or attacks were recorded that day. Iraqi National Guard and US troops secured the area shortly after the blast.

There was a slight breeze and partly cloudy skies. Body parts were scattered across the intersection. Blood stained the streets.

When none of us talked, Alison would make us listen. During one session, she told us how Post-Traumatic Stress wasn't a disorder. "A disorder," she said, "is an abnormal reaction to normal circumstances. What you've experienced is a normal reaction to *abnormal* circumstances." She told us that war isn't normal; especially the full-spectrum shit that we saw. She said that the amount of stress we experienced had effects that scientists could measure. Effects on the brain. The irreversible kind.

One day she told us about the history of PTSD, how there were different names for it in the past. They called it "soldier's heart" in the Civil War. The idea that heart rate and pulse had something to do with the change men experienced after combat. It changed to "shell shock" during the First World War, and then "combat fatigue" in the Second. But it wasn't until Vietnam they gave it a scientific name. Only they called it a disorder, and that kind of shit doesn't fly today so now they call it Post-Traumatic Stress *Syndrome*.

That's all kind of funny when you think about it. I can't help wondering who came up with the names, because it's civilians that are always trying to label shit. Give it a name and you can wrap your head around it. All of them sounded that way, except for maybe shell shock. That's a true grunt's term. A no-shit description of trench warfare. I said that to the group and then Alison asked us to come up with our own word. A word to describe post-millennial war trauma. All I could come up with was "disillusionment."

"How about, 'moral oblivion,'" said Aaron.

Aaron was the SAW gunner for a fire squad based out of Samarra. He'd come back to therapy after his wife watched him threaten to beat their two children. He talked more than the rest of us combined, and this time he started by recalling his first month in country, when he was "fresh meat."

"Here we go," said Martinez.

Aaron mouthed something in the direction of Martinez, but Alison spoke over him. "Martinez," she said. "If you have something you would like to share, it can wait until after," but Martinez was already waving her off.

"I was about a month into my tour," said Aaron, turning back to Alison. "Anyway, we were out on patrol outside of Kandahar. An IED detonated under the Humvee in front of us—shower of sparks and so on—except that the whole vehicle got lifted onto its side."

He nodded as if this was a thing not many people could wrap their heads around. "The Humvee was completely wrangled," he said, "but it looked like everyone survived the blast. The gunner – he got knocked out of the turret chamber. Shot across the pavement, skidding on the metal plate in his armor for about a hundred yards."

Martinez scoffed at the exaggeration, but Aaron kept going. He said that he watched and felt sick about it because they were just starting to get along, him and the gunner; that they were from the same region of Tennessee. Aaron couldn't remember the guy's name anymore, but, apparently, he got back on his feet and while they waited for a Medevac, Aaron came up with a nickname for him. "Leo," he said, "after the ninja turtle, because of the way he skidded like a turtle on its shell." Aaron's team loved it. Even "Leo" smiled at his new call name. Granted, he'd just been diagnosed with a concussion. The medevac came soon after, but by the time everyone else returned to base Leo's concussion had developed into a traumatic brain injury. He was flown to Germany that same day. He died in surgery three days later.

Aaron didn't cry when he told us this. He laughed. It was genuine laughter, too, remembering the way that Leo shot across the road with his legs up. But there was something beneath the laughter that made the rest of us quiet. Even Martinez, who'd been rolling his eyes when Aaron started, was listening at the end. Because all of us knew that it was stuck in him—that he was trying to get it out—and he's ashamed that, on lazy Sunday mornings, he still won't watch "Mutant Ninja Turtles" with his two and four year-old sons.

The press release helped.

Four men stop-lossed so many times that two months before their tour ends, they can hardly believe they're going on leave. To get to the airbase they have to wait for an armored Humvee or Stryker to return from patrol because there are no spare vehicles. The only ones that are not in the field are being repaired in the motor pool, busted up from IEDs. But to catch their flight to Kuwait they have to leave now. Missing their flight means a three-day layover in Kuwait City. That's three days of their ten-day leave that could be spent at home, with their families and friends, rather than in the 130-degree heat and sand and shit.

They decide to take a civilian bus to the airfield, which is okay because it's after the Surge. Iraqi Security Forces have assumed more responsibilities. The roads are safer, and patrols are sweeping the streets every few hours. But the bus hits an IED. It's a big one. The trigger's connected to a pile of artillery shells buried in the road, and they aren't wearing armor or helmets or carrying weapons because they checked them all in before heading for the airport and now they're dead.

I tried telling this version of the story to my aunt in Hoboken, but she's a southern belle without the stomach to sit down and hear about the real war. I got into such a hurry spilling it out that I failed to clarify that it was Jenson who'd been torn up and spilt across the street. Because if you hadn't known—if you had just shown up from some other fucking planet and seen the mess—you'd have thought that it was a trailer full of bulls, cattle, or some other beast on its way to the slaughter. Because nobody would expect that much blood to have come from *human* bodies. Because there is no way that an explosion like that, so simple and vulgar in the middle of a city intersection, could have been felt ten thousand miles away in New York, Texarkana, and Alameda County.

It was our platoon that got called in to clean up. We were tasked with washing away the stench. Only, we couldn't. Not right away, at least, because blood is the stuff of life and it never rinses off the first time.

I met David Jenson in basic training and disliked him—he was too handsome, too charismatic—but he was one of the only guys to stay in my unit all the way to Iraq. I'd known him for three years when he died.

Still, I had only a vague notion of who Jenson was. I remember him being sarcastic, but he'd bury his head when there was work to be done. He was older than most of us in basic, and all of the drill sergeants loved him because he was a physical machine. A guy from my squad later said that he ran toward a burning vehicle in Iraq, just to drag out a pair of civilians.

I had one conversation with Jenson that stuck. It was in the smoke pit with the fireteam. We'd always gather after a patrol or OP and sit on rocks, chain-smoking until we ran out of cigarettes. After an hour, everyone else had drifted to the gym or to jerk off, but Jenson stuck around. He lent me a cigarette, and I kept smoking until it was just us.

The drag was like sitting in a sauna after the gym, the chill of warm air in a hot shower. The sky above us was dark when Jenson started on about his brother at West Point. "He's in his third year," Jenson said. "Set to graduate with honors." His father, he told me, had led a whole company in Vietnam. Later he mentioned that his fiancé had stocked up on lingerie before his leave got pushed back, and now they were just waiting.

At some point I told him about my stepdad being a doctor in the Army. I didn't mention my biological father because he wasn't relevant to the military, and after a while I showed him a picture of my girlfriend. She wasn't really mine—just a girl that surrendered a yearbook photo of herself a few days before I shipped out—but he looked at the photo and said, "Nice, bro," flashing his straightened teeth. "Looks like a real catch."

Jenson was a classic California kid. Tall and blonde—he even talked slow—and if he wasn't smiling about something, he was laughing. Except, now I can't really picture him. You know, how he really was. All I can picture is what might've been him. Or pieces of him. Because it had to still *be* him. Even after that. Because why else were we ordered to pick up the parts?

The other guy in our group told a story. His was bad. Worse, even, than the sergeant Martinez told me about because this was him and he was right there telling us about it.

His name was Matthews. A biblical name. He even went a few years in seminary before meeting a girl that changed his mind. He enlisted, he said, to provide for his family. It was what he felt God was calling him to do. Four months later, God razed the Twin Towers and deployed Matthews to the land of Genesis.

Matthews was the first in our group to talk. He was from Georgia and shorter than the other guys but with deep, brown skin. You could tell he had his shit together because there was a whole story and he could finish telling it. He later claimed to have told his wife, but now he was talking like it was a thing he'd never wanted to say again, something he didn't want to talk about at all.

"We were driving this convoy through Iraq," he said. He leaned forward to the edge of his chair. They were cheap classroom chairs, and the foldable desk pushed him left so he was facing me more than the others. "It was in the middle of the Surge and we're carrying a lot of equipment, a lot of stuff, to guys desperate for resupply." He started rubbing his hands together. The fluorescent lights made even Matthews look pale, and as his fingers locked, they went white and then a kind of reddish brown.

"I'd just been promoted, bumped up to E-4, and we were about to go through a small town along Highway One. I was in charge of driving this huge truck. And it was weird. Because they didn't give us a mission brief, or a convoy brief. Instead, my sergeant just kind of walks over to me and tells me how he knows my position—you know, that I was Christian—and he gives me the option to back down. To let someone else drive. He tells me that kids were doing this thing where they'd line up in the streets and hold hands so that cars couldn't pass, but when the convoys stopped they'd all jump on the trucks and start stealing equipment."

Matthews looked at me and I nodded because that sounded like Iraq, but my gut was churning. It sounded too familiar, like I already knew what he was going to say.

"For me," he said, "I'm carrying the MREs. Our food. And he tells me, my sergeant, he says, 'Look, Specialist. You can't stop. No matter what happens, you keep going.'"

Someone walked into the gymnasium. The door slammed and we all looked up to see a man crossing the back of the gym. He wore a lanyard around his neck, head bowed. His footsteps echoed in the bleachers, even after the door shut.

"I told him I'd do it," said Matthews. "Probably because I just got E-4 and was proud of it, so I didn't want to back down or disappoint anybody, but also because I figured if it wasn't me driving then it would have to be some other guy. In a way, I thought I was doing something good. Like a sacrifice."

He let out an empty laugh and looked up at the lights. We could hear the quiver in his voice.

"We're driving into town," he said. "There's no line of children or anything, but there's this one—I dunno, a kid, maybe thirteen or fourteen—and I see him down the road. He's reaching up and touching and, I could see, he's up and jumping in front of every vehicle." His fingers locked, pulling violently. "This kid, he moves mostly at the last second. But we slow down and some of the Humvees swerve out of the way, but I... I can't do that!" he said. "I'm in a huge-ass truck with 3 axles and it doesn't *do* that. It can't move like that. And before me there's this huge howitzer being towed. This big cannon with the barrel facing me. And the kid has a lot of room... he has a lot of room, then, to squeeze in. To get between us. And he moves behind the truck and there's that barrel and he's beside it. He's right there standing beside it, and he's trying to get me to stop when—"

His voice caught. We could see his shoulders vibrating, hands shaking. "I don't know," he said. "I don't know what happened. The adrenaline. It's like a black spot in my mind. I think he tried to get out of the way, but—"

Matthews wanted to stop, to keep the pieces from spilling onto the floor, but he couldn't. Nobody spoke. Martinez and Aaron were both frozen still. Even Alison was quiet. All she could do was make this cooing sound like she might touch him on the shoulder but couldn't.

Not that any of us blamed him. I would've done the same thing—a story that makes sense—but I remember watching him and wondering, "*This* is what healing looks like?"

The next time Matthews told the story, he added the part that he'd blacked out. He hit the kid. "Clipped him," he said. "Probably crushed his legs, something like that." By the fourth time, he said it without breaking. Told us he ran straight over him—the kid—only it wasn't a teenager, anymore. It was an eight-year-old boy.

The telling gets easier over time.

Our platoon arrives on site after a perimeter's been established and most of the debris has been cleared away, leaving us with the cleanup. It's one of those rare days in spring where clouds spatter the sky. Shadows move in soft and slow, carrying a wall of shade across the bloodstained pavement. Wind moves dust and smoke and light. Shade, I learn, brings a vivid kind of detail to death.

There's so much silt in the air that the buildings around us are blurry. Their plaster façades look like a boxing knife had been used to cut out the windows. Everything is dull in the blurred light. A bus is at the intersection. It's grey and has a stripe down the length of it like a winding road, only where the center would've been there's a crater the length of a car. Body parts scatter the pavement. Limbs, mostly. A few scraps of meat. Some are surprisingly far from the blast, but most are concentrated. Blood catches in dips and potholes around the blast to form puddles, only the street's so damn hot that the water has evaporated and—where it's too thick to absorb into the pavement—the blood cooks into a coagulated slime that crumbles at the edges.

"Saying it out loud will make it easier the next time," Alison told us, "like muscle memory." But what she didn't say was *why* it got easier; how when you learn a story by heart you don't have to think about it anymore when you tell it; you don't have to relive every word that you say; your mouth just moves and the words come out without registering. The numbness empties you, because after seeing that much gore—after stooping in it, scraping at the meat and bagging up the limbs to ship home for the families to bury—nothing is gruesome anymore.

Martinez would arrive late to our sessions and leave early. He almost never talked, and after skipping two weeks in a row he showed up to a meeting halfway through and hungover.

This triggered something in Alison. We could all sense the time bomb there, but this week she stopped halfway through a speech about traumatic processing to drag a whiteboard across the gym. She had it propped on a classroom easel and didn't bother lifting it off the ground to bring it over. Rubber stoppers squealed across the flooring, and with our attention set she began listing examples of how regret manifests itself in our daily lives. She got halfway down the board with things like "obsession," "neglect," and "denial," when she decided to go in a circle and have each of us say a thing that we regretted from the war.

Matthews and Aaron answered with direct answers, but when she got to Martinez, Alison crossed her legs and said, "So? We haven't heard much from you yet, Martinez. Is there anything that you regret from your deployment?"

"Sure," he said.

The Expo marker in Alison's hand squeaked between her fingers. Each of us went still. Even the gym held its breath, the hum of the air conditioner hesitating in the summer heat.

"I regret getting my leg blown off," said Martinez. He grimaced, hearing the words, and his whole body seemed to sag forward. I thought he was going to continue—to admit that he'd been careless on patrol, that he'd veered off course during a ranger file march—but instead, he looked up and with his jaw set, he said, "Because if I still had my leg, I wouldn't have to sit through all of this bullshit."

The air conditioners kicked on in the silence that followed, and the entire space groaned.

"Well," said Aaron, as if he'd just proven something. Even Matthews, who was the voice of reason and patience between the four of us, clenched his fists. I wanted to punch him in the face, too, but Alison, she just sighed. There was a resignation in her response that I hadn't seen before. She always sat upright in her chair, legs crossed or pressed together at the knee. Now her spine was curved, and her feet spread with the toes pointed in. She capped her marker, placed it heavily on the easel shelf, and said, "2009. Last year, in 2009, more military personnel committed suicide than died in combat."

Alison looked up and Martinez shrugged. He pulled his feet beneath him and the pole of his prosthetic shin clanged against the leg of the chair. A metallic ring cut across the gym.

"Every sixty-five minutes," said Alison, "another veteran commits suicide. That means that since we started our session today, a veteran just like you took his own life. That's a suicide rate higher than any war before it. Compared to Vietnam, the amount of deaths at home are startling." She paused to look each one of us in the eye. "I'm not saying this because I think that any one of you are at risk," she said. "I'm saying it because *all* of you are."

Martinez grunted.

"Do you know what the leading cause of suicide is?" she asked. She was looking at Martinez, but my own fingers whitened in my lap, interlocked and tense.

"It's depression," she said. "Do you know what causes depression?"

She stood up, straightening her skirt to face the board. "Namely," she said, and began writing out:

feelings of isolation

a lacking sense of community

not feeling understo—

"Do you know why I'm here?" said Martinez. Alison was in the middle of writing the word "understood" and had to twist her body. Her hand was still resting on the easel, her back arched to reach the bottom of the board.

202

"I'm here because I have to be," he said. "Because if I don't at least show up, the VA will cut my disability and I'm left with one good leg and a severed compensation."

Alison stopped writing. She was perched above the chair and when she dropped to sit down, the metal frame creaked. Her forehead wasn't creased anymore, her jaw was unclenched, but in the fluorescent light and the way that her head was tilting I could see dark shadows carving a ring beneath her eyes. She looked broken, as if that one statement—uttered so casually by Martinez—had undermined her entire career.

There was a fire in my face after that. My jaw clenched shut and I could tell by the stiffness of Matthews and the way that Aaron gripped his knees that they could feel it, too. Martinez was alone in this group. He'd lashed out at his only ally, and now she wanted nothing to do with him.

Alison went on to finish her list of regrets. She wrote the words from her seat without responding. Martinez spent the next few minutes bent forward, picking at his fingers. He might've felt ashamed, but he appeared to feel nothing else. He wouldn't meet my gaze or anybody's. He didn't look up for the rest of the session.

Alison made us exchange information at the end of the night. "You looked after each other in the war," she said, the four of us scribbling with our pens. "You can do it back home, as well."

I scrawled my phone number onto cardstock and tore up slips to give each member of the group. Aaron and Matthews gave me their cellphone numbers, and Martinez scribbled a Hotmail account in half-legible cursive across a torn 7/11 receipt. We went our separate ways: Martinez to Brooklyn, Matthews and Aaron into the city, and me on my trek uptown. None of us ever saw Martinez again.

Alison gave out homework. One week, she told me to write down my story. She had a typical shrink mentality—that everything circled back to childhood—and she had me start from the beginning. "Writing – the physical act of it," she said, "is tied to memory." Then she told me that if I could write the words in order, if I began at the beginning and continued to the end, I would be able to add in the bits between.

I found a café one morning after a night shift and ordered a black coffee. I was right off of the Hudson River and still in my work uniform—black slacks, white button-down and a black coat—but once I started writing, I couldn't stop. That entire morning and afternoon I spent hunched over a pile of notebook paper. My hand cramped from the effort. The sweat made my fingers stick.

What happened was I started to notice things. It wasn't remembering, really. I was re-remembering, adding things together, drawing parallels with David Jenson: like how my life could've been his if maybe my stepfather had walked into it sooner. I wrote about my parents' divorce: how my dad, with his backcountry cooking, and my mom as a New

Orleans native, tried to open a Cajun restaurant in Jersey, and how after it failed my father drank himself into depression until my mom left. She married Tim, a black man from New Hampshire, and when I turned sixteen, we moved into a nice home in a good neighborhood. Tim was a doctor. He did his residency in the Army and spent four years in Germany. I wrote that he made me want to live better, but that it was too late to fix my grades, so I did the only thing that made sense. I joined the Army.

Writing that part was easy. I wrote it out ten more times before the end of the week, digging deeper into the narrative with each version. I kept brushing against the story of David Jenson—the cleanup, and picking up the parts—until, finally, I was able to keep writing.

We arrived on site at eleven hundred hours. It was late in the morning and the humidity was so dense that it held the stench in the air and made it hard to breathe. A perimeter had already been established, and most of the initial debris had been cleared away. We'd never done anything for forensics before, so when HQ called in to tell our LT that we were left with the cleanup, it didn't really register what that meant.

Our sergeant passed out the body bags and the first of us vomited. The wet sound of it hitting pavement made me gag, and as we moved closer to the wreck more of us threw up. We wore gloves and put plastic bags around our boots. There were a few cars lining the road where the explosion had been, but most of the civilian population had cleared out. A few guys from my fire team went straight for the middle, where the bulk of limbs and dead meat was, but I found myself straddling the perimeter. An arm lay somewhere against the curb. It'd been blown off at the bicep, and the tissue was stiff but warm from the sun. The end of it, where the meat was charred and the bone came out, reeked of burnt BBQ. I tried lifting it up by the wrist, but the end of it stuck to the pavement. I had to yank at it, the tearing greasy sound of it, in order to put it with the smell into my bag.

The rest of the afternoon was a blur. I remember a civilian woman rushing the street. She'd found her son, maybe, and was scraping at the pieces of him. Somebody went to pull her away so that she didn't take any of the wrong parts. There's no way to tell, said the LT. Get the parts to forensic and let those guys put them together. Our job was to bag it all up.

By fourteen-hundred hours, the explosives investigation team was done, and we were able to start the deep clean. The bus got towed and the chemicals came out, but the smell remained. Water washed chemicals with stains on the pavement, shade passed overhead, and the scent of charred meat hung in the air like the 4th of July.

When we returned to the FOB, it was dusk. Everyone had skipped lunch, but when we passed the chow hall, I felt my stomach pang. There was a buffet line with burgers and pizza and grilled meat. I filled three whole trays of it: ribs with BBQ sauce, pulled pork and rib eye and seasoned chicken wings. It wasn't until I finished my second tray that I began to gag.

My therapy ended the moment Alison could answer why I'd passed out at my aunt's rooftop barbeque. Then the VA traded our therapy sessions for a Valium prescription I threw away. A few weeks later, I threw a glass table piece to the left of my aunt's head and it shattered against the kitchen cabinets. She kicked me out after that, and I started living on whatever funds I had left while waiting for my disability application to be reviewed.

Meanwhile, I did the one thing that calmed me down. I continued the story of David Jenson. By this time I'd written it out so many times that his tragedy had become mine—his death my own—until, after months of writing, I was able to share the story with a girl I was seeing. It ruined our relationship, but I discovered that my writing was good.

I spent the next three months honing down applications to writing programs. I hadn't spoken with anyone from our therapy group since I was cut, but the loneliness chipped away at me until one night I found myself drinking bourbon and digging up an old 7/11 receipt with an email address scribbled across the top. I spent the next half-hour drafting an email to Martinez, and seconds after clicking "send" the thing bounced back with a Failure Notice.

I called Aaron after hearing Matthews had left town. It was a Saturday night and he was at a dive bar off of Amsterdam Avenue. I met him there to talk about Martinez and Matthews and our therapy sessions, but I found him squeezed between a pair of young women in heels longer than their necks and skirts just as short. He bought a round of jaeger bombs right off, even though the bourbon had set in and I was already walking through a haze. It was the haze of the city that made me follow him and the girls to a cocktail bar a few blocks south.

"C'mon," said one of the girls, grabbing my wrist. "It'll be fun."

There was a new tattoo on Aaron's bicep. It looked like a bear had clawed at his arm, and when he reached to silence the ring of his phone—still glowing in his jean pockets—it stretched with the flex of his muscle. "I can't handle these two broads alone," he said, leaning to whisper in my ear. "Wingman me."

I thought of his wife and his two sons watching cartoons, and then I said okay. Outside the air was thick with exhaust fumes and wet pavement. We passed an open door with dim lighting and a tall, long bar. I looked in and recognized the headboard. It was the sake bar I'd visited with Martinez a year before. My feet stuttered, and through the window I caught a glimpse of metal.

The others had kept walking but stopped and were looking back. "Zac," called Aaron. And then all of them, "What are you doing?"

I didn't budge. There was this overwhelming certainty that he would be inside, perched against the bar.

"Is he hallucinating?" asked one of the girls.

Her voice leaked through a veil of sounds: the creak of a prosthetic shin, the whisper of a sergeant from the invasion. It occurred to me, then, that Martinez might not have known the sergeant, but that the sergeant might've represented a part of him, or else Martinez had related to the sergeant in some way. I wanted to hear him say it. I wanted to tell him that it was okay to talk about it, that the telling made it possible to move forward and that my writing was proof. I wanted to show him that I was better.

My hand found the handle of the door. I pushed it open, felt the rush of warm smoke and dull light, the harsh whispers of a forgotten evening in December.

Before me sat an old man drinking sake from a straw. In the corner was a young Asian couple, annoyed by the draft of air I brought in. The bartender, at least, acknowledged me. But there was no Martinez. There was no conversation of troubled veterans. No echo of a sergeant and bleeding young girl. There was only a row of barstool legs, glimmering with metallic symmetry.

THE MANIFESTATIONS OF WAR

The audience enters a short but wide space with a low ceiling. Seats against the back wall are elevated by a platform, and a single esplanade divides the four rows of chairs below. Lighting fades to dark and the curtain is pulled back. A single spotlight illuminates a woman in a chair. She is wearing green scrubs, leaning forward with her hands clasped between her knees. Before her, angled to the right, is another seated figure, silhouetted by the light. The figure faces the woman and appears to hold a pen and a pad.

■■ı

Jennifer: I suppose I should start with who I am? Right. Well, my name is Jennifer Sabates. I deployed to Iraq in January of '06 and finished my tour as a military physician the following November. You could say that was a particularly rough patch of the war. We saw a lot of patients. We were the place to be, you know. The center of Baghdad, in the middle of a civil war. They brought a lot of upper-end guys to our table. Colonels, generals, the like. But, let's see – should I just start from the beginning?

Without a response from the figure, Jennifer continues.

Okay. We arrived at the end of January during the rainy season. Everything was wet and grey. And the base we were on—we basically had to blow it up to take it—so everywhere were crumbled buildings, remnants of the enemy base, and between were scattered blocks of concrete for buildings. Like our hospital, which was right against the wire. I mean *right* against it. And everything was entirely lifeless. No one spent time outside when they didn't have to because it was always grey and there were mortars. They shot all of the birds. You know, to prevent them from nesting in the engines of jets and Humvees and the like. There were no birds singing. Just the sound of machine guns firing and the occasional rocket.

I was stationed as a physician at a forward operating base in the middle of Baghdad. And—well, I guess I could start with a normal day. Not that there were any normal days. There were average days. There was a general routine and we followed it and that helped to pass the time. I'd wake up early and ride my bike to the hospital. About halfway through the tour I found a pretty rusted bicycle, and I'd ride it to the hospital everyday. I got very strong, you know, wearing Kevlar and all. About sixty pounds of armor. I was in fantastic shape. Very health conscious. I even picked out my meals at chow to avoid nitrates and packaged foods and what not. The irony of which... well, now it's just painful.

I'd arrive at the hospital and immediately see patients. Check on those from the day before, seeing how they did overnight, or if there were any new admissions I'd divvy them up first. Then we'd do rounds with the whole team: the ICU staff and physicians and respiratory therapists and the high chain of command would come through. We all had our tasks for the day and, if we weren't on call, we'd leave. I'm not really sure when we finished; I never looked at the time. But after my shift I'd usually go workout at the gym, then spend my evening reading or writing—I wrote a lot in my journal—and try to get as much sleep as possible. And the same thing would happen the next day, and the next; unless I was on call, which was every fourth night. That's when I'd be the only ICU attendant to cover every patient and new admission. That was overwhelming because *all* of our patients came in at night. They'd come one after the other the whole night through. Sure, it could be hard. I told you earlier that I've had, well, "experiences" with PTSD.

But I also have physical symptoms from the war. Things that might've developed from various causes: mental, and circumstantial. Like from the burn pits: the way the military disposed of jet fuel and the like. All of it has had a measurable influence, you know, on my condition. And it's strange because I'm a doctor in the west, so I was brought up in this system—*sweeping a hand across the audience*—a system that preaches physical sciences to be the "end-all" in medicine. You know, chemistry, pharmaceuticals, etc. That there are cells inside of the body and there are cells outside of the body, and the way those various cells interact with each other determines the condition of the body and the mind and health in general. But, the reason I maybe found myself affected more, or the thing that made my experience of war particularly unique— other than my being a woman—is my experience with eastern cultures, and my, I guess, "belief" in the powers of holistic medicines.

(*Laughing*) I know! That's the reaction I always get. "But you're a doctor!" they say. "You're a leading voice in medicine and science and reason!" And I know all that and I pride myself on my knowledge in the field and of medicine in general. But I also believe in, I guess, a sort of balance.

I finished my undergraduate degree in the winter, and I spent the few months I had before Tulane travelling around Southeast Asia. Thailand, Cambodia, Malaysia, New Zealand at the end— Actually, I did it alone. My parents, they practically had an aneurism over it. I didn't tell my mom until I was in the airport. She's a big Cuban lady and my god you should've heard her go off. But once I was over there, on the other side of the world, she was able to block me from her mind, I think. I've got plenty of siblings. Plus, there were always other travelers, people I'd pair up with. You know, students from Australia, British tourists, a few Europeans that were generally older. We'd roam about the sites, living cheap and soaking in the culture. And that's how I learned about the medicinal practices of that region. By experiencing them firsthand. Like in Thailand. The people there go to these Buddhist temples to get massages from the monks – I know, right. But it's not a relaxing massage like how we think of it in the west. You don't go there to unwind. These monks basically double as massage therapists, and they're climbing all over you. You don't know the ways your body can bend until you've had some Thai guy climbing all over you. And they did this as part of their daily ritual, go to the temple for a massage. People there are probably more likely to see a Buddhist monk than a doctor. And it's all tied into a bigger philosophy. That the mind, spirit, and body are all connected. That you can't treat the mind without addressing the body, and the body the mind.

In light of modern medicine, it's hard to explain—their practices, I mean—they're almost impossible to defend. But I came to a level of understanding, a kind of acceptance, of the effects that the mental and spiritual have on the physical. On our bodies. It's a philosophy that, as a doctor in the United States, I could never implement or promote in my own practice. But it's something I've carried with me, all the same.

I guess what I'm getting at is that it affected me. In Iraq, and as a doctor in general. Because the things that I saw there, the things that I experienced, it was just really hard for me to isolate medical conditions. You know, to separate the physical mutilations from the person, to step back and say "this is a leg" or "this is a skull with an impairment to the cerebral cortex," and that's all—that there's nothing *more*—like I was working on a crumpled Humvee instead of a 19-year-old boy. I don't think that's how most surgeons would say they make their living, but it is. It's how they get through the day. It's how they deal with the idea of cutting off a leg just above the knee or sewing up a chest cavity or relieving the swelling of a brain by drilling a hole and seeing it—the delicate grey ooze seeping out the skull—as gelatinous matter and not the stuff of *life*.

With my background and my beliefs as they were, it became fairly difficult. Because these weren't natural injuries we were dealing with; these were combat injuries.

Injuries from guns and shrapnel and machines. Injuries caused by men. And after I returned from my tour, I experienced side effects. PTSD. You know, anxiety, nightmares, flashbacks. And it wasn't just from the things that I saw. No, it was more like my proximity to the war. Don't get me wrong, my experiences of combat were limited—I never even left the base—but the attacks were almost constant. Mortar and rockets, bullets zipping through medical tents. Enough to cause chronic anxiety, a prolonged type of stress that has physical effects on the brain—measurable effects, like cerebral deterioration—and after the war it got to the point that I had to quit my practice.

Jennifer adjusts in her seat. Her gaze angles upward, toward the ceiling, before coming back down.

I suppose I should explain that. I'm back at the university now, focusing on medical research. "The Effects of Free Radicals in Polymers on Living Tissue." That's the name of the article I just published. I've removed myself entirely from practicing, and I think it's good. I mean, I miss it. I do miss it. But it – I – was suffering, and I was putting my patients at risk. It's good, what I'm doing now. It's good to be a researcher, and to see the effects of your work on a larger scale. And it's good to take a break from surgery. Sure. I sometimes see myself recovering, returning to the practice. But right now, what's best for me is to stay in the field of research.

You see, I'm still piecing together my own PTSD. And a part of me wants to blame what's happening to me, what I'm experiencing, on the war itself. Because, well it's not just mental. And western medicine says it can't be all mental because there are physical effects: the kind of effects that, quite honestly, feel like I'm falling apart. Physically, I mean. My organs and immune system. My thyroid, for instance, shut down a few weeks ago. Failed completely. And, you know, a part of me—the Westernized part, maybe—tells me that it's from the effects of the burn pit, from all of the chemicals that were in the air. Or else it's the physical manifestations of stress; having that high a level of cortisol in your blood stream for such a long period of time. That has effects on the body. But it's strange, because I don't remember being scared. I never really thought about dying over there. I was only doing my job. I'd go to work every day and there was mortar and gunfire, but I adjusted and never really thought about it if there were patients in front of me. And there were always patients in front of me. I guess the one time I even really stepped back to say, "Okay, I'm in a war. This is a war," was when we had a four-star general in our hospital.

That was a hectic period. Intel must've leaked out, because we started getting mortared like crazy. I mean, the fear was palpable. It was in the air and it was hindering my ability to work. I was struggling to breathe, at times. But eventually we sent out a predator—a big tank-like vehicle— and about an hour later they brought us one of the enemy combatants. He's wounded, but there's this nurse under me who's refusing to help him. The combatant's kicking and screaming—behaving exactly, I guess, as you would expect a captured combatant to act—and this nurse is in a kind of shock. All of us were overwhelmed by the mortar, by the fear of it, and now he's saying, "We're supposed to help this guy? He tried to kill us!" And I remember thinking to myself, I remember being confused as to why this insurgent was alive. It didn't make any sense to me. I'm thinking, "This is the enemy. He was trying to kill us, and our guys went out there to kill him first, but now he is here, and he's alive." And it was my job to *keep* him alive. I'll never forget how... strange that was: witnessing, or enforcing, the rules of modern warfare. He went with our security forces afterward; I'm sure they wanted to interrogate him.

After a pause, Jennifer stands. The spotlight follows her to the left, away from the figure.

Do you have any water I could – ah.

She approaches a mini-fridge embedded in the counter and squats to peer at the shelves within. Pulling out a bottle of water, she straightens and twists off the cap before taking a long draught.

I'm sorry, I just... I get a bit tense, recalling some of this stuff. There's plenty that sticks. Patients, mostly. And I'm not sure why they stick. I think, I guess it was the ethical aspect. Because there were lots of events, decisions that we made, that the military made, that were unethical. And that's a part of war, and it's unfortunate and some of it needs to be addressed—like the burn pits—but in medicine, there were moments like that enemy combatant that really made you stop and think.

She leans against the counter, holding the water bottle by her side.

We still helped him. Even the nurse, he helped us patch up the enemy for questioning. But there were plenty of other times, less clear times, like when... well, there was this American soldier—a kid, really—he'd lost both of his legs from an IED. And he wanted me to kill him. I remember, he should've been in shock. Sedated and out of it. But his eyes were the clearest I'd seen, and I remember he addressed me by my name. "Dr. Sabates," he said. "Let me die." He begged me to kill him. And in that moment, I didn't know the right thing to do. I didn't let him die. I couldn't, even if I'd wanted to. But you just have to hope that they'll want to live again farther down the line. That one day they'll be grateful you didn't listen, grateful they're alive.

Moments like that affect you. Mentally and physically, I believe. And that's what's hard for me because there's the war and the burn pits, and then there's my PTSD, which is... well, the symptoms of my PTSD are complex. And having complex PTSD makes it hard to determine the direct cause because there isn't just one thing—a single event, say—that I have to overcome. There's no "confrontation" where I can recognize a certain emotion and then face it head-on. So it's hard dealing with my condition because I can't really know what the cause is, and it's embarrassing because the symptoms are there. They're tangible and they're real and they affect me every day. Me living with PTSD is me living in fear. It's me being useless, really, because I can't do anything other than work and sleep, and even then, I find myself struggling. I mean, thank god I didn't have a family before, because me living with PTSD... well, it's changed me.

She pushes off of the cabinet and begins to walk back to her seat.

It's changed me physically, too. Even though it's difficult to say, because... well, because I don't know where to draw the line. There's the PTSD, the overall effect of the war and being constantly surrounded by death. But then there's the burn pits. And the burn pits – well, I suppose I should explain about the burn pits.

Jennifer returns to her chair, setting the water bottle on the floor beside her. As the spotlight follows her, it becomes clear that the seated figure has disappeared. All that remains is the silhouetted chair across from her.

On any given FOB, the burn pit is where the military disposes of their waste. They burn it. They burn everything. Even the shit and piss. It was, it smelt, horrible. And there are always these huge wafting clouds of black coming across the base, to the hospital of all places, but generally all around the base making everything dark and grey and just sitting there in the heat. And when I say they burned everything, I mean jet fuel, plastics, chemicals. You know, bio-hazardous material that's illegal to dispose of without careful regulation in the States, but that they burn out in the open there. The air on base, our toxicologist measured it one day and found it to be the most toxic air he had sampled in over twenty years. And this was air we were breathing every day. We adjusted to it, sure, but here, now, almost seven years later, my body is failing. Like my thyroid that failed: my immune system shut it down. I have no history of autoimmune disorders and I've never had allergies or respiratory issues before the war, but I came back with asthma. My bone marrow's decaying, and I was recently diagnosed with early-onset menopause. My husband, he still hopes there might be a way for us to have children. It's difficult for him, you know, to process that I'm thirty-five and barren.

There's a good chance that it's all tied to the burn pits. But our minds, you know, we search for patterns. We try to make connections, any connection, to make sense of it all. That's what "this" is all about, I suppose. This interview. Talking about my experiences. For me, there's the burn pits and the cortisol—you know, the physical cause of my PTSD—but in the back of mind there's always that question of "What if it's not just chemistry?" What if, as a human being, this is what happens when you bear witness to so much death and violence?

Like in Fallujah. Bear with me here.

Jennifer stands, approaching the edge of the stage:

I know, I go off on tangents. But for my research I dug up a study from the University of Ulster. They collected data on the amount of cancer cases in Fallujah following both battles. The study happened six years after the First Battle of Fallujah, and what they found was a fourfold increase of cancer in adults—this is all types of cancer—but the stumper, the truly bewildering part, is how the cases of children showed a twelvefold increase.

She begins to pace, eyeing her feet.

I mean, can you imagine that? A twelvefold increase of cancer in kids. And there was a decrease in the birth rates of males, higher susceptibility to illness for all children, skyrocketing infant mortality. All of these are symptoms shared by survivors of Hiroshima—the effects of radiation, right? —but this was on a scale even greater than that. Anyways, the whole big conclusion was that during the Battle of Fallujah in '04 we used this incredibly radioactive weapon called depleted uranium, and we used White

Phosphorus—the stuff in smoke grenades—but as an offensive weapon. The military denied this, at first. They always deny everything until it's absurd for them to deny it any longer. But a year after the study the evidence became overwhelming and they came out about it, admitting to the use of white phosphorus as an incendiary. It creates a lot of smoke, you know. But it can also be used as a combustible. To burn down buildings and homes, or to set a room of insurgents on fire. The stuff hadn't been used offensively since Vietnam, but it was used in Fallujah.

The argument was all about White Phosphorus and how that plus depleted uranium caused the cancer spike in everyone. You see, phosphorus under the right conditions can release radiation, but it's even more complicated than that. What makes phosphorus dangerous is its allotropes. An allotrope is the form a compound takes when an atom binds to other atoms like it. White phosphorus is an allotrope of the phosphorus atom, which is the most reactive, toxic kind of allotrope because of the way electrons repel each other. It's all based on the structure of the phosphorus atoms when they come together—their tetrahedral shape, if you want to look it up—and it pushes the electrons out.

Now, when compounds like phosphorus react they create an ionizing radiation that penetrates the body and then stays inside of the body. And these atoms, once inside, they can damage whatever they touch. And they can cause free radicals. What happens is atoms in the body lose electrons to the phosphorus allotropes—because of the tetrahedral shape—and those electrons can go on to harm the DNA of other cells. The DNA is what contains the transcript for cell replication. And that's what cancer is: the infinite, unregulated replication of a cell body. When it's left to reproduce for a long time, you get tumors.

All that is to say the presence of white phosphorus in Fallujah created free radicals in the bodies of local residents, and those free radicals increased the quantity of cancer cases. And, to us scientists, it makes sense. Molecules on the outside of the body cause changes to the molecules on the inside of the body. That's chemistry.

She slows to a halt.

But isn't that the problem with modern medicine? That we see the results *first*? That, knowing what happened, we go on measuring the means by the end? We think we understand the root cause because of the molecular interactions that support preexisting notions and data, but there's still a gaping hole in this whole study. Inconsistencies overlooked by scientists and doctors and, perhaps most conveniently, the people who conducted the study. Inconsistencies like how there's no evidence of lingering radiation from white phosphorus *anywhere* in Fallujah; or how there's no direct link to white phosphorus as a cancer-causing agent; or how cancer itself is as illusive and inconsistent as any of the most ambiguous of nature's manifestations, and finally—the part that was screaming at me from the start—how children experienced a *twelvefold* increase of cancer, over the adults' fourfold. Isn't that a lot to just shrug off?

Now I know what you're thinking. That children are growing and that their cells are still developing and thus more susceptible to all that allotrope business. And that is partially true, children *are* more susceptible to free radicals.

What you're overlooking here, though, is how the body accounts for this. Our bodies at that age know to catch unregulated cell growth and nip it at the bud. Why else do you think cancer in children is so rare? If it isn't just their natural susceptibility to free radicals, what else could it be? That's the question that needs to follow. What else, if *not* the free-radical-causing allotropes of white phosphorus. Because the explanation has to correspond with precedence, with previous studies. And in this country, any proposal beyond the boundaries of modern medicine would be absurd and out of the question, right?

But—and this is where I'll lose most of you—what if it weren't.

Jennifer grabs the chair behind her and pulls it to the front of the stage. Swinging a leg over, she straddles the backwards chair and scans the audience.

What if the cause of cancer was something more conceptual? Something more intuitive. Because what happened at the Battle of Fallujah was the annihilation of an entire population. You know the numbers. You've seen the statistics on Wikipedia, in the New York Times: thousands of enemy combatants killed, 300,000 civilians uprooted and tossed aside like weeds. And you *know* there were people who stayed. Families that neglecting the call for evacuation. Kids who got mixed in the crossfire; or, perhaps worse, witnessed to it all.

I mean, what if that's all it takes? The witnessing of it? We've always known that proximity to death can have a physiological effect. Especially when that death is unnatural – manmade, so to speak. The memory of that death lingered in Fallujah. In the minds of those who survived.

And yes, in their bodies. Because wouldn't the experience of death on that scale—on a scale resembling Dresden, even—be enough to manifest itself as a disease more synonymous with death than war itself? Because how else do you explain the children?

Jennifer tucks in her arms, hugging herself behind the chair.

There was a twelvefold prevalence of cancer in kids aged fourteen and younger. By that study, the oldest of these kids would've been eight years old during the Second Battle of Fallujah. Eight years. At that age and younger, witnessing that amount of violence, that amount of destruction.

Jennifer rises, dragging the chair back to its place and reclining in the seat across from it. Her hair is disheveled, arms heavy.

It's all nonsense, of course. "Hearsay" compared to Western medicine. Physiological conditions are caused by measurable stimuli. The mind and body are separate. Radiation causes cancer—the same that affected Hiroshima survivors after World War II—and if we could create safer weapons then we could make war more "humane."

You can see how this train of thought is popular, and why it's propagated by the military. But for me, it's just not conducive to my experience of war. I struggle with it. I struggle with the displacement of responsibility, and the cancer in those children. Not because, at least I don't *think* it's because of my own inability to have kids—god knows how they would've turned out otherwise—but I think it's because of what's happening to me. To my organs. My thyroid, and my immune system. You know, whether the cause was the burn pits and the stress, or whether the cause was my proximity to so many violent deaths.

To be honest, I haven't a clue. And I think that's why I'm here, talking about it. To figure it out. To remember what it was like, or who I used to be. To figure out whether any "good" can come out of my experience of war. My husband, Zac, he wanted me to come here. He's a good man, a kind of idealist. But he's changing. My parents, my sister, they're all changing. Turning cynical. Who knows. Maybe that's my fault. Maybe I've been compromised—a rogue electron, free radical—damaging everyone I come in contact with. Sure, sure. I know it's not the same. "It's not my fault" and so on. But you've got to see the irony of it.

It's like what Jason, our toxicologist, told me after we got back from Iraq. He'd moved to the Pennsylvania countryside, to recover from a year of incessant gunshots, mortar and rockets exploding through the night. He thought the peace and quiet would help him sleep. Anyway, he called me the other day and I asked if it worked. "Did you get any sleep?" I asked.

He said, "Hell no. I didn't sleep a wink." I thought he was referring to the nightmares—that's what I was struggling with at the time—but, as it turns out, it wasn't the nightmares at all. He couldn't even sleep enough to dream. "You know what it is?" he said to me, finally. "You want to know what it is? It's all the damn birds."

Jennifer starts laughing. Her laughter grows until her voice cracks and she has to reach for the water bottle at the leg of her chair. She unscrews the cap, lifting it to her lips, but stops short. Her laughter stops. She looks up from the bottle's rim as the light begins to fade, and her body slumps against the back of the chair. Her arms fall and the water bottle jostles above the ground, splashing her hand and the stage below.

WORDS

The last time that I told the story of David Jenson I was reading from my book at a symposium on the post-Westphalian system of warfare. After questions, people tend to approach me with a few words or thoughts. Usually they're older women. They come up and say, "thank you for sharing that," or "that was very brave of you," and so on. Other people thank me for my service, which is a nice thing to say when you understand what they mean by it. I'd rather they just bought my book, but there were no books to sell at this conference and when I finished reading the only person to approach me was a middle-aged man a few years older than myself. It was a conference for academics and PhD students, but this guy was wearing jeans and a khaki coat. A patch on his sleeve read Hempstead Electricians. Most of the other attendees wore slacks and coat jackets, so he stood out like a fiberglass leg even before I noticed the prosthetic boot beneath his jeans.

"I read your book," he said.

It didn't really register that I was supposed to recognize him. The crowd had thinned—there was a coffee break before a Slovakian philosopher, Matej Novák, spoke—and there was no line of fans waiting for my signature. It was just him and me, and while every indication pointed at his connection to my book, it was his voice that triggered a name.

"Martinez," I said.

He laughed because his real name wasn't Martinez. It was Martin, and he wasn't Mexican; he was a second-generation Venezuelan American. The character and the person had become so mixed up in my mind that I was confused as to why his skin wasn't darker, why his eyes were brown instead of hazel.

"Martin," I said, shaking my head. "Martin Ramirez. Christ, how are you?"

He grabbed my hand and his weathered palm swallowed mine, plush and worn as the carpet between us. "I read your book," he said again, and he allowed those words to expand in the pause. "I liked it."

The lines around his eyes wrinkled and I sagged forward a bit. I hadn't expected to ever run into Martin again, but those were the last words I expected to hear from him.

We walked together to the porte-cochère outside of the Hilton foyer. It was early in the evening, but I was eager to escape the plastered formality of academia. "Let me buy you a beer," I said.

I was in no rush to get home, but Martin had to drop off his kids at school the next morning. We were in Riverhead on Long Island, and his home was in Hempstead. "It's another ninety minutes home without traffic," he said. "My wife's expecting me for dinner."

I let him go but insisted on seeing him again. The door to his car was open, and I held my hand against it. "I owe you," I said.

He gave me his card, which read Master Electrician, and I called him to set the time. We decided that he should come to my house since he had three kids—a six-year-old girl and two younger boys—that he said, "tend to overwhelm people." That was fine by me, since my wife had just succumbed to another spell and it was better if I stayed at home while she was ill. "We're in Queens," I told him. "Take the train. That way you don't have to worry about driving home."

I planned on getting drunk with him. I hadn't gotten drunk in almost a year, and the idea of drinking with Martin Ramirez from my old therapy group promised boundless material for writing. Three years as the resident writer of Long Island University had drained me of inspiration—along with a few of my favorite vices—but it also happened that my life at that point was in desperate need of a good binge.

I was hoping to talk about my book the most. It'd been published as a series of short stories nearly six years before, and I'd written only one book since—a novel about a soldier returning to a broken family, a disillusioned country, the works—but I still considered David Jenson's story to be the catalyst for my career, my most inspired piece of writing perhaps ever. I spent the next week anticipating the direction of our conversation, planning how I would delineate discrepancies between the reality and his character: everything from why I'd chosen him to tell the story of a sergeant shooting an unarmed girl, to why I wrote him storming out of our therapy group at the end. There was no telling how that might've made him feel, but I doubt "good" was anywhere on the spectrum. What I wanted now was to show him my reasoning, the sincerity behind my intentions, and that his character had been the price for a deeper truth. In any case, if things became tense there was always the whisky.

Martin didn't take the train. Instead, he spent a good thirty minutes searching for a parking spot outside of our apartment. In the end, neither of us could be sure if he'd left the thing in a tow-free zone or not, but it was getting dark and my wife was waiting up for us so I offered to pay the ticket if his car was gone, afterward. He said no—that he would pay the ticket himself if it came to that—and then he parked the car.

My wife greeted us at the door. She's a small woman, Jennifer, and Martin is a head taller than me so she naturally struggled taking off his coat. We had a modest flat, the two of us, with only one spare bedroom and a kitchen that was more spacious than the living area. Jennifer had arranged a space in the kitchen for us to talk. Two chairs had been set across the table from each other, with two placemats before them. In the middle of the table was a bottle of Scotch with two empty glasses, and above the table hung one of those fake chandeliers that tints the light bulbs yellow.

"Here we are," said Jennifer. She sagged forward after pulling Martin's chair back. Jennifer was only a few years older than me, but she'd grown frail in her middle age. We met while I was studying at NYU, and although she was half Cuban and normally a soft shade of brown, her face looked paler than mine. She was still recovering from her latest spell, but she'd read endless drafts of my David Jenson story and, determined to meet Martin, she'd put up her hair and put on her makeup. Once the two of us were seated she forced the color into her face and said, "I hope you like scotch!"

Martin winced.

"He has to drive home tonight," I said.

"Work tomorrow."

"Well," said my wife, unblinking. "With water, then!" She grabbed a wine basin from the cabinet, filled it with water from the sink and brought it to the table. When she set it down, her grip slackened, and the basin slammed against the table. Water drenched her hand and splashed onto the table.

Jennifer cocked her head, taking a moment to acknowledge that her hand was wet. Then she wiped it against a kitchen towel and apologized. "You'll have to excuse me a bit early, tonight," she said, returning to the table. "But I feel like I know you already, Martin, so I'll give you a hug. Make yourself at home."

She gave me a goodnight glance, but her expression was blank and before either of us could reply she had turned and dismissed herself from the room.

"She's not feeling well," I explained.

Martin nodded.

I settled across the table from him and immediately decided that the light in the kitchen was too bright, that the table was too bare. The conversation I had in mind was meant for a den with armchairs and a nineteenth-century musket hanging over the fireplace. What I had was a living area with a couch, desk, and piles of books; along with my wife in the bedroom next door, sleeping. I didn't want to disturb her with our talk, so we stayed where we were.

"Jennifer does research at LIU," I said. "She was a trauma surgeon in Baghdad for ten months."

Martin didn't reply. He was looking at the center of the table, feeling probably as out of place as I did. "In fact," I said, reaching for the whisky, "the book I'm writing just now has nothing to do with the war. It takes place during the Great Chicago Fire. It's a mystery novel." I poured us both a glass.

"That sounds interesting," said Martin. He reached for the basin and filled the remainder of his glass with water. I'd been prepared to bear the brunt of the talking, as I often had during our conversations in the past, but now that he was here I'd no idea how to begin.

I swallowed down my whisky and filled the glass again. It burned my throat and stomach. This wasn't the smooth kind that you find on sale in an airport. It was a peaty brand, the type of whisky that tastes like the smoke of a cigar when you breathe it out. I'd bought the stuff with clenched teeth at a high-end liquor store. The war had made us hard, I thought, waiting in line for the cashier. This wasn't going to be a casual night. It was going to be a spinal tap. A tearing at the roots.

Meanwhile, Martin was sipping his glass as if it might jump at him. He cringed afterward.

"Guess I'm out of practice," he said, noticing my expression.

"You and I both."

He laughed, then. It was good to hear him laugh, and I joined in. The whisky had loosened the muscles in my neck and I've always felt that words came easier if it hurt more to drink. "So!" I said, clapping my hands together. "Let's talk about life."

Martin blinked.

"Your family, your job," I said. "I want to know how you've *been*."

Martin was confused. He glanced to the side and shrugged. "Well," he said, "I met my wife while we were in therapy. The job I've been working for about ten years, now. But listen, Zac—" He said this with an intensity that stilled the whisky in my glass. "What you said before. You don't owe me anything. I finished reading your book a long time ago. I only came to that symposium because of something I read, recently. I thought it might be good to see you again."

When I still looked stunned—unconvinced might be a better word—he said, "I got it, though. Your whole book. I understood it."

"You understood?"

"Sure," he said. "I mean, I knew which character was based on me. And I get why you presented him that way. Really. It's fiction. You have to tweak things to fit the mold."

He was wafting his hand in the air as if to say "and so on," but I struggled to believe that he could understand the intricacies of the creative process, or my internal struggle to produce a rounded story rather than sticking to the actual events: making Aaron a tattooed thug instead of the thin, wired up paranoid he was; painting Matthews out to be a born-again Christian instead of a clichéd preacher's son.

"But you don't have any questions?" I said.

Martin cocked his head to the side. His shoulders rose, and he looked ready to shrug, but at the last moment his face brightened and he leaned forward. "Actually," he said, thrumming the table. "What happened to our therapist. Did she really burn out and quit the VA?"

It took a moment for his question to settle. There was a garrulous quality to it, like gossip. "Alison?" I said, eyebrows slanting. "Well, I don't know actually—"

"Oh. That's a shame."

"But, Martin," I said. "Aren't you curious about anything? Like the story that your character told in the sake bar about the sergeant? Don't you wonder where that came from?"

Martin crossed his arms. His lips and brow were tightened with thought. "I liked the story of the sergeant," he said. "I didn't mind being the voice for that one. It made me sound... poetic."

I threw back the whisky remaining in my glass and held it in my mouth. It took a few seconds for the numbness to set in. I even poured myself a new glass before swallowing.

"As for the rest of it," continued Martin, "look. I may not always know what's going on behind the curtain, but I got the gist of it. It's true I never talked about my leg, and I get why that became a theme. Even though I didn't lose my leg how you implied."

He eyed me and I went stiff, clenching the glass in my hand.

"But that's fine. You wanted to tell a story that you know. That most people know. If it'd been a grunt who set off an IED while running to help his blown-up Lieutenant in Afghanistan's Green Zone, well... that wouldn't have resonated the same way, I guess."

His words reached me after some time, through the gap between us.

"Right," I said. The whisky swirled in my stomach. I hadn't eaten dinner—Jennifer usually forced me to, but she'd only stomached a few bites herself that night—so I was already beginning to feel a buzz.

"That's good," I said again, wondering if I should ask what he meant. But he spoke in such a way that I believed his tone. He understood. He'd forgiven me. Which was great, except that the rest or our night would have to be unscripted. I'd dedicated the entire evening to explaining his character and the story of David Jenson and we'd zipped through all of that in the first fifteen minutes.

Movement flickered across the corner of my vision and I looked up to see my wife in a cotton robe with her hair down. I stood up and Martin turned around. The whisky rushed to my head, spotting my vision.

"I'm so sorry," she said, ducking toward the stove. "I just can't find my medicine. Zac, honey, have you seen my Levothyroxine?"

Martin was watching Jennifer sift through a drawer at the back of the kitchen. She'd washed her face and the rings around her eyes looked darker than eye shadow. You could see patches of her scalp where the hair was falling out.

"I don't know," I said, standing between her and Martin. "Did you check the nightstand?"

"I thought I left them in here—"

Her voice shut with the kitchen drawers. I placed my arm around her waist and felt her weight shift. "Well let's check again," I said, leading her back to our bedroom.

When I returned to the kitchen, Martin's whisky glass was empty. He'd been skimming emails on his phone and he only looked up when I sat down across from him.

"Everything alright?" he said.

I told him everything was fine. "She didn't get much sleep last night," I said. "Delirious, I think. The fatigue."

I poured myself another glass and handed him the bottle. "How about that whisky?"

Martin was inspecting the label. "I almost expected sake," he said.

I forced a laugh. "Came all the way from an island in Scotland," I said. "Some place with the highest concentration of whisky distilleries in the world."

"Hmm," said Martin. He rolled the bottle in his hand and squinted. "Is it very strong?"

"Not as strong as Japanese whiskey," I said. I was rambling again, but I wanted him to get drunk. We had a spare room he could sleep in overnight and I got the feeling his work in the morning wasn't compulsory. Mostly, I just wanted him to get drunk because I was getting drunk myself.

"Go on, pour yourself a glass."

He did, and when he was done I pulled the water out of his reach. "You should try it straight," I said. "Came all of the way from Scotland."

Martin sighed. Then he drank straight from the glass. He coughed almost immediately afterward and we both laughed. "Crazy, isn't it?" I said, "Twenty years ago we would've drank pisswater if it had alcohol on the label. Now look at us."

Martin had to sip the whisky again to settle his throat. We were doing good now, talking about nothing. Even the light in the room seemed less, as if there were a haze around us that softened the glare. Martin's grip on his glass slackened and he slumped against the back of his chair. He was sipping his whisky and talking more often, and at some point he looked up and said, "I really liked your book. The writing, I mean. It was very good."

I'd been in the middle of swallowing, and when he said this the whisky got stuck in my throat and burned up my nose.

"No," laughed Martin, seeing me flinch. "Really. Talking to you now with your book and your position, I can't say a bad thing about it. I look forward to your next one."

He toasted his glass with mine but, having nothing else to say, I asked: "Do you read a lot, then?"

Martin shrugged. "I do now," he said. "It's easier on the eyes than television. Helps me fall asleep."

"Huh," I said. "And what was it that reminded you of me?"

Martin cocked his head.

"You mentioned reading something," I said, skeptical of my own memory. "You were reading something that inspired you to come to my symposium."

"Ah, right. Well, I wouldn't really call that reading," he said, rolling his glass on it's edge. "More like skimming. See, it was a collection of essays—I know, I know; even I had no intention of slipping down that rabbit hole—but I'd been motivated by some political meme about ignorance killing democracy, so I bought this book and one of the chapters caught my eye. I actually read it all of the way through. It was titled 'On Cultural Narrative.'"

"Cultural narrative," I said.

Martin laughed. "To be honest, I'm still not even sure what that means. The book as a whole was too dense for my taste. But there was this essay about how the media and the public tell a story that over time becomes a kind of history for current events." He paused and looked at the gold in his glass. "I'm really starting to enjoy this whisky, you know. It grows on you."

"It does," I said, refilling his glass.

"Just let me know if I'm talking too much."

Laconic might not have been as much of a characteristic of Martin as it was Martinez, but this was possibly the most I'd ever heard him speak. I wasn't going to slow him down.

"This essay, though. It wasn't so much the article as it was the thoughts that it sparked. I don't know. I started thinking about the story people tell about war. You know the one I'm talking about—the one featured in every book and portrayed on the media since Vietnam—the line that war is horrible and destroys everyone and everything it comes in contact with. And I can tell you think I'm crazy," he said. "But I'm not disagreeing with that. I get why your book had that whole 'lost innocence' theme, and I believe that it's bad to glorify war and paint it in any kind of light that might inspire young people to join up. But fuck me if I didn't lose my leg in Afghanistan and consider it the best thing that ever happened to me."

I knocked my knee on the table and the bottle of whisky wobbled between us. It was half empty, and I had to reach out to keep it from falling. Martin hardly noticed.

"I mean, I was a rat of a kid. I was cocky, I was an asshole, and I bullied the smaller boys. Do you know why I signed with the marines?" he said. "I joined because I wanted to kill hajjis. That's the truth. I mean, who *knows* if I hadn't lost my leg. I might still be that guy. I might still be bitter and angry and violent for no reason. I definitely wouldn't have met my wife or fathered my kids. And I wouldn't have been caught dead reading essays on cultural narrative and history."

He laughed after that and took a sip from his glass, but when he saw my expression he said, "I know, I know. You think I'm crazy. And maybe I am. But wouldn't it be something if somebody told a different kind of story? If somebody told *that* story? Not one that glorified war or told kids that getting your leg blown off is a good thing; but a story that showed how—even in the most fucked up situations—some *good* can still come of it all."

He was smiling, waiting for me to reply, but I was watching his hands. I hadn't blinked and my eyes were drying out. Then, being the author, it struck me that this whole message was directed at me—that it was me who should've written that story, and that this is what he'd come here to say—but when I looked back at Martin he must've seen this in my face, because his smile flattened and he looked down at the table.

"Don't pay any attention to me," he said. Shadows from the fluorescent light cut a line through his lips, under his nose and eyes. "I didn't see the things you did. I blacked out after the IED went off, so somebody else must've picked up the parts. Christ, I haven't drank this much in ages." He stood and reached for the water basin. He filled his glass to the brim.

I shook my head and smiled. "Nonsense," I said. "I'm just drunk. I need more time to process these kinds of things when I'm drunk."

Martin relaxed and we kept drinking. He took control of the conversation and, as the bottle of whisky drained, he probed me more and more about my residency at LIU: the potential for settling down and tenure. He asked about Jennifer and our plans for children, whether my next book would be more genre or literary, and so on. My own thoughts were sparse and preoccupied. I kept slipping back to his spiel about narrative, but anytime I began tying it in with my own writing Martin would ask another question.

And the whisky flowed. I couldn't feel it in my throat anymore, but I could taste the smoke of it and see how every time I breathed out it added to the haze in the room. We drifted quietly through a cloud of conversation and my mouth grew dry and tired of moving. I spent a moment holding the bottle after it emptied when finally I looked up and said, "There is no book about the Chicago Fire."

Martin waited, and when there was nothing more he said, "Well, that's alright." He was fingering the glass in his hand, guzzling water like he'd just finished a patrol through the desert. "It's the idea that matters? Once you've got the idea, a little bit of guidance and motivation—"

"Martin," I said. "There are no ideas. There's no book, and in three months my residency at LIU will end."

Martin froze. I could see it even through the haze: his shoulders tensing, his neck twisting so that he could look away if just for a second. I wanted to keep going. I wanted to tell him about Jennifer's early onset menopause because of the burn pits in Iraq, and how her thyroid had shut down. I wanted to tell him that my second book had been a dud and that there was not an agent in all of New York willing to commit to another. I wanted to tell him that I had nothing lined up after my residency ended, and that in approximately three months I would be living off of savings.

I didn't say any of these things, though, and don't really know why. Maybe it was because I didn't want to burden him with all of it. And maybe it was because, in the smokiness and the haze, I thought it was Martinez sitting across from me—Martinez, with his intolerance for sharing, his unwillingness to speak or heal—Martinez who would've mocked me for spilling my guts after just a few glasses of Scotch. My mouth was dry and tired and I kept it closed, wafting my hand in the air as if to say, "and so on."

Martin responded with a mass of reassurances: "Good ideas for your book will come with time," he said. Then, "Tenure's overrated." I was so drunk I don't even remember him leaving. I mentioned the spare bedroom and that he shouldn't drive home drunk, but he'd switched to water long before I drank the bottle dry. I fell asleep like a schoolboy at a school desk, bent over the table and flattened across my arms, nuzzling into the smoke of my sweater. When I dreamt, the burn in my mouth became the war and David Jenson.

My wife had to peel me off of the table the next morning. I called Martin to apologize but reached his voicemail and when he called back he told me that there was nothing to apologize for. I insisted that we meet again. "Without the whisky," I said, "so that I can't embarrass myself anymore." He said okay and I never heard from him again.

His spiel about the war, though—how the whole country was painting it in a narrow light—that stuck. I remembered parts of it in the evening, my head panging with hangover. The next morning it hit me like a mortar shell. It hurt so much, I think, because he was right. Because there was a truth to what he'd said; the kind of truth that you didn't need to quantify, you just knew. I'd known the night of our conversation, struggling to keep it at bay—fighting the inevitable force of epiphany with eyes closed so hard I could've squeezed out shrapnel—but it sunk in eventually. It always sinks in eventually. And it stung like hot metal because it meant that reimagining *itself* corrupts reality; that there's no point to fiction; and that the part of my life I'd viewed as a kind of personal catharsis might also have been a means to capitalize on David Jenson's death: framing it with a narrative that was popular, that would sell.

Stephen J. O'Shea

I persisted in this state until one morning, weeks after my night with Martin, Jennifer woke up to her alarm. She crawled out of bed without my help and prepared herself for lab. I watched her put up her hair through half-closed eyes, applying foundation to hide the pallid tone of her skin, and when the bathroom door shut, I sat up and let my uselessness set in. It was a magnificent, crushing weight, and it pressed me against the floor of the room. What strikes me now, though, is that after it passed I was able to get over it. I dried my eyes and threw back the sheets. I even cooked us both breakfast, despite not eating breakfast together in about six months. Then, cleaning the dishes after Jennifer left, I realized that I could move my hands. I could think words. I could write.

I went back to the drawing board and began picking apart the story that I'd read at the symposium. The reality, though, is that I'd written and rewritten the story of David Jenson a hundred times since therapy. I never sat on it long enough to incubate a Vonnegut-esque *magnum opus*, but before Martin's visit I'd held that story to be the most important and inspired work of my life. Writing it had allowed me to confront the weight of my trauma—the inhuman gurgling of stomach acids to the smell of burnt meat—and though it had been a revolting and morbid scene to relive, the writing of it had allowed me to move forward: to talk openly and creatively about an experience that, for an enormous chunk of my life, had been unspeakable. And yet, despite five or six years of writing and refining, the first line of that story had never changed. "The first time that I told the story of David Jenson," I wrote and that was my springboard into every draft since. It remained

245

untouched throughout my masters at NYU, rounding out characters and narrative and place, until—along with a larger narrative—I submitted the story of David Jenson's death for publication.

Now, weeks after Martin left my wife to peel me off of our kitchen table, I'm sitting down to a blank page. "The Parts – Rewrite," I ink across the top. But, before the first line, I stop. It's Martin that comes to mind: what he said about narrative and history and the way that he said it. Staring at the page, I realize that I can't "fix" this story. There is no "deeper truth" that I can uncover by writing the perfect version; no edits I can make that might do justice to David Jenson. So, instead, five years after its publication, I'm setting out to write the imperfect story—a kind of redemption; a restructuring of words—to, if not create a new truth, then to at least address the existence of one. My pen touches the page, and striving for that same sense of honesty I felt from Martin in my kitchen, I write: "The last time that I told the story of David Jenson…"

IN WILDFIRE COUNTRY

What nobody tells you about marriage is that it can leave you stranded in the Jemez Mountains of New Mexico, listening to the dead sound of a disconnected phone line for thirty minutes in your car. That's where I was, at least, when I decided to call up my younger brother. There was no reception on my property, and I had to drive the mile and a half down to Highway Four just to check my voicemail. When there were no new messages, I decided to call my wife. She hung up on me after two minutes and forty-three seconds.

I had braced myself for a longer conversation. In my lap was a piece of notebook paper outlining what I'd meant to cover during that phone call, all of it culminating toward a promise for the future. "I'm doing much better here," I was going to say. "The isolation has been good for me." If it went well, I planned on inviting them to come visit: my wife Alice and Ellie, my daughter. I'd even scribbled in the margin: "Invite for visit." The call didn't go well. I mentioned Skyler and my wife went off. "Fuck you," she said, but in a tone that told me to chip my teeth on the barrel of a shotgun.

After that, I drank from my flask like it was the first inspired thing I'd done in months. The truth is, I wasn't doing any better. My life was on fire and the "mountain home" I'd bought to fix up required a steep learning curve. Since I was a journalist, and not a handyman like my brother, I spent most of that first month intoxicated. Parked along Highway Four—with the passing headlights highlighting the lines in my face—whiskey seeped out of my pores more pungent than the B.O. build-up from three days without a shower.

My phone was burning a signal through the leather of the passenger seat when I decided to call up my brother. Normally, it'd take more than a flask of whiskey to inspire a conversation with him. We stopped talking casually after he dropped out of Penn State to join the Navy, but when I got back from my embedded stint in Iraq there was a new kind of tension. See, our father had earned a Purple Heart in Vietnam. He made a full recovery but died after refusing chemo for colon cancer. It was a messy death, and our mother held his hand through the end, praying all the while that her own death would be peaceful. Then she married a drunk and died in a car accident a few years ago. Looking back, it adds up that I would go to war as a journalist while Chandler spent his tour of the military in the Pacific, baking on beaches in the sun. The only miracle is that he didn't die from a stray bullet during a drill somewhere.

Not that I was thinking about any of this when I decided to call him up. I'd been soaked with depression for thirty minutes, and once the whiskey kicked in, I rebounded with nostalgia for the time Chandler and I had built a tree house in our Connecticut backyard. We'd followed the juvenile tradition of scavenging wood and tools from a nearby construction site, tearing trim from framed houses and breaking into storage sheds for nails and the occasional handsaw. Our foundation was a beautifully convoluted layer of plywood, slanting across three branches about ten feet up a precariously bent oak tree. We were even done building the back wall when our father found out. A man named Payton Landry tipped him off. Landry owned the construction company we'd been raiding; he was also the main referral source for our father's pool service.

We were made to disassemble the fort and return everything in person. The plywood was frayed and broken. The 2x4s had an excessive amount of nails poking through that we hadn't bothered to remove, and the 4x4 foot beam we'd used to prop up the back wall cracked when we dropped it down the tree. Landry burned the wood in front of us. Then he told us to go home. We must've looked as wrecked as we felt because our father promised to make us a new one. He built it two feet above the ground with splinter-free wood and we immediately lost interest. Two years later, he was diagnosed with cancer. Weeds grew through the floorboards of that old fort, and brown recluses claimed the corners. It didn't take long for the wood to start sagging into the earth again.

My mountain home was in a similar condition to our childhood tree house. The floor sagged into the pier-and-beam foundation, and the walls were a splintered mess. It was almost November, and unless I started storing firewood in my car, I'd never have enough to last through winter. The image of me freezing to death in that place filled the space of my mind until finally I lifted the phone and called my brother.

A series of ringbacks followed. After the fifth or sixth, I began to wonder if he'd changed his number. I hung up and waited five minutes to call again. He answered after the first ring.

"Monroe Remodeling, this is Chandler," he said.

It stung at first that he hadn't saved my number. But then I realized it would be just like Chandler to try and impress me that way. He'd a family now, started a remodeling company outside of San Diego, so I stifled a laugh and said, "Monroe remodel, want me suck you off?"

"Oh," said Chandler, breathing into the receiver. "Max. What's this about?"

"What's it about?" I said. "What do you mean, 'What's this about.' I'm just calling to see how my little brother's doing." My voice had a tendency to climb in pitch whenever I called Chandler, but there was a dryness to it that made my voice click. I sounded about as drunk as I was.

"We've just finished dinner," he said. "This might not be the best time—"

"Who's that?" I said. There was the sound of a child crying in the background.

"Casey," he said. "Adrian stole her spoon again."

I laughed too long at this, stalling to remember their age. "That's my nephew, alright," I said. "Takes after his uncle."

Chandler grunted, maybe prying the spoon from Adrian's fingers. "*She* certainly has an older-brother maliciousness about her."

There was a familiar aggression to his tone, but I didn't let it phase me. Chandler had never invited me to meet his kids or stay with his family, so how could I have known that Adrian was a girl? Instead I said, "Hey, you know what I was thinking about just now? You wanna guess?"

Chandler jostled the phone. Scratching noises came through the receiver like it was wedged between his shoulder and chin. "Not really," he said. "Look, Max—"

"Come on," I said. The whiskey was leaking out of me, now. "When's the last time I called you like this, out of the blue like this? Humor me for a sec."

Chandler's silence was so complete that I had to pull the phone back and make sure he hadn't hung up. The truth is that we might never have talked like this, out of the blue with nothing to say except, "Help." I had called him once several years ago—drunk after an argument with Alice—to tell him about the EFP that almost split me from crotch to throat during my two months in Iraq, but he had been in Thailand with his buddies on leave and when he answered it was to say, "Go fuck yourself." He'd changed since then. Had a few kids, found Jesus, the works. And as the background noise flooded back, it wasn't disdain that saturated his voice. It was reluctance. "Alright," he said. "What were you thinking about."

"Well," I said, "I was *thinking* about that tree house we built in our backyard. Remember? That old fort we wedged in the middle of an oak tree. Couldn't have been more than ten feet up, but I swear that thing swayed in the wind."

Chandler was quiet. It was as if the words reached him after a delay. "Sure, I remember," he said. "It's a miracle that thing didn't collapse and kill us."

"Right? Those were some good times," I said. "We really got along back then."

"Sure," said Chandler. "Right until you hammered that nail into my hand."

I think it's safe to say that all of us harbor childhood regrets. This, however, wasn't one of mine. Not because I stand by what I did or was proud of it, but because I'd forgotten about it entirely. There was a darkness in me then that I still can't defend, and, while I was trying to show him that I'd outgrown that phase, a shadow of my younger self welled up inside of me. His hand had been splayed across a 2x4 plank, exposed and trusting. Afterward, he yelped like a dog. I took heavy breaths over the phone to not choke with laughter.

"I'm sorry," I said, wheezing. "I was a little shit, it's true."

"I couldn't write for a week," he said. "Mrs. Etheridge wrote me a referral and made mom get me a tetanus shot."

My laughter came out in stifled bursts. I tried to make myself stop, but it felt so damn good to laugh after sitting in that car with thoughts of my wife and daughter and blowing my brains out. "Mrs. Etheridge!" I panted. "How do you even remember her? Christ, Chandler…"

"Well, it's hard to forget when there's a scar on the back of your hand," he said. Chandler wasn't laughing. Instead, there was a bitterness to his voice that sobered me up fast.

"Well look," I said between breaths. "I only meant to bring that up because of this idea I had."

"Here we go."

"Sure," I said. "I'll give you that one. I deserve that one. But hear me out, okay? I've got a feeling you're really gonna like this."

I was stalling to catch my breath, but when he didn't say anything back, I knew that I had him. His wife and kids had faded into another room, and I took a long pause before pressing on.

"So I bought some land in the Jemez Mountains," I said. "It's a great plot of land. One hundred acres of pine surrounded by national forest. Hell, it's a mile to my mailbox. A mile of gorgeous land. And the house I'm living in—"

"Living in?" said Chandler. "You bought a hundred acres in New Mexico and *moved* there?"

"Sure," I said. "Blew my load on this place. But it's a gem, Chandy, and I got her at a steal. I mean, you should see the trees up here: tall and looming, hundreds of years old. Not like the palm trees in Southern California. This place is all natural. Running streams, mountains, rock formations like you've never seen. And I know how you used to love climbing."

"What the hell are you talking about? What about your job? What about your *family*?"

"Well," I said, and stopped. It was at this point that I realized Chandler would know nothing about my job or separation with Alice. The last time we had talked was after I clogged our dishwasher in Newark where my wife still lived. That call had lasted six minutes and consisted of troubleshooting and a list of instructions. Now, rather than diving into how I'd fallen in love with a younger journalist and was being sued for sexual harassment, I told him that it was an "overdue life change."

"I embedded in Iraq," I said. "I was a war correspondent. You can't spend the rest of your life sitting at a desk after that, coaching doe-eyed millennials on how to write a tabloid."

"But what about Alice?" said Chandler. "And your daughter, Max. Are they still in Newark?"

"It sounds bad," I said. "I'll give you that. But Alice and I talked it over and decided that a little distance might not be a bad thing. Besides, once I've got this place all fixed up they're going to move out here and we're gonna start over. Raise Ellie in the country, away from the city. Which leads me to my idea." I could hear Chandler inhale. "The place I've got, it's a bit of a fixer-upper. Nothing big," I lied. "Nothing I can't handle on my own. Some patchwork, you know, to make it presentable. But I was thinking you could drive over and join me for a while."

"Drive over?"

"Sure," I said. "You're two states away. What's that, ten hours?"

"In a helicopter, maybe."

"Well I was thinking you could come out for, say, a month."

"Max," he said.

"Now hold on, I'm being serious. It'd be like a vacation. This is beautiful country. There's hot springs and trails to hike on. Hell, there's even trout in the streams. We could go fly fishing like we did at Lick Creek." I said this even though I didn't own a single fishing pole. "You wouldn't have to lift a finger if you didn't want to. Just point me in the right direction and watch me work."

"Max, I can't," he said. "I've got a business, a family. I can't just leave for a month."

"Bring 'em along!" I said.

"Out of the question."

"I'll reimburse you for everything," I said, and regretted that, too.

"It's not a question of—"

"Chandler, look," I said, and the desperation in my voice was enough to cut him off. "I'm in a bad place. I wouldn't be asking, otherwise." My voice broke in the middle, and I realized that this was true: that it was the most honest thing I'd said in months.

A long silence followed. Lisa, his wife, called out to their kids in the background, but a grinding sound muffled her voice. It was Chandler, dragging his hand across his face.

"Alright," he said. "I'll see what I can do."

"That's all I'm asking."

"But there's no way I can stay a month. A week, tops."

"Two weeks," I said. "We'll make it work." My excitement was steaming up the windows of the Altima. "Listen, Chandler ole boy. We're gonna have a great time. We're gonna have the greatest damn time in the world, you wait and see."

Chandler planned to drive up the next week. That gave me six days to clean and get sober. The house was so littered with clothes and empty liquor bottles that you could hardly make out the flooring beneath. Meanwhile, there was a propane cooking stove I'd yet to install. We were going to need wood. Wood, nails, screws, and plates. The morning after our talk, I even tore up a few floorboards in my room to scope out the rotted base beam underneath. Then I traced the walls for cracks in the shiplap and measured the ceiling for plywood and replacement rafters. We'd need slats to replace the middle wall, as well, and 2x4s for the porch.

Combined, it was more wood than I could ever transport in my Altima—I'd been living out of the backseat of that car for the past month, stacking everything else in the trunk—so the day before Chandler arrived I got Hugh, my retired neighbor, to join me in picking up a few slats and beams from a lumberyard in Albuquerque. Hugh owned a new F-250 from when he'd moved with his wife, Joy, from Cleveland. Since he rarely got to use the truck, he was happy to volunteer. We piled the payload alongside my house. I'd no shed or overhang, yet, but the whole state was in the middle of a decade-long drought and there was virtually no chance of losing the wood to snow.

I got in bed that night at 10pm. Chandler wouldn't arrive until noon—he'd left on Thursday and decided to break up the drive by sleeping in Flagstaff—but when he arrived I wanted it to look like I'd been at work for weeks. The only problem was that I didn't sleep a wink. I lay there with my mattress in the main room staring up at the rafters and thinking about Alice and Ellie and Skyler.

I hadn't tried calling Alice since she hung up on me because I planned to call her while Chandler was in town. The idea was to prove that I had reconnected with my roots, but even as I planned out what I would say my mind drifted to Skyler: to the brush of her hair in my face, how when she moved on top of me it felt like I could wrap my hands around her entire waist. The first time I kissed her, she bit my lip so hard that it bled. I let her do it again right after. I can't really say what appealed to me about that, other than it reminded me of what it meant to feel alive.

Skyler got caught misquoting a handful of sources and fabricating others. But I was the one who printed her work as a headliner, without checking her references. I fired her in a last-ditch effort to save my own skin, and a week later she sued me for sexual harassment. The fire spread. "They're going to ask you to resign," my boss and longtime friend, Gary Jackson, told me. "Just promise me one thing. Promise me you won't make a scene."

I promised him that much, but when they wanted me to leave the office with my few possessions in a box like some scene from a film, I put on the "PRESS" Kevlar vest that I'd worn in Iraq and wore it out. The idea was to remind everyone of how much I'd given to that newspaper, how I'd been a yard away from getting split by an

Explosively Formed Penetrator, but the message got misconstrued. For one, the vest smelled terrible. I'd never washed it, see, and it was still stained with sweat and dirt. It'd been framed—hanging above my desk for the past fifteen years—but after wearing it out of the building, everyone thought I'd gone homicidal. "He's at war with the media," somebody said, and rumors spread that I was going to go all Charlie Hebdo on everyone's asses.

Four months passed and I still couldn't land a job interview. My freelance work wasn't enough for groceries, and my life savings—the small amount untouched by Alice—was being funneled into the black hole that is a Hoboken apartment. The night before I bought the Jemez property, I dreamt I was burning alive, disintegrating into the impeccable white fire of my apartment with no money, no family, and no legacy.

Chandler arrived the next day. I'd given him my address, and he was going to use satellite GPS to navigate. I didn't really think twice about it until he still hadn't arrived by 2pm. That's when Hugh drove up to check in, popping his head out of the truck.

"Where's the little brother?" he said.

I was removing the chicken wire that skirted my house's foundation. Hugh's wife, Joy, had lent me some gardening gloves that I wore with a shrug. They were speckled with flowers and bumblebees, and it took a moment for me to remember how I'd gotten them.

Hugh was a clean-faced man with long, silver hair. His gut spilled over the front of his belt like molded clay, and his shoulders had the tendency to slump forward if he stood upright too long. Although we both had properties of around a hundred acres, our houses were pinned into the same corner. From the window above my stove you could glimpse the metal of Hugh's roof glinting through the trees. His house was also pressed against the Jemez National Forest, but unlike mine it had three stories, WIFI internet, satellite television, central heating, and a wall of double-paned insulated windows that faced Mount Redondo. Despite this, Hugh's favorite pastime was finding fallen trees for firewood. He'd weave his truck through the forest looking for thick old pines to haul home. After sawing the logs into stumps, he would roll them over to his F-250 and use a makeshift pulley system to lift them into the bed. Then he would stack them in his yard until the first snow buried them.

Hugh was amiable enough, though, and he always brought an extra mug of Nespresso coffee over on weekday mornings. He'd brought three this time, since I'd told him about Chandler coming. "Hard at work?" he said, handing me the drink.

"For once," I said. It was November in the mountains, but it was still New Mexico and the afternoon heat was enough to dampen my shirt. I took a swig and sweat dripped down my neck. There was a restlessness about me that I wanted to ride out, though, so I placed the mug on the ground and went back to the chicken wire.

"You think he got lost?" said Hugh.

I yanked at the skirting and a staple flew across the space between us. It bounced off of Hugh's tennis shoe, and he looked up toward the sky, like it'd been a rogue snowflake that fell.

"He's got GPS," I said. "Should be fine."

"Alright," said Hugh. He stood there a moment longer with a mug of coffee in each hand. Then he turned and looked at the bald cap of Redondo. It was a landmark you could see from both of our houses, and one that Hugh always turned to when he didn't know what else to say. "I'll get out of your way," he said. "Check up on you in a bit."

I grunted again and Hugh climbed into his truck. Ten minutes later I heard him pull up to his house next door. He never walked the fifty yards separating our two homes. I think he liked the idea of it taking ten minutes by car, driving down his driveway to Spring Creek Road, then up the mile and a half to mine.

Two hours later, my brother still hadn't arrived. I'd torn off the skirting around the entire house and set to tearing up floorboards in my bedroom. I'd no idea how to replace a base beam, but that seemed the natural first step. Once I had the old hardwood piled up outside of my house, with the 2x12 replacement beam propped against the wall, I finally resolved to drive down to Highway Four and give my brother a call.

"Hello?" said Chandler once I got through.

"Chandler, it's Max."

It only took the sound of my voice to set him off. "Damnit, Max," he said. "I've been calling you for three hours. I had to pull into a diner and ask for an outlet just so

I could recharge my phone. How on earth did you not think I'd be lost?"

He was right, of course—it should've clicked a long time ago—but I was tired from work and not sleeping, and the high pitch of his voice made me irritable. "I dunno," I said. "Maybe you slept in, alright?"

"Slept in?" he said. "*Slept in?*"

"Look, you said you had GPS. If you had GPS, how the hell did you get lost?"

Chandler was quiet for a moment. I knew he was fuming, but I couldn't hear it through the phone. "Look, I don't know," he said. "The signal gets dodgy after Jemez Springs. But either way, there is no 1411 on Spring Creek Road. I drove up and down that road for an hour. I even knocked on somebody's door to ask about it. They said the only other house on that road was a Mormon family."

I'd pulled over onto the highway shoulder and could just make out the road sign in my rearview. It read Spring Creek Drive, not Road.

"Shit."

"What," said Chandler.

"Nothing. Look, can you get to Jemez Springs?"

"That's where I've been the past three hours."

"Great," I said. "Meet me at the gas station. There's only one, so try not to get lost."

I heard static as Chandler swiveled his head around. "Fine," he said. "But look, Max. I was *this* close to driving home. I'd given myself another five minutes, and if you hadn't called I was gonna—"

"I'll see you in five," I said, and hung up.

I didn't mean to seem short, but the light was falling faster now and I really wanted to get that base beam installed before dark. I'm not sure what possessed me, going from zero to sixty on productivity that day, but when I saw my brother parked in the gas station with his window down, I didn't bother getting out of the car. I didn't even stop, really. I just rolled by and honked. His little Acura jumped to life and he flashed his lights, pulling out after me.

Chandler threw up his arms after we passed the sign for Spring Creek Drive: I watched him through my rearview mirror. My driveway was unmarked, too. The pair of parallel ruts that served as a road wound behind a patch of pine trees right off. Meanwhile, parts of the road were cut so deep that if Chandler hadn't known to straddle the ruts he might've bottomed out. But he followed my lead and we arrived at the hill where my house was perched.

I pulled over to the right of the place. Chandler parked beside me, and I got out to watch his reaction. Whatever aggravated or frustrated him on our drive up was replaced by a childish disorientation.

"This is it?" he said, leaning to the side as if to spot whatever was hiding behind my boxed up shed.

"This is it," I said.

To be fair, my house was a dilapidated mess. The front porch was more of a block platform. It dipped forward and to the side so that if you placed a can in the middle of it, the thing was as likely to tumble headfirst as it was to roll off the edge. The outer walls were cracked shiplap, which wouldn't look so bad except that Hugh'd had the idea to cover some of the openings with old 2x4s. They sat pinned against the façade like ladder steps to a tree house. The roof was rusted tin, the one hole having been patched and restored before I moved in. The only good window faced our cars—the other one I'd boarded up—but the size alone was enough to cause alarm. It took up four hundred square feet, at best: a kind of toolshed turned guesthouse.

Chandler blinked twice and shut his eyes, concentrating as if to process it. Meanwhile, I moved to the back of his Acura and looked him over. We'd skipped greeting each other, but I couldn't help taking him in. He stood a half-head taller than me, his shoulders filled from years of deployments with nothing better to do than gym, eat, and sleep. He was tan as well, with jet-black hair that curled above his ear. He'd grown into middle age handsomely and had a presence that suggested *he* was the older brother between us. This was unsettling mostly because I still remembered things like the time he got caught masturbating to porn at our neighbor's house while babysitting their kid.

"So," I said. "Whaddayou think?"

Chandler crossed his arms. "I think that you told me 1411 Spring Creek Road, not Spring Creek Drive," he said. It was the first time he'd spoken to my face since our mother's funeral, before I skipped out on the reception.

"I meant about the house."

"You call that a house?" he said.

"Okay, fine."

"'Nothing I can't fix up by myself,'" he mocked. "That's what you told me."

Chandler was scowling, and while I hadn't expected him to be ecstatic I had hoped that the wildness of everything would impress him.

"It's no vacation resort," I said. "But with a bit of work, it could be livable. I just need it to last the winter."

Chandler walked around my car. He looked up and down the house, peering around at the empty rainwater tanks pinned to the frame. Then he circled back and paused on the porch.

"You've been"—he paused— "living here?"

I laughed. It was a forced laugh, and it sounded strange in the forest, amplified by the type of tree that looms overhead through a fish-lensed camera.

"For the past month, yeah."

"Shocking."

"Jesus, man," I said, throwing up my hands. "I thought you might at least appreciate its potential."

Chandler looked over his shoulder and for the first time his expression softened. "Don't get me wrong," he said. "It is beautiful. And the drive up from California: it's desert for two days and then *bam*, all of this green pops up out of nowhere. But…"

"But what?" I could see the rest of the sentence on his lips, but I wanted to hear it.

"But I've seen your house in Newark, Max. The pool, the flat screen TVs. I guess I never pictured you out here, living off of the grid like this. Living out here like some kind of woodsman."

"*Woodsman?*"

He grinned at this, and I closed the gap between us. "I'll take that," I said, clapping the rock of his back. "Now, it's time for this woodsman's here to give you a tour."

Chandler followed me into the house. I'd removed the door to fit the propane stove inside, but the missing floorboards overshadowed this: they'd been peeled back like autopsied flesh. There was still a floor in my living room. I'd maneuvered the stove to beneath the window, and on the back wall sat a mop sink attached to the rainwater tanks. Beside that was a wood stove, still warm from last night, and my mattress. It was a flimsy spring bed, not unlike the cots you'd find in a military barracks, and I'd propped it in a corner so that we could move around. The air mattress I'd bought for Chandler's visit. It was folded and tucked into a corner. I still hadn't figured out how we'd both fit in the one room, but I was prepared to crash in the backseat of my Altima if it came to that.

The only other objects in my house were the electric lantern and my rifle, a .30-06 propped against the corner. Chandler moved timidly across the space, his fingers reaching for the gun with a casual familiarity. He'd handled rifles and .50 cals in the Navy, flying combat drills and rescue missions as a helicopter crewman. I knew that much. But after touching the barrel he withdrew, turning instead to the ruined wall that separated the living space from my bedroom.

"You hunt out here?" he said.

I watched him move around my house. "Not really," I said. "Nowhere to store the meat."

In reality, I didn't know the first thing about hunting. I'd gone to a sports shop looking for a 12-gauge shotgun and I came back with a hunting rifle. The plan had been to blow my brains out in Hemingway-esque fashion, but when the retailer asked what I wanted it for I couldn't tell him that, so I said, "Hunting." Thirty minutes later, I'd bought a .30-06 bolt-action rifle with a free-floating barrel. "Here's what yer after," said the attendant, glowing. "Reliable. Accurate. The perfect starter gun." Afterward, the image of gore splattering shiplap was replaced by a punctured hole lobotomizing my frontal lobe. With my family's luck, I'd survive to become the next Phineas Gage.

"What kind of game you got out here?" asked Chandler, running a hand along the skeleton of my wall. His scar glinted on the back of his hand, a knot of pale skin.

"Elk, moose," I said. "They're all over the place."

Chandler squeezed through the vertical 2x4s into the floorless bedroom. 2x12s crossed the ground from the front of my house to the back, and he had to straddle these for his feet to reach the earth below. "Are you allowed to hunt this close to a national forest?"

"Sure," I said. "So long as they're on your property. You can shoot any animal that wanders onto your property." In reality, the thought that it might be illegal had never occurred to me.

"This 2x12 is rotted," he said, stooping to inspect where it sagged into the earth.

"Correct." My pitch rose, as if intentionally contrasting his. "That's why I removed the flooring."

"Well, you didn't have to do that."

"What?" I said.

Chandler didn't look up. He kept his head bent and stepped over 2x12s like it was a football drill, disturbing earth that hadn't been moved in years. I envied him that: his familiarity with the bones of my home. It wasn't a malicious envy. It wasn't like what I'd felt in high school when—even though he was younger—I'd seen him talking to a girl in my grade who wouldn't be caught dead talking to me. It was more a forlorn type of jealousy, the realization that his hands were more industrious than mine. I was mystified by the way his fingers brushed wood, how his eyes spotted rot as quickly as mine found a comma splice. He peeled at the corner of the base beam and wrapped his hands around it, tugging to test the stability. His palms were weathered and red, accenting the scar on his right, but his hands had produced real work: tangible structures that existed outside of a word document or printed page, things far more resilient than the dated periodicals of a New Jersey newspaper.

After years of working behind a desk, I had little to show for it. Only one of my articles, a reflection piece on surviving the EFP attack in Iraq, had been printed by the New York Times. But I'd never written a book about it. I'd never had a product to physically hold. The only tangible work I had left were a few laminated cover stories and a *Letter to the Editor* from "Local Bill" thanking me for embedding in Iraq. Otherwise, my stamp on the world had been recycled or dissolved, leaving me jobless and penniless and wanting more than ever to have calluses on my hands, to thicken fingers that—after years of running over a keyboard—resembled the sinewy legs of a marathoner. It was one of the reasons I'd taken on this project: to build up something structural, something with purpose. To leave a legacy.

"Well, for one," said Chandler, gesturing at the beam, "we don't actually need to cut this guy out."

"Chandy," I said, softening my tone. "This 'guy' is rotted through. It's practically touching the ground."

He smiled. "That's true. But the edges are alright. Where it's notched into rebar is alright."

I crossed my arms.

"It's just a lot of work to replace a base beam," he said. "We'd have to get a wet saw to cut through the rebar. We'd have to prop up the house to fit the new beam in that space, and we'd have to screw plates into the concrete to pin the new one down when really all we need to do is slide that fresh 2x12 under the foundation and pin it here." He pointed to the space alongside the rotted beam.

I brought a hand to my chin. My beard was patchy and rough, even though I'd trimmed it before Chandler arrived. I'd kept it rough because I wanted him to grasp the magnitude of my transformation. Now, though—in pretending to weigh a clear decision—I felt a little ridiculous.

"Okay," I said at last.

"Okay?" he said.

"Okay, let's do it." I lowered my hand and shrugged. Then I dropped down between the beams and grabbed his shoulders. "This great, isn't it?" I said. "Just like the old days."

We worked through the afternoon at a relentless pace. Chandler was less excited than me. I sensed it in his expression, the movements of his body—he was still cooling off from getting lost outside of Jemez Springs—but as we worked, an amazing thing happened. We started to sync up. Our hands moved in time, and our voices loosened. The resentment and disagreements of our past were dissolved by brute physicality, the penance of labor.

By the time we finished, a bruised sky was creeping overhead. I turned on my headlights so we could clean up in the dusk light—there had been a few last-minute improvisations—and with the sun falling, the temperatures fell. We traded our sweat-drenched shirts for fresh ones, and I grabbed us a pair of beers from my cooler outside. We sat listening to the trees and the wind with the buzz setting in.

"How've you been cooking your food, then?" asked Chandler, maybe realizing that my propane stove had been unused. I said I'd been cooking over a campfire. What I didn't say was that most of my meals only needed reheating: ready meals from the grocery store, leftovers from Hugh and Joy, if not sandwiches or canned ravioli. But I had no food in my cooler that night. Just beer, warm from a week of neglect. It went well with the first cold night of fall.

We'd been prepared to drive into Jemez Springs for takeout when Hugh pulled up with dinner. I thought maybe my earlier curtness would keep him away, but he'd a resilient good nature. Hugh ambled over to us with a stack of Tupperwares balanced in one of his hands. We could see condensation on the inside of the tubs, steam rising from the top. Inside was a ground-beef and macaroni casserole.

"Homemade hamburger helper," he said, passing them around. "Joy wanted to have you boys over for dinner, but I saw you were working so I told her maybe tomorrow. 'Tonight's a boys night,' I told her."

I laughed, mostly at the image of Hugh's wife hosting the three of us for dinner. Joy was a plump, small woman with a tireless energy for conversation. The first time we met, I was waiting in their front yard for Hugh to return from Los Alamos. She spotted me loitering and invited me inside. "If you see anything you like," she said, "just take it. It's yours." That's how Joy was. She'd say things she couldn't possibly mean, but with the conviction of a therapist talking about childhood trauma. "We're open nesters," she said, clutching my elbow like a lost child. "Everyone who enters this house is family." She once sat across from me at her dining room table and—right after saying she wanted me to feel at home—grabbed my wrists, twisting the palms until they faced upwards. Then she grated her grip up my forearms to the elbow, tearing my arm hair with the dampness of her hands before pulling back down. With her grip on my wrists, she arched her back like a cat and pulled until my elbows popped. Afterward, she looked at me with the air of someone commenting on the weather. "You keep too much of your pain bottled up," she said.

It was hard to blame Hugh, in that regard, for eating with us. He was constantly searching for ways to spend his retirement outside of the house. He even volunteered at a nuclear facility in Los Alamos three days out of the week, working the security gate. On other days, he would go scouting for firewood or drive to my house, offering Nespresso coffee and leftovers in exchange for sanctuary.

"Hugh's an engineer," I said. We were shoveling macaroni into our mouths like children at the dinner table. "He used to design detonators for nuclear warheads."

"That's right," said Hugh. He laughed, but we didn't. "Worked on the detonator frames. I didn't design the mechanism that triggers atomic reactions or anything."

"Oh yeah?" said Chandler.

Hugh kept smiling. He enjoyed our company about as much as we were enjoying the food. He'd been in a fraternity at Ohio State, and the level of nostalgia he had for his "glory days" I'd only seen matched by retired marines. The first night we got drunk together, he told the story of how he met Joy. She'd been in his frat's sister sorority and they'd thrown a joint party. When Joy went up for a keg stand, one of his frat brothers grabbed her ass. Joy thought it'd been Hugh, so mid-chug she raised an arm and started swinging. She punched Hugh so hard in the balls that his eyes watered. Someone told Joy that it hadn't been him, that it had been some other guy, and instead of chasing down the culprit she brought Hugh a pack of ice from the kitchen and nursed him to health. "Best first kiss I ever had," he'd said.

Now he was talking about his job at the security gate. "It's a rush," he told Chandler, "working that close to so much power."

Chandler wasn't listening, though. His head was lowered, and he didn't even look up to crack open his next Milwaukee's Best. It occurred to me that he might've skipped lunch.

"You know what?" I said, setting down my food. I was full of beer. "I've just had an idea."

"Well, what is it?" said Hugh. He was giddy and silhouetted by the headlights.

"I was thinking," I said, "and bear with me here, because I know there's been a drought and all. But I was thinking, 'what if we had ourselves a bonfire?'"

"A bonfire?" said Chandler. It was the first time he'd looked up since our food arrived.

"Sure," I said. "We're gonna have to throw out that hardwood, anyway. Might as well burn it."

Chandler nodded. "Haven't had a bonfire in years."

I turned to Hugh. The smile plastered across his face reminded me of when my daughter Ellie smiled at a joke she didn't understand. "Sure," he said, clearing his throat. "Sounds fun. I'm just not sure if it's the right idea."

He said this last bit as an afterthought, and I let out a groan. "Hugh," I said. "Hugh, Hugh, Hugh."

"Yeah," said Hugh again. "What a buzzkill, right? But the last forest fire out here… it wiped out a thousand acres of pine. Almost blew through the Caldera Preserve."

"Well if there's a burn ban—" said Chandler.

"There's no burn ban," I said. I hadn't been drinking all week, and although I wasn't drunk yet, the exhaustion of labor and not having slept made my voice loose. "Look, we'll move it to the clearing behind my house. There's no wind back there. Hell, we'll line the edge with stones if you like."

Chandler shrugged, but Hugh didn't respond. I was grateful for Hugh in a lot of ways: for his company when there was no one else, for the food he brought and his coffee in the morning when I was so hungover that it hurt to breathe. He might've been my only friend in the world, but with my brother in town and after so much time apart, I wanted Hugh to leave.

"Fine," I said. "If you don't wanna partake, that's fine. But my brother's up from San Diego and we're gonna have ourselves a bonfire."

Hugh stiffened. It took a moment, but instead of taking the hint he clapped his hands together and stood up. "Aw, hell," he said. "Let's do it."

We got the fire going easy enough. Hugh had a canister of gasoline in the bed of his truck and we doused the wood with it. Chandler gathered brush to plug the gaps, and I arranged the wood into a teepee-like structure. Nobody had a proper match, so we got Hugh to use a lighter. He leaned toward the edge with his head facing away. It lit with a bang and Hugh was knocked onto his ass. A spray of embers caught fire a few feet away—we hadn't found any stones to trap it with—and Chandler had to rush and stomp to put them out. I was tending to Hugh, meanwhile. The hair on his fingers and the back of his hand had been singed off. I thought maybe his eyebrows had been singed as well, but after staring at his hands for a long time he looked up and I could see the white line of hairs glowing in the light.

There was a thrill to it all, from igniting the blast to how our fire burned like an effigy, blotting out the lesser stars. I could see it on my brother's face, the flames in his eye, and I was reminded of the campfires we'd built with our father on weekends at state parks. It had always been the wilder places, the open space, where our blood flowed equally. In the suburbs, there wasn't room enough for the both of us, but now I was looking at him and the fire and my house and I was glad that he'd come. I wasn't sure where I'd be if he hadn't—if I'd be drunk or hungover or dead—and staring at the moonless night, a punctured dome of darkness, I felt something shift. It was hope, I think, and it was the first optimistic thing I'd felt in months.

"You know what?" said Hugh, breaking our trance. We were sitting on a line of tree stumps around the fire. Chandler and I faced the fire; Hugh faced us. "I just remembered something. I just remembered this beer that I've got at the house. It's a real good beer. Beer that I've been saving for a special occasion," he said. "Whaddaya think? What better time than now?"

Hugh was a beer buff, and while I didn't mind the IPAs and nitro porters he'd force on me during my visits to his house, I also enjoyed a lukewarm lager on a cold night. But I egged him on and the two of us listened to the hum of his truck fade down my driveway.

I was a bourbon man myself, and the minute Hugh left I got up to dig a bottle out of my trunk. I'd been saving it for later in the week, when Hugh wasn't around, but we were getting a good buzz going, and with the fire lit it felt like a good time. I spent a minute sifting through the trash and clothes in my trunk, then turned back with the bottle and two plastic cups, sticky and thin from overuse.

"What's that," said Chandler.

I handed over the bottle. "That's the best damn bourbon on the market."

Chandler held it up to the fire and the bottle tinted his face red. He gestured to it and the forest around us. "You've really committed to this whole woodsman role," he said.

I laughed and took the bottle back. I could tell he wasn't as excited as I was, but it didn't matter. I'd already mapped out our schedule for the next two weeks. Tomorrow we would go to Los Alamos and pick up the replacement floorboards for my bedroom. Then we'd build up the middle wall and line the rafters with plywood, fill the attic with insulation. After that, we'd expand the porch and build an overhang to store firewood on, maybe even an outhouse so that I didn't have to shit in the snow, come winter.

"You know," said Chandler. I'd filled his glass to the brim, and he sipped it with caution. "I promised myself I wouldn't be seduced by all of this."

I breathed in the whiskey. "It's not too bad, eh?" Chandler tilted his glass in response, the bourbon shimmering gold. "Better than a tour in the Navy, I hope."

Chandler laughed, but it came out forced. "I read that article you wrote, by the way," he said, tilting his head. "The one that got published in the New York Times."

"Oh."

"You never told me about that," said Chandler. "That your Humvee got hit. That you could've died."

The fire flickered with a stop-motion abruptness, two-dimensional against the black night. "Not much to tell, I guess." I lifted my glass and held the bourbon in my mouth until the sting of it settled against my gums, between my teeth.

"Maybe," said Chandler. His hands clenched the plastic of his cup, warping it enough for bourbon to dribble onto his fingers. "You know, I was curious"—he said, pausing to absorb the bourbon from his hand— "about that Specialist."

"MacElvaney?" I said.

"Yeah. You said he started chanting something. Like a prayer."

"Sure. I know what I said."

"Well," said Chandler, shifting toward me. "What was he saying?"

The fire shifted and a flurry of embers flew up. We watched to make sure a patch of needles or wood didn't catch fire, then turned back to our drinks. The conversation was wanting to take a religious turn. I knew through his wife's Christmas letters, through our dead mother, that Chandler had turned evangelical, and so a part of me wanted to say that it was gibberish—that he'd been repeating the last five words we'd heard on the radio—but I was too damn grateful that he'd come all of the way out here to help me. Besides, after twelve years I'd written so many versions of that story I couldn't even remember what

276

actually happened. I couldn't distinguish between the experience and the narrative it had become.

"I don't know," I said, shrugging. "Maybe it was a prayer. Maybe it was nonsense."

There was more that could be said, but my pulse had spiked in the remembering. I hadn't put myself inside of that Humvee for years, and it took a few pulls of bourbon to calm myself down.

"Okay," said Chandler. The fire cast a shadow across half of his face, deepening the lines around his eye. "Okay."

He began picking at the plastic rim of his glass. I could tell that he was embarrassed for me, that he didn't know what else to say, so I shook myself and said, "I'll tell you what, though"—stretching my arms wide—"I'm gonna sleep like a baby tonight."

It's not what I was supposed to say. It's not what Chandler had expected me to say, either, or what he'd hoped I would say, but I was still surprised when he didn't reply. Neither of us spoke for a while. In the quiet, we heard Hugh's truck pull up next door. I could see the glow of his headlights through the trees, the gleam of it on his roof before he pulled into the garage.

"You know, I've never told you this and I probably won't again," he said, laughing so I wouldn't take him serious, "but I'm proud of you. I'm proud of what you did over there, covering the war. It was brave."

Hearing it like that seems harmless enough. But there was something in the way that he said it—like I needed him to be proud; like *he* was the older brother—that made me laugh. I laughed at him, and then I whistled slowly. When I spoke, it was to tell him that he could forget it. "Save your pride," I said.

"You deserve it," said Chandler. "You risked your life out there, for something bigger than yourself."

He was speaking earnestly, like he had scripted this speech in his head, but I was drunk and tired and wanted to remind him that I was older. "If you believe that," I told him, "If you really think I was there for something other than myself, you're about as naïve as I always knew you were."

I drained the rest of my bourbon and reached for the bottle. "I wasn't there to find the 'Truth.' All of the articles I published were screened by the military and commissioned by the journal. The only thing I wrote that mattered—a piece about homeless boys getting picked up off the street by wealthy old men, raped, and then returned—my editor refused to publish. Said it wouldn't 'resonate.'"

Chandler's eyes narrowed in the dark, the fire expanding its hot lungs beside us. "It's not too late to try again," he said. "Write it freelance. Write a book."

"No, no," I said. "I surrendered that right when I flew home."

Chandler glanced at the fire before looking back. The flames were burning brighter, hotter, than before.

"Can you believe," I said, draining more of the bourbon, "I mean, *can you believe* that, before I almost got blown up, I'd been hoping for something like that to happen? To get hit by an IED or sniper shot. Take a bullet to the arm, say; a piece of shrapnel to the hand." I pricked my arm to demonstrate.

"A million-dollar wound," he said.

I laughed. This time not at him, but at how backwards it all was. "Sure," I said. "But not to get sent home. I wanted to get hurt for the story. When that EFP went off, it was like an answer to a prayer. Everyone else in my Humvee, well they were praying for the opposite. But instead of making something out of it—instead of staying and writing that story as a downpayment on whatever I wanted to write afterward—I fled. I ran home."

"You could've died," said Chandler.

"But I didn't."

Chandler was staring at me. He leaned forward on his tree stump, his eyes boring into me. "You did the right thing," he said. "For Ellie. For your family."

I met his gaze. There was a clarity to the way he spoke that made me tense up. When I looked at his hands, I could see that he'd hardly touched his bourbon.

"You were right to leave Iraq," he said. "But you weren't right to leave New York." He'd changed his tone, the way he was sitting, so that the weight was in his legs.

"What are you talking about?"

"About this," he said, gesturing to the woods around us. "Isn't that what you're doing out here? Running away again? From your daughter? From New York and the lawsuit?"

"Look," I said, raising my hand. "Ellie knows full well—" but I froze. The words caught in my mouth like ash, because I'd never mentioned the sexual harassment suit to him. I hadn't even told him about my affair. "What do you mean, lawsuit?"

Chandler stiffened. He looked away and after a long moment his breath came out white.

"How did you know about that?" I said. The heat of the fire was in my face and on my hands. "Did you call Alice?"

"Max," said Chandler.

"Did you call my *wife*? Is that why you came out here? To punish me?"

"You know that's not it," he said, spreading his arms. But the revelation had already sparked a web of implications.

"You're on her side. You want me to sign the papers."

I felt a crumpling in my chest, a pit opening in my stomach that I hadn't felt since Alice hired a legal process server to deliver the divorce forms. It struck me then that if I didn't move, if I didn't stand up and walk around, I might spill out into the dirt.

"I'm here to help," said Chandler. "But honestly Max, did you expect me to come all this way without knowing what state you were in?" He stood up too but moved behind his stump and away from the fire. "We can still fix this place up, buffer the resale price."

"Resale price?" I said.

"Sure. I've got a few more days before I have to head back—"

"A few days," I said. My neck was pulsing hard, my breath sharp in my chest.

"I never agreed to two weeks. Come on, Max. I've got a company to run, a family."

The crackling of fire drowned out the rest of his words. I was pacing so close to it that I could feel the lick of every flame against the back of my hand. Chandler continued to speak in the background, facing me with his palms out. Looking at him there with his arms wide, I realized how everyone in my life—my brother, my wife and daughter, even Skyler—had made me out to be their Judas. I was the villain in their life's tragedy. And yet Chandler, my only living relative, my own blood, had betrayed me. Full stop. I wanted to hit him. I wanted to pick up a burning piece of wood and sear my hand just to strike him with it. But right then—when my face was boiling with rage, my arms trembling in the act—a car door slammed behind us. We'd been so caught up with each other that neither of us heard Hugh's truck pull up, noticed his headlights bleach the forest with an LED glare.

"Sorry that took so long," he called, trotting around the corner of my house. He had two bottles of beer in one hand, and a third tucked under his arm. "Got held up by the missus."

Hugh slowed to a halt when he saw us. Chandler turned to face him, standing a few steps from the fire. I was pressed against it, the heat searing my arm. I had to step back and look up at the sky just to breathe. Hugh handed Chandler a beer. Then he moved toward me.

"Here," he said, passing the bottle from a distance. "I got these from an annual beer festival in Albuquerque." He leaned in with a bottle opener and popped off the cap. The smell of hops filled my nose, bitter and sour beside the bourbon. "Won't be finding this batch within five thousand miles."

I took a sip. The stuff made my cheeks tighten, my tongue curl into the back of my mouth. Without trying it again, I dumped the rest onto the ground.

"Honestly, Max," said Chandler.

Hugh took longer to react. He cocked his head to the side, his smile arching like an open wound. When it dawned on him what I'd done, the sheer waste of it colored his face.

"I hadn't even opened mine," he said. "If you didn't like it, I could've just—"

"Go home," I said. They were the words I wanted to say to my brother, but I looked at Hugh instead. "Nobody wants you here."

Hugh took a step backward. He glanced at Chandler and raised a hand to his gut as if it might come away covered in blood. I'd wonder later if those were the cruelest words I'd ever spoken in my life.

The bonfire shifted beside us. I considered falling into it, finishing what Skyler had started so many months ago. But I didn't. Instead, I tossed the empty bottle into the flames. A shower of embers rose into the sky like dying stars.

"We're all just burning slowly," I said to nobody. Then I turned and walked into my house. The mattress barely fit between my two stoves and the sink. Without undressing or pulling up the covers, I collapsed in a deep and empty sleep.

My dreams that night were a vivid kind of remembering. I dreamt of Skyler crying in my office the morning I confronted her about the sources scandal, the articles she'd fabricated. I held her in my arms, promising to take the hit even though I knew that it was over. Then I dreamt of the first time I said "I love you" to Alice. How she didn't say anything back, she just placed her head on my chest and, for an entire minute, listened to my heartbeat. When I told her about my affair, about the sexual harassment suit and losing my job, she was similarly stoic. Our lives were on fire, but she didn't even cry. Instead, she left with Ellie and wrote me a letter two days afterward. It said that I was on a path to self-destruction and that she couldn't stand in my way any longer.

It was an hour before I realized that dawn had come and gone, that it was only dark because the sky was cloudy. My phone had died, and I'd no way of really knowing the time, but I forced myself out of bed to look for Chandler. My air mattress was still folded up in a corner, and the house was empty except for my gun. There was no sign of him outside except for his car and the bones of our bonfire, smoldering nearby. They would've put it out the night before; Hugh would've made sure of that. But I couldn't imagine where they'd found the water.

I settled onto the porch, looking at the grey sky and recalling how I'd taken my anger out on Hugh. My hangover was the world-ending kind, the type that used to leave me in bed for days wondering how I would make it through the week without offing myself. But instead of crawling after my gun or back into bed, I spent a long time basking in it. In the pain. It was ceremonial—the whip of blood against my throat, inside of my head—and I wondered if this was the same feeling that had appealed to the Flagellants: syncing the pulse of pain with the beat of life.

There was water in my car, a discarded bottle of Aquafina, discolored and carbonated from weeks in the sun. I used it to wet my lips. Then I took several meditative breaths before pulling out of the driveway. Chandler and Hugh would be around soon. They would want to check up on me or reprimand me. Either way, I didn't want to be there. What I wanted was for Chandler to go home, for him to call Alice and tell her that I wouldn't budge, that I was set on my path and that I was determined to see it through.

I hadn't a destination when I drove off, but I needed floorboards for my bedroom, so I headed for town. It was a forty-five minute drive to Los Alamos. The road climbed up the Valles Caldera Preserve, with Mount Redondo beyond, before dropping down a wall of switchbacks to a plateau of dust and rock. The city was only a few hundred feet lower in elevation than my home, but wildfires had knocked out the whole forest there sometime in the late 80s. All that remained of the once pine-rich oasis was the bare hand of a plateaued peninsula, reaching toward the desert with long, extended fingers. There were no trees or grassy lawns; there was only dust as lifeless and barren as modern-day Mesopotamia.

An Ace Hardware store sat right off of Central Avenue. The attendant had so many wrinkles weighing down his eyes he could barely see out from beneath them. He would've been living in that town long enough to watch the first fires sweep through, to see the earth go bald with ash. When I asked about buying floorboards, he looked through me, as though he'd had that conversation a hundred times already. "Won't have any of those in stock until next week," he said, "assumin the weather holds."

I imagined he saw me as a man who would chase a mirage off a highway, but I held his gaze for a long time, challenging him to explain how commercial trucks won't carry stock up the icy switchbacks of Highway Four. I was another yuppie in a mid-life crisis to him, but he didn't know that I was living in a floorless cabin without insulation. He also didn't know that my own daughter had refused to speak with me, that I'd heard her mumbling "no" like a two-year-old when my wife asked if she wanted to talk to her daddy.

There was a McDonalds right off the exit from Highway Four. I ordered two breakfast sandwiches, but my stomach writhed, and I couldn't finish the first. My mind was clogged with logistics. There were lumberyards in Albuquerque. On days the roads were plowed and not frozen, I could make a round trip in six hours. I'd need to borrow Hugh's truck, and that would require reconciliation, but Hugh was a simple man. I would placate him with an offer to wood-hunt one afternoon. My brother would leave the next day—I'd make sure of that—but I would have him prioritize our tasks, first. "It's the least you can do," I'd say without forgiving him. And even if he didn't, there was Hugh and small-scale contractors and YouTube.

The food amplified my headache, but over coffee I felt a shadow of the momentum from yesterday building back up.

Chandler had helped at least with the base beam, even if last night had been a setback. I'd get the hardwood before the end of the week. In the meantime, I'd build up the middle wall, insulate the ceiling, maybe even start on the porch overhang to store firewood under before the first snow fell. My rainwater tanks were empty as well, so I picked up water on the way back.

My hangover subsided slowly. It was a miserable day, but the dimness of light and the coolness of air soothed my head. It also made the pine green a shade darker—deeper, even—as if the trees were absorbing more light than usual. The hills were blanketed with a bed of mahogany needles, the cold rock summit of Mount Redondo faded into the clouds, and the Valles Caldera Preserve opened up in a golden bowl, sinking into the forest like an inverse dome. Winter would pass wet and lonely. But I would work on my book, and, in the Spring, I would set to expanding the house. Alice would forgive me in time. She always did. And when she saw this place, when she saw that I had rebuilt it with my bare hands, she would visit with Ellie and they would move in. Ellie would go to school in Los Alamos, growing up among the trees and the forest and away from the city grime. Alice would work from home with me, in the cabin I had built. Everything would fall into place with time.

I'd just about reached the entrance road to the Valles Caldera Visitor Center when a dagger wedged itself between my right eye and forehead. My vision flickered and then went out, so that I had to pull the car over and close my eyes. When I could finally see enough to blink, it was all I could do just to squint with my eyes.

I rested that way for a time. The image of Chandler and Hugh on my porch ricocheted across my mind until I turned off my engine and sat there in silence. Beside me, a dirt road led to the Valles Caldera visitor center. My gaze was always drawn to that basin—to the sublimity of so much space opening up in the midst of a mountain range—but for maybe the first time I looked opposite, to the woods that lined the left side of the road. There was something strange about the trees there, about their depth, and as my vision crept back I noticed that beyond the first row of pines the trees were branchless and black. They rose up, masked by the speed of travel, like the menacing spines of a porcupine.

I stepped out of my car and the humid air slapped my face like a cold rag. There was no passing traffic when I crossed into those woods, so I moved slowly. I expected something different, I guess—an ashy plume to rise up with every step; grey dust settling around me, and my breath disturbing the haze—but the air was crisp and clean: the crunch of death, cold. It was only when I pushed my hand against the trunk of a branchless spine that it came away smeared with black.

"Probably isn't the safest place to be." A park ranger stepped over a fallen tree on a path from the road. He moved carefully to avoid brushing his uniform against the charred wood. "Saw your car from the visitor center," he said. "Hope you don't mind me following, but these trees are prone to fall any day now."

I kicked the base of a nearby spine for him to watch. A shower of ash flitted down, but the tree didn't budge. "Seems firm to me."

The ranger laughed, his head down. He stopped a few feet away from me and eyed the tree I kicked. His beard was white, lining his jaw and lips, but the tone of his voice was harmless, and his eyes smiled. Even his lips curled upward in thought.

"'Brittle' is probably a better word," he said.

There was a melody in his voice that made me want to lean against one of the trees and rest.

"When did it happen?" I said.

The ranger widened his eyes. "A while ago," he said. "Five years, maybe?"

"Five years?" I said, looking up. The trees around us pierced the sky like a set of sterilized needles.

"Five years last month," he smiled. "Worst one in these parts since the Los Alamos Fire."

I watched him nudge his boot into the ashen floor, then flinch at the black stain it left on his toe. He was waiting for me to leave, for me to laugh and say, "Well, sorry for crossing over." But there was a gravity to the place that weighed me down. "How many acres?" I said.

The ranger paused to think. He was anxious about us standing alone, exposed to the brittle trees. "A few thousand."

The figure meant little to me, but I whistled anyway.

"Lost a pair of Fire Angels, too," he said. "You know, firefighters that parachute down and fight the fire from the inside." I nodded gravely, but his words were soothing and fell on my face like snow. "Made our final stand right here, off of Highway Four. If the fire'd jumped the road, it would've wiped out the whole preserve."

"Unreal," I said, looking past him. Behind us, the black spines rolled away as far as the eye could see, a cancerous splotch on the otherwise uniform green of the forest. "It takes five whole years? Just for these trees to fall?"

"At least," said the ranger. He shifted again, moving a few steps to the side.

"How long until they grow back? The trees, I mean."

"Oh, well that's hard to say." He was closer, now. I could see the grey specks in his eyes when he looked up. "The old ones have to fall before the new ones can grow in. That could take another twenty years, maybe."

"Huh," I said. In twenty years I would be retired, a grandfather, divvying up my land for Ellie and her family.

"But these here," said the ranger, "they won't be growing back at all."

He was ushering me toward the road, but I stopped and looked back. "Won't be growing back? What do you mean?"

He paused. "Well, the climate, I s'pose. These pines need a certain amount of precipitation. Less heat. That's why there've been so many fires, lately."

"But the drought won't last forever."

"No, you're right," he said. "But this forest has been thinning out for decades. The older pines are dying off and the new ones aren't growing back the same."

He smiled an apology, as if embarrassed about the climate changing, but I couldn't wrap my head around it.

"If temperatures keep rising," he continued, "fifty years from now this place'll be as barren as an Iraqi desert."

He meant it as a shrug, but I stared at him with such incredulity that he took a step back. It was impossible that he had fought in the war—that he had meant those words in that order—and yet they filled my head like the blast from the EFP. My hangover flooded back and I brought a hand to my eyes. I pictured the peninsula at Los Alamos, the tumbleweeds and rock gardens of people who'd given up on grass lawns. I saw abandoned gas stations and empty schoolhouses and then I saw my new home, my dilapidated cabin, sprawling and dead as the dead woods around us.

"You alright, son?"

I tried to respond, but at that moment a cold sting hit the back of my neck. I lifted my hand and it came away wet.

"Well would you look at that?" said the ranger. Flurries of white ash were falling from the trees, settling onto our jackets and feet. When they settled onto my hand, they felt wet and cold.

The ranger grinned openly, but I wasn't looking at him anymore. I was watching the ash collect on my hand. They obscured the skin of my palm, calloused from a week of handling splintered wood. They smeared the black ash from when I touched the dead tree, and as the snow fell faster, in larger clusters, it melted and washed away the stain altogether.

My hand went numb, the collar of my shirt damp and cold. In the distance was Mount Redondo. I could just make out its summit through the flurries, draped in white.